The Fix

The Fix

K'wan

www.urbanbooks.net

Urban Books, LLC
97 N18th Street
Wyandanch, NY 11798

ISBN 13: 978-1-60162-642-4
ISBN 10: 1-60162-642-8

First Mass Market Printing December 2014
First Trade Paperback Printing March 2014
Printed in the United States of America

10 9 8 7 6 5 4 3 2

Distributed by Kensington Publishing Corp.
Submit Wholesale Orders to:
Kensington Publishing Corp.
C/O Penguin Group (USA) Inc.
Attention: Order Processing
405 Murray Hill Parkway
East Rutherford, NJ 07073-2316
Phone: 1-800-526-0275
Fax: 1-800-227-9604

My mother always told me that my goodie box was a home, not a rest stop.

—Persia

PROLOGUE

Persia felt like she was falling forever. The wind felt good, like it was caressing her tenderly. For a few seconds all was right with the world and she was wrapped in her mother's love. That came to a crashing halt when Persia hit the ground and it felt like she broke every bone in her body.

She lay there, in too much pain to move, watching the snowflakes fall across the glare of the dirty yellow streetlight. It made them look like pretty yellow diamonds. She wanted to reach up and grab a handful, but her arms didn't seem to work anymore. As she lay there, feeling her life drain away, she thought about her mother and how she'd treated her. She wished she'd understood that all Persia wanted was a little love and one grand adventure. Persia would've given anything to be able to hug her one more time and tell her that she loved her and wished that she had been a better daughter, but she would never have the chance. She also thought of Chucky, and how he hadn't been there to save her from this horrible fate. She wondered if he would cry when he found out what happened. There was so much that they still hadn't had a chance to do. Tears of regret began to roll down Persia's face. She didn't want to die alone in the snow.

The bells of the church rang loudly. It was midnight . . . her eighteenth birthday.

She began to weep heavily and sang. "'Happy birthday to me . . . happy birthday to me . . . happy birthday, dear Persia . . .'" Her words trailed off as the darkness claimed her and ended her adventure.

PART 1

DADDY WAS A GANGSTA

CHAPTER 1

Harlem 1990

Face sat in the passenger seat of the Audi, staring aimlessly out the window. He caught a glimpse of his reflection in the window, black ski hat rolled up, sitting cocked ace-duce on his head, bloodshot eyes from the weed he'd been smoking and an unmistakable look of uncertainty on his face. For the millionth time he wondered what the hell he was doing in the car that night.

"You nervous?" Monk asked from behind the wheel. He was a brutishly built man, with long arms and hands the size of baseball mitts. He had gotten the name Monk as a kid because of his close resemblance to a monkey, but when puberty hit he blossomed into a full-grown gorilla. He and Face had been friends since they were ten years old.

"Nah, I'm good," Face lied.

"Bullshit." Monk gave a throaty laugh that sounded like something out of a scary movie. Face hated when he laughed. "You been my ace since free lunch, you know I'd never put you in harm's way."

"I know it, Monk, but it just seems like we're taking a big risk doing this shit all out in the open," Face said.

"Yeah, it's risky but it's our best chance. If we try to do it in the building we can get trapped off," Monk explained. Face still didn't seem convinced. "Dig, I know you ain't no stick up kid, Face, but we need this paper. I got a kid to feed and you got one on the way. You're always talking about how you don't wanna raise your seed in the hood, but you ain't gonna get out no time soon selling packages for Neighborhood. We need this paper . . . our kids need this paper."

Face thought of his girlfriend, Michelle, and his unborn child. When Michelle told Face she was pregnant, he started hustling like a man possessed. He made decent money hustling coke for Neighborhood, but it wasn't enough to build the type of life that he wanted for his family. For as long as he was eating from the next man's hand, he would be behind the eight ball. He needed to gain his independence, but to do that he needed seed money, which was what placed him in the car with Monk about to pull a caper.

"Yo, that looks like his whip right there," Monk said, pointing to a green Jeep that just pulled up in front of the building they had been staking out.

The kid they had been plotting on was named Sonny, a dealer from Harlem. He ran a few spots north of 145th Street. He wasn't a heavyweight, but he tried to carry himself like he was one. Sonny thought he was a made guy and had a tendency to treat people like they were beneath him, especially his workers. One night he'd slapped one of his workers around in front of a bunch of people, and as revenge the worker told Monk about Sonny's collection route and the bag of money he retired with every night. It was said to hold between $10,000 and $20,000 nightly. It wasn't much, in comparison with the competition, but it was enough to put Monk on his ass and drag Face along for the ride.

Sonny was just climbing out of his Jeep, when Monk rolled up behind him, brandishing the .44. "You know what it is, nigga. Let me see those hands," Monk ordered.

Slowly Sonny turned his head and looked at Monk, and Face, who had just joined them. He knew their faces, but not their names. "You little niggas know what you're doing?"

"Yeah, robbing you! Now hand over the money," Monk demanded.

"I got a few hundred dollars in my pocket. You can have that," Sonny said, keeping his voice even so as not to provoke the young gunmen.

"You think I'm stupid? I want that drug money you've been riding around all night collecting," Monk told him.

"Listen, I don't know what you're talking about. All I have on me is the money in my pocket," Sonny said.

Monk swung one of his meaty hands and slapped Sonny. The force of the blow sent him crashing into the Jeep. "Stop playing with me and set that cake out before I put a hole in you!"

"Leave my brother alone," a voice startled them. A teenage boy, who they hadn't noticed, jumped out of the Jeep and rushed them.

"Chill, shorty." Face grabbed him in a choke-hold.

"Tim!" Sonny yelled and made to move for the boy, but Monk's gun to his head stopped him. "Chill out, man, don't hurt my little brother."

"I'm gonna put this ugly little nigga in a bag unless you give me what I want. I know about that bag of money you bring home every night," Monk said sinisterly.

Sonny calmed himself before speaking again. "Look, I don't know who you've been getting your information from, but they're wrong. I don't have any money, but I can get you some. I just need a few hours."

"Unfortunately, time is not your friend," Monk said. "Check the Jeep," he told Face.

Still with Tim in a chokehold, Face backed up toward the Jeep and peered inside. When he saw the black duffle bag on the floor his eyes got wide. "Jackpot," he said, shoving Tim on the floor and retrieving the bag. It was heavier than he expected, which meant there was potentially more money in it than they had been told.

"You're making a mistake," Sonny said.

"Shut the fuck up." Monk slapped him to the ground. "I should shoot your bitch ass just for lying to me. How much you think is in there?" he asked Face.

Face nervously unzipped the bag, and when he peeked inside his face went slack.

"How much?" Monk asked. Seeing his partner's facial expression made him anxious.

"You gotta see this," Face said, still staring into the bag in shock.

Keeping his gun on Sonny, Monk moved to looked over Face's shoulder into the bag. Sonny hadn't been lying about having any money, but what he did have was about several neatly wrapped packages of cocaine.

Monk's lips parted into a wide grin. "Santa done bought a white Christmas to Harlem."

Sonny felt like the bottom of his stomach had just been ripped out. He had been given the assignment to deliver the drugs by a very powerful man, as a test of his loyalty and he had fucked it up. Not only was he getting robbed for his package, but he'd gotten his little brother caught up with him.

"Listen, y'all can have my money, my jewels, and my Jeep, but those drugs belong to Pharaoh," Sonny told them.

At the mention of the name Pharaoh, Face immediately began having second thoughts. Pharaoh was an urban legend in the hood. Nobody was quite sure where he came from or what his story was. It was as if one day he and his crew had just popped up out of thin air and started moving major weight. More than few cats had tried to challenge Pharaoh's claim and it ended ugly for all of them. Pharaoh's men murdered his enemies in the most gruesome ways, and always made sure the bodies were left in plain sight, so that it sent a message to everyone else who thought to test him. After a while, cats either steered clear of him or got down with him. Nobody fucked with Pharaoh, not even the police.

"You mean they used to belong to Pharaoh," Monk corrected him. "You and that nigga better chalk this up to the game."

"Pharaoh is gonna kill you when he finds out what happened," Sonny spat.

"Good thing you ain't gonna live to tell him about it," Monk said, before pulling the trigger and blowing Sonny's brains out all over the sidewalk.

"Sonny!" Tim scrambled over to his brother.

"What the fuck did you do, Monk?" Face grabbed his friend.

"Dead men tell no tales." Monk shoved him away. "I should've beat him to death instead of shooting him for making me go through all this trouble and not having no paper on him." Monk kicked Sonny's corpse.

"Let's get the fuck out of here." Face scooped up the duffle bag full of coke.

"A'ight, let me just tie up the loose ends." Monk aimed the gun at Tim.

"He's a fucking kid, Monk," Face said.

Monk looked at Tim, who was cradling his brother's corpse and staring daggers at Monk. "Kids grow up to be men." He cocked the hammer.

Face laid his hand on his friend's arm and lowered it. "We got the bag. Nobody else needs to die tonight," he said softly.

Monk cut his eyes at Face then back to Tim. After a few long moments, he lowered the gun. "You got that, Face," he agreed, right before he kicked Tim in the face, knocking two of his teeth out. Tim lay on the ground, unconscious and bleeding. Monk turned to Face, who was looking at him like he was stupid. "Just a li'l something for him to remember me by." He snickered. "Let's boogie." He darted back to the car with Face on his heels.

The whole ride back to the block, Face kept looking over his shoulder as if the police would jump out behind him at any moment, or worse, one of Pharaoh's hit squads. His heart had been in his ass ever since they'd left the crime scene. Monk had gotten Face into some messes, but this one trumped them all. It was too late to cry about it at that point. What was done was done.

"When we get back to the block, I'm killing John for that bogus tip," Monk said casually. "This nigga told me Sonny was gonna have cash on him, not powder. I ain't got time to stand around and try to sell all this shit off. I got some homeboys in New Jersey I can call and maybe they'll buy all this shit from us if I give them a deal on it. I'm thinking for seventy cents on the dollar. We won't get street value for the coke, but at least we'll be able to get rid of it all in one shot and have some money in our pockets."

"We keeping it," Face said, unexpectedly.

Monk took his eyes off the road and looked at Face. "A little while ago you was acting like you didn't want nothing to do with is, now you talking about we keeping it?"

"It's like you said, hustling for Neighborhood ain't gonna get me and my family where we need to be, but what we got in that black bag will," Face said coolly.

Monk smiled. "Spoken like a true gangsta. We about to own all this shit, Face."

Their moment was broken up when Face's pager went off. He looked at the screen and saw Michelle's number, followed by the numbers 000.

"Oh shit, take me to Harlem hospital," Face told Monk franticly.

"Something wrong?" Monk asked.

"Nah, everything is right for once. Michelle is in labor. I'm about to be a father," Face said proudly.

"Hot damn, it's about time," Monk said, making an illegal U-turn as if they didn't have a bag full of cocaine in the back seat. "I guess it's true what they say, huh?"

"What's that, Monk?"

"One life leaves the world, so another can enter it."

CHAPTER 2

1995

"What do you think of this one, Persia?" Face held up a tiny pink fur coat that he had pulled off the rack. He had cut his braids and now wore his hair in a low Caesar, with a half-moon part. His face was covered in a faint coat of hair, but he still didn't look a day over twenty-one. Dressed in a fitted black button-up shirt, blue jeans, and Timberlands, which he refused to tie, Face looked more like a male model than the trafficker of poison he had become.

Persia cocked her head to one side, causing the white beads braided into her hair to rattle. Her lips twisted like she was in deep thought, making her look even more like her father. "I think that one is really pretty."

"If you like it then it's yours," Face said, which made Persia clap excitedly. She loved when her daddy bought her gifts.

"Face, put that coat down because we're not getting it for her." Michelle came from the back, wearing a tight-fitting, off-the-shoulder dress she was thinking about buying. She was a pretty, light-skinned girl, with short cropped hair and a bright smile. Since Michelle had given birth to Persia she had put on a little weight, but mostly in the breasts, hips, and thighs so it looked good on her.

"Why not?" Face asked.

"Because, it's a waste of money. You brought her a fur coat last year and by the time she got around to wearing it, the coat was already too small," Michelle reminded him.

"Hush and let that man spoil his child if he wants," Charlene said. She was behind the counter ringing up some items a lady had just picked out. Her long box-braids were pulled back into a ponytail, drawing attention to her angelic face. She was as dark as onyx, with smooth, blemish-free skin, an ode to her Kenyan heritage. Charlene was Michelle's best friend and the mother of Monk's son.

"You mind your business. Of course you don't care if he blows money unnecessarily in here because it's going into your purse," Michelle said.

Charlene's was Charlene's love child: a boutique on 125th Street that specialized in customized women's and children's clothing. While Monk had been spending money, Charlene had been stacking it and managed to save up enough to open the boutique. Monk always felt like it wasn't necessary because he was getting enough money in the streets to support them, but Charlene was no fool. She knew that fast money didn't last forever and she wanted to make sure they had something to fall back on.

"Okay, let's get a neutral opinion. Li'l Monk, what do you think about this coat?" Face asked the little boy who was sitting on the stairs near the register with dazed look on his face.

Li'l Monk jumped. He was pretending to be reading a comic book but was secretly watching Persia and he thought they'd caught him. "I dunno." He shrugged his broad shoulders. He was only six years old and already the biggest kid in his class. He had his father's brutish genes and thankfully his mother's good looks. He was a handsome young man with thick black hair and long, dark eyelashes.

"Of course he doesn't. All boys are dumb except for my daddy," Persia said.

"I ain't dumb," Li'l Monk said heatedly.

"Are too," Persia taunted.

"Shut up, Princess P," Li'l Monk called her. It was a nickname the kids on the block had given her when their family moved from Harlem to their new house in Queens. Persia hated the name.

"Don't call me that, dummy!" Persia said heatedly. Tears formed in her eyes, but she refused to let them fall.

"Okay, the both of you knock it off," Michelle ordered.

Charlene came from behind the counter, smiling and shaking her head. "Those two argue like an old married couple."

"Might be a sign. What do you say, Li'l Monk? You gonna make an honest woman of my baby girl when you're all grown up?" Face asked teasingly.

Li'l Monk's brow furrowed and for a minute it was almost like looking at his father when he and Face were that age. "Make an honest woman of her? How am I supposed to stop her from lying when it's her mouth?" he asked, obviously not getting the joke.

The adults laughed while the children looked at them as if they had lost their minds.

"I swear if he ain't his father's child." Charlene kissed Monk on the forehead.

"Speaking of which, where my nigga at?" Face asked.

"Your guess is as good as mine. Monk spends more time in the streets than he does at home with us," Charlene said with a slight attitude.

Face shrugged. "You know how the game goes."

"Yeah, I've been playing it with him since I was a little girl and it's getting boring. I sure wish he would grow up one day like you did, Face," Charlene said.

"Don't think living with this one is a cakewalk." Michelle spoke up. "I get more than my fair share of bullshit from Face, but I have to admit he's getting better with it. My training is paying off." She laughed.

"Trained my ass. I do what I wanna do," Face boasted.

"Yup, that's exactly what I allow you to believe." Michelle kissed Face on the lips.

Face's sky pager went off on his hip. When he read the message across the small blue screen he smiled. "Speak of the devil. This is Monk hitting me up right here. I'm about to go meet him in the hood."

"Wait a second, what about Persia?" Michelle asked.

Face was confused. "What about her? You got her, right?"

"Come on, Face, don't even play me like that, baby. I told you that me and Charlene were going to the movies and I needed you to stay with Persia," Michelle reminded him.

Face sucked his teeth. "Why don't you just take her with you?"

"I am not taking Persia to see *Higher Learning*. That's too grown up for her. Now stop acting up and take your daughter with you."

Face let out a deep sigh. "I can't believe you're doing this to me when you know I'm trying to hit the block."

"And I can't believe you're complaining about watching your own child," Michelle shot back. "If you're just going to the block then it shouldn't be a problem, unless you've got something going on that you shouldn't." She raised her eyebrow.

"You know damn well I ain't got nothing funny going on. Stop acting like that, Michelle."

"Then stop acting like you're having a problem helping out," Michelle told him. "When the movie is over we might stop off and get something to eat. I'll page you when I'm on my way home." Michelle kissed Persia on the forehead. "Be a good girl for Daddy, okay?"

"Okay, Mommy." Persia beamed.

"Face, since you're going to see Monk anyway you may as well drop Li'l Monk off to him," Charlene suggested.

"Aw, come on. I ain't Mr. Mom," Face said.

"Don't be like that; I'll even pay for the cab." Charlene pulled a twenty from her purse and extended it to Face but he didn't take it.

"A'ight, but y'all owe," Face conceded. "The next time me and my nigga wanna hit the town I don't wanna hear shit from either one of y'all."

Michelle sucked her teeth. "Y'all do what y'all wanna do whether we complain or not, so stop it."

"C'mon, y'all." Face took both kids by the hand and left the boutique to catch a cab on the Avenue.

As Face was standing on the curb trying to flag down a taxi, a car pulled to a stop at the red light. There were three people inside: Shaunte, who was a chick known for boosting in the hood, her man Tim and his little brother Chucky. Normally Tim wouldn't let Chucky mob out with him, but his mother had made him promise to take the twelve-year-old along because she had to work a double shift and didn't trust the troublesome child to be home by himself. Ever since the death of her oldest son, Sonny, she had become increasingly worried about her other children, praying they didn't get caught up in the same madness. Grudgingly, Tim let Chucky roll out, which pleased Chucky to no end. He had been trying his hardest to follow in his big brother's criminal footsteps so actually being able to ride around with him made his day.

"Shaunte, why the fuck did you come across 125th Street instead of taking 126th? You know traffic is always fucked up," Tim complained.

"Tim, stop being a damn backseat driver and let me do what I do. I been driving in New York since before your ass could ride a bicycle," Shaunte teased him.

"I hear that, old timer," Tim teased back. He pulled a rolled blunt from his pocket and proceeded to spark it.

"Tim, why you lighting that shit while we got Chucky in the car? I don't wanna hear no shit from your mom if he comes home with his clothes smelling like weed," Shaunte said.

Tim sucked his teeth. "Shaunte, you my girl not my moms so why don't you chill? Besides, this li'l nigga smokes too and think nobody know it. Ain't that right, Chucky?" He turned around to face his little brother.

"Yeah, I got blazed a few times," Chucky said proudly, trying to impress his brother.

Tim laughed. "That dirt y'all be smoking in the park don't even count as getting you blazed.

This"—he held the blunt up—"is that real shit." Suddenly Tim had an idea. "You wanna hit this?" He extended the blunt to Chucky.

"Tim, don't give that boy no weed," Shaunte warned.

"Shaunte, he gonna smoke anyway, but at least if he's smoking with me I know ain't nothing gonna happen to him," Tim reasoned. "Here." He forced the blunt on Chucky.

Chucky took two pulls and began coughing. Tim laughed and tried to take the weed back, but Chucky wasn't quite ready to let go. He took another pull, this one smaller and softer, and held the smoke. Within seconds Chucky's bright eyes became red and lazy. Wearing a dumb grin he handed the blunt back to Tim.

"Yeah, that's that shit right there." Tim smiled.

"You are such a bad influence," Shaunte said, before snatching the blunt from Tim hitting it.

Tim was lounging in the passenger's seat, enjoying his buzz when he saw a familiar face that made him sit upright. He squinted to make sure his eyes weren't playing tricks on him. The man was older than last time he saw him, but he'd know his face anywhere. "Pull up on that dude right there," Tim ordered, pointing to a man getting into a taxi with two small children.

"What's going on, Tim?" Shaunte asked nervously. Something about the look in Tim's eyes frightened her.

"Stop asking me so many damn question, and pull up!" Tim shouted. He reached into the glove compartment and pulled out a small .32.

"Tim, please don't start no shit," Shaunte pleaded.

"I ain't starting nothing, but I'm about to finish some shit," Tim told Shaunte, but kept his eyes on the man.

"What's going on?" Chucky asked from the back seat. He had never seen his brother so mad and it made him nervous.

"You wanna know what's going on? That faggot right there is one of the dudes who killed Sonny. They shot him down like a dog in the street and now it's time for payback."

Chucky's mind immediately raced back to the day he had come home from school to find his mother crying, and Tim sitting on the floor, still wearing the shirt stained with Sonny's blood. At the time he was too young to really understand what was going on. "Should we call the police?"

Tim laughed. "The police don't give no fuck about kids in the ghetto. This gotta be handled with street justice." Tim reached for the door handle.

"Tim, don't, he got kids with him." Shaunte grabbed his arm to try and stop him from getting out of the car.

Tim snatched away from her. "Fuck him and his seeds, he killed my blood and I'm gonna kill him."

"Tim, we're on 125th. If you shoot Face your ass is going to jail before his body hits the ground. Don't be stupid," Shaunte said.

"You're right," Tim said as her words sank in. "I ain't gonna do nothing to him on 125th, but his ass is going to sleep today. Follow the cab."

"Tim—"

"Bitch," he cut her off, "you either drive this muthafucking car or get the fuck out so I can handle what I gotta handle, but Face is outta here either way."

Shaunte was hesitant. This was not how she had planned her day going when she came out of the house. All she wanted to do was swipe a few pieces of clothing from the local stores that she could sell in the hood so she could have some party money that night, but she now found herself on the verge of becoming an accessory to a murder. She looked to Tim to try to reason with him, but the hurt expression on his face after seeing his brother's murderer said it wasn't up for debate. Reluctantly, Shaunte did as he had ordered and followed the taxi.

CHAPTER 3

Face got out of the cab in the street and walked around to the curb to open the other door for the children. As soon as the neighborhood kids saw Persia with Li'l Monk they came running, glad to see their chums. Face had moved his family off the block when his name started ringing in the streets, so Persia didn't get to see as much of her old friends. Monk had moved too, but only a few blocks over and he was a constant fixture in the hood.

"What up, Big Face?" A young boy named Charlie greeted him by slapping his palm.

"Chilling, shorty. What's up with you? I hope you're staying out of trouble and staying focused on school?" Face quizzed him.

"Yeah, I'm doing great in school. I got four As and two Bs on my last report card," Charlie said proudly.

"Good shit, man." Face smiled.

"Since I'm doing so good in school, can I hold something?" Charlie asked, with his hand extended.

Face shook his head and reached into his pocket. "I swear if you ain't your mother's kid," he said playfully as he peeled off a five dollar bill and handed it to Charlie. Face and Charlie's mother had dated back in the days but she was always begging him for money and it was a turn-off so he stopped messing with her.

"You know you can't give one without giving the other," Karen said, with one hand on her hip and the other one extended. She was Charlie's little sister and even at an early age the fresh little girl showed signs that she would likely follow in her mother's footsteps.

Before Face could get back into his pocket he was surrounded by the rest of the neighborhood kids, all wanting their cuts from his bankroll. Face broke all the kids off with dollars then watched as they all went running down the block to the bodega. In them Face saw how he and Monk used to be: dirt-poor kids who dreamed of having something in life and escaping the ghettos they were born in. He only hoped that they make better choices than he had in their quests for freedom.

Face didn't see Monk immediately, but he knew he wasn't far. Cats like him never ventured too far out of their comfort zones. Face waved to some of the people he knew and snubbed others. When he was still making hand-to-hand sales, he was always on the block, but with more money came more problems, so he played the block less and less. People started whispering how Face thought he was too good for the old neighborhood, but that was hardly the case. He just knew better than to continue to shit where he lived. No matter how some of the locals felt about Face they knew better than to try him because whereas Face was seldom seen, Monk was always around, lurking and looking for a reason to hurt someone.

"Yo, Face . . . Face!"

Face turned to see who was calling his name and spotted Neighborhood coming in his direction. Neighborhood was what you would call a landmark in the hood, meaning he had been there longer than most and had no desire to go elsewhere. He would live and die in the same hood that had birthed him and he was totally fine with that. Face and Neighborhood had history. It was Neighborhood who had taught him how to survive on the streets and turned him on to the drug game. He was the man who had given

Face his first package when he was starving, and his blessings when he wanted to strike out on his own. At one time Neighborhood had been a sporting young cat who showed plenty of promise in the drug game, but Neighborhood's downfall had been the fact that he loved a good time more than the money. When he fell off, the hood had turned it's back on him, but Face still had love for the man who had taught him the hustle.

That day Neighborhood was sporting a pair of green Boss jeans with the beef-and-broccoli Timbs and camouflage army jacket. His jacket looked like it could've benefitted from a spin in the washer and his boots weren't the crispest, but he could fit in with most crowds without raising a red flag.

"What's up with you, Neighborhood?" Face gave him dap.

"Same shit, different toilet," Neighborhood replied. "I see you shining like new money, as always." He eyeballed the thick bracelet that Face was rocking.

Face brushed invisible lint off his sleeves. "You gotta dress for success, you know how it go."

"Listen to you spitting my own lines at me. Face, I can remember when you was just a nappy-head young nigga out here begging to hold a package, now you handing them out. I'm proud of you and how you came up to play this game," Neighborhood said, beaming like a father who had just watched his son graduate from high school. "I swear, I never could figure how you came up so quick after you left me."

That was a secret only known to Face and Monk. After they'd taken Pharaoh's drugs, they knew the streets would be buzzing about the robbery and missing product. They had to move smart so as not to give themselves away. Face was messing with a girl who lived in Richmond, Virginia, who he knew could help them move the drugs down there. It took a minute, but they were able to sell off all of the coke. With the money they made in Richmond, they went to see Neighborhood's connect, Flaco, in Washington Heights and started buying cocaine in small amounts at a time. Over the course of a few months, when they had worked their way up from grams to weight, nobody gave them so much as a second look. They were just two young cats who were on their grind.

"Well, I did have a good teacher," Face played it off.

"Indeed you did, Face. You were always a smart kid, good with money and knew how to fly under the radar. I just wish some of that could've rubbed off on your buddy Monk. I love the youngster like I love you, but Monk is out here moving sideways." Neighborhood shook his head sadly.

"What do you mean by that?" Face was now serious. Neighborhood was his OG and he respected him, but Monk was his brother.

"Same shit, man." Neighborhood shrugged it off as if it was nothing because he didn't want to create tension.

"Don't start speaking roundabout now. What's up, Neighborhood?"

Neighborhood hesitated for a few minutes, searching for the right words so as not to offend. "Dig man, word on the streets is that your boy Monk is out here on some gorilla shit. I heard a few cats whisper tales that it was him who robbed them Jamaican cats up on Boston Road for all that cocaine a few nights ago."

Face had heard the story like everyone else, but it didn't make sense for Monk to be the culprit. "Neighborhood, that don't even sound right. Me and Monk get our work from Flaco, so why would he be stealing coke instead of just seeing our man for the re-up?"

"Because Monk owes Flaco money for that heroin he gave him on consignment," Neighborhood informed him.

"Bullshit, we don't sell heroin, only cocaine," Face reminded him.

"*You* only sell coke. Monk will sell anything he can turn a dollar from. The way I hear it, he got the dope to try to make some side money off these dudes some bitch turned him on to. Of course the deal went sour and Monk got burned for the dope," Neighborhood filled him in.

Face shook his head. "Monk is always doing some dumb shit over pussy. If Monk wants to sell a little dope on the side, it's his money to spend and fuck up. I got no beef with that; it's the consignment part that's bothering me. From our very first package, we've always paid for everything up front. No debts, that's the rule."

"Face ain't you realized yet that you're the only one playing by the rules?" Neighborhood asked. "You better open your eyes to what's going on around you, Face."

"I'll get in his ear and see what the fuck is good," Face said.

"You can talk to him all you want, but he might be more inclined to listen to that white bitch who been whispering in his ear than me or you."

Face was shocked. "What white bitch? Monk didn't tell me he started fucking with . . ." Then it hit him. "Nah, you got it wrong, Neighborhood. I know Monk toot a li'l bit, but so do a lot of cats.

Monk sniffing a little coke here and there ain't about nothing."

"That's the same shit I used to say when I started dipping and look at me now." Neighborhood opened his jacket so that Face could get a good look at the tattered Iceberg sweater he was wearing.

Face didn't even want to get the visual in his head of what Neighborhood was insinuating. "I'll talk to him. Where is he?"

"I seen him earlier down by the basketball courts 'round the corner," Neighborhood recalled.

"A'ight, let me go holla at my nigga." Face gave Neighborhood dap. "You good? You need a few dollars?" He pulled out his bankroll.

"C'mon, Face. Don't insult me like that. I'm a little down on my luck right now, but my hands still work and I'd rather use them to earn some money than take a handout. You wanna do something for me, put me on a package and let me rock for a few hours," Neighborhood told him. He had always been a proud man, even being down and out.

"I'll have one of the young boys bring you something tonight that you can knock off," Face told him.

"That's what I'm talking about." Neighborhood rubbed his hands together in anticipation. "And don't worry, you know I'm gonna bring all your money back straight," Neighborhood assured him.

Face waved him off. "Don't even worry about it. I'm gonna lay a half of a G-pack and you can keep whatever you make from it. That should keep you straight for the next few days."

Neighborhood was so happy he looked like he would burst into tears. "Thanks, Face." He hugged him. "I swear they don't make real niggas no more. You gotta be one of the last."

"It is what it is, but if you fuck that up don't come back around me singing no sob story, Neighborhood. I'm serious."

"Face, don't even play me like that. I'm an addict, not a creep. Now let me hold twenty dollars so I can get my day started. I ain't had my wake-up yet." Neighborhood gave him his best slave grin.

"Same old Neighborhood." Face laughed, while peeling him off two twenties.

"Ain't nothing changed with me, baby. For as long as the neighborhood stays the same, so will Neighborhood." He capped before vanishing into the hustle and bustle of the Avenue.

***

Face took his time walking down the block, as he had a lot to process before he saw Monk. He was trying his best not to digest what Neighborhood was telling him, but it made sense as he thought about it. A week or so prior when Face had been in the Heights, Flaco had offhandedly asked about Monk. Face hadn't paid it any mind when it happened, but in light of recent information he was forced to reevaluate everything. Though Face hadn't taken anything from Flaco, Monk was his partner so it looked bad on both of them.

Face and Monk and had been making money hand over fist over the last few years from selling cocaine and crack. Face was hustling under Neighborhood; it was strictly coke. Neighborhood and some of the other cats didn't want to bother with crack because they looked at it as a poor man's drug. To them, smoking lacked the elegance of snorting, but Face saw it differently. He predicted that crack would spread like wild fire and he was right. It started in the hood, decimating households and breaking up families, but it eventually spread. Dudes who were once on top of their game were now walking around like zombies, selling their jewelry or whatever they could get their hands on for a hit of crack. Nobody was exempt, including the white kids who were once buying grams of cocaine in clubs bathrooms. They were now buying boulders of crack for half the price and double the blast. It soon got to a point where people from all walks of life now flocked to urban ghettos to pay homage to the new king of the slums . . . the crack man.

Face heard his friend before he spotted him. Monk's voice boomed from the basketball court, shouting profanities to get his point across. It was chilly out, but he still had his shirt off wearing nothing but sweatpants, Nikes, and a white du-rag. Steam came off his coal-black chest as his hot sweat met with the cold air. His every movement was primal, dribbling the ball awkwardly between his legs, glaring at the other young men on the court, challenging one of them to guard him. All ignored the challenge, except for one young man by the name of Rafik.

Rafik was a schoolboy and only came outside to go to the store for his mother or play basketball. He occasionally sat out on nice nights to sip a few beers or smoke weed, but other than that he didn't normally play the block.

Monk dribbled hard to the hoop and as he passed Rafik, he slammed his elbow into the man's gut hard enough to drop him. "Shaq style, nigga," Monk snarled, bouncing the ball hard on the ground for emphasis.

"Damn, you a butch," Rafik said, picking himself up off the ground.

Monk stopped his dribbling and turned toward the kid. "What you just call me?"

"Chill, Monk, he didn't mean nothing by it," Scooter intervened. He was one of the young boys who hustled and did dirt with Monk.

"Nah, let the nigga speak his mind." Monk pushed Scooter to the side and confronted Rafik. "What did you say?"

Rafik was clearly nervous, but he didn't want to seem like a punk in front of everyone who had been watching the pickup game. "All I'm saying is, you be out here abusing niggas on the court. I didn't mean nothing by it; learn how to take a joke."

"You know what, you're right. I do take things too seriously sometimes and I need to learn how to laugh more," Monk said before hitting Rafik in the face with the ball and busting his nose. "See, now that shit was funny!"

The whole park erupted in laughter as Rafik stood there with his nose leaking like a broken pipe. Face had seen enough, so he stepped in. "Monk, you bugging." He got between his friend and Rafik. "You good?" he asked Rafik. He simply nodded and walked off in shame. Before he left the park he glared behind him at Monk who was still laughing. If looks could kill, Monk would've dropped dead.

"Pussy!" Monk called after him.

"Cut that shit out, man. You supposed to be a boss and you acting like the schoolyard bully." Face slapped his friend's palm in greeting.

"I don't know how they do it on your side of Seventh Avenue, but on this side the strong survive. I keep the fear of God in these nigga to squash any big ideas," Monk told him. "What you doing up this way? I thought you'd be out in Bellport at the Country Club or something," he joked.

"Knock it off, acting like the hood don't still pump through my veins. I just like to keep a little lower profile, unlike yourself. I hear you been pretty busy lately."

"Where you hear that?" Monk asked.

Face shrugged. "Streets are talking."

"That ain't new. Streets been talking since the beginning of time, which is why snitching is at an all-time high," Monk shot back.

About then Persia, Li'l Monk, and their crew came into the park with the bags full of candy they'd brought from the store. Monk kissed Persia on the top of her head and greeted his son with a jab to the chest, staggering him.

"You know the rules, protect yourself at all times," Monk reminded him and threw another jab. This one Li'l Monk blocked and came back with a combination. "That's my li'l soldier." Monk rubbed the top of his head. "Go grab Daddy's hoodie off the bench; it's getting chilly out here."

"Okay," Li'l Monk said and skipped off to retrieve Monk's hoodie. When he picked it up off the bench, a small handgun fell out of the pocket. The other kids wisely backed up, but Li'l Monk scooped the gun up and wrapped it in the hoodie as if it were normal.

"Boy, what the hell is wrong with you?" Face snatched the hoodie and gun from Li'l Monk and shoved it in Big Monk's chest. "Don't you know that loaded guns are not toys? They're dangerous."

"Uncle Face, why you bugging? My daddy showed me how to handle a gun. I even help him clean them sometimes," Li'l Monk said innocently.

Face looked to Monk for an explanation, but he just shrugged. All Face could do was shake his head. "Y'all go play over there so the grownups can finish talking." He shooed them away. When they were out of earshot he turned his attention back to Monk. "Is everything good between you and Flaco?" He was frustrated now and wanted to get right to the point.

"That wetback muthafucka been talking about me? Flaco out here kicking dirt on my name?" Monk immediately got defensive.

"Monk, you need to chill. Flaco ain't said nothing about you to me, I'm just asking if everything is all good between y'all?" Face explained.

Monk searched his face for signs of deception. When he saw none he managed to relax a bit. "Ya man Flaco had fronted me something and I got burned for it on the street, so I owe him a little change."

"Monk, you know the rules. We pay for what we get. We don't play consignment," Face said disappointedly.

"Some of us play differently than others, Face. I'm in the streets with it, B, sometimes shit happens and we have to move accordingly. That's how it works when you're on the ground floor and not watching from the sidelines."

Face didn't miss Monk's slick tone when he said it, but he let the slight go. "Monk. You been my ace since we was kids and you always gonna be my ace, whether you're right or wrong. All I'm really trying to break down to you is that it's important for all of us to keep business relationships good so that everybody keeps eating."

Monk didn't want to admit it, but Face had a point. He knew if things went sour between him and Flaco it'd be fucking both their pockets up and that wasn't honorable. "You right, Face. I'm gonna make it right with Flaco this week." He gave Face a pound and hug to seal the deal. "Yo, walk with me to the store. Playing ball with these young boys got my mouth dry as hell."

The two men started toward the park exit, talking among themselves. When they got the mouth of the park, Persia called Face back. Monk kept walking while he met Persia near the fence.

"Daddy, if you're going to the store can you bring me something back?" Persia asked.

"Girl, didn't you just come from the store?"

"Yeah, but I forgot to get something to drink. Can you bring me a soda?" she asked in her sweetest voice.

"No, you can have a juice," Face countered. He and Persia stood near the fence haggling about soda versus juice when Face heard the rapid slapping of feet on the sidewalk behind him. He turned around and saw a man rushing toward him with a gun raised. His lips were pulled back into a sneer, showing the space in the front of his mouth where his teeth used to be. The man shouted something, but it was distorted, as if the world had slowed down. Face looked over his shoulder at Persia, whose eyes were locked on the gunman. *Not in front of my baby girl,* was all Face could remember thinking before everything went black.

When Face got his wits back about him, he was being thrown roughly on the ground and having his arms forced behind his back. For a few seconds he was confused about what was happening until he saw the cold, dead eyes of the gunman, staring at him from a few feet away where his body lay. When the police yanked him to his feet he was able to really take in the scene.

The shooter was stretched out with two holes in his chest. Face would find out later that the man he'd shot was the boy he'd made Monk spare five years prior. Tim had come back seeking revenge for Sonny. The officers kneeling around Tim's body were holding two guns, one a .32 and the other was the .44 Bulldog Face carried with him religiously. He didn't need the police to tell him what had happened, and he didn't need a trial to know that he was fucked. A few feet away Persia screamed frantically, while Monk tried to keep her from the crime scene. Face's heart broke into a million pieces when he saw his daughter hysterical. Knowing he was going to prison for a very long time didn't hurt him half as much as the thought of him letting her down.

"It's gonna be okay, Persia!" he called to her, as the officers shoved him toward the car. "You hear Daddy talking to you? It's gonna be okay! Persia! Persia . . . Persia!"

PART 2

THE PRINCESS AND
THE PAUPER

CHAPTER 4

2007

"Persia . . . Persia!"

Persia woke from her sleep with a start. Her heart beat so hard in her chest that she felt a mild headache coming on from the overflow of blood to her brain. Her fingers gripped the sweat-soaked sheets so tightly that she had broken a nail. The haze was slow to roll back from Persia's brain, as she looked around expecting to see a Harlem street corner, but instead found floral-papered walls lined with pictures and awards from school. Standing in the doorway with a worried expression on her face was her mother, Michelle.

"Are you okay, Persia? I was coming to wake you up for school when I heard you screaming," Michelle asked in a concerned tone.

"I'm fine, Mom," Persia said, pushing her sweat-dampened black hair out of her brown face.

"Are you sure? You look kind of pale." Michelle sat on the edge of the bed and placed her hand on Persia's forehead.

Persia pulled away. "Yeah, it was just a bad dream."

"The nightmares back?" Michelle recalled the horrible nightmares Persia had suffered from for years after what had happened that day. "How long?"

"Not like before when I was having them almost every night, maybe for a week or two, off and on," Persia told her.

"When you used to get them the doctors said it was stress that was likely causing them; maybe the adjustment of transferring to a new school is what's causing them. I'm sure if we spoke to Father Michael at St. Mary's he'd let us transfer you back."

"No, mom. I've been in Catholic school all my life and its driving me crazy. This is my last year of high school and I want to enjoy it wearing my own clothes instead of a uniform, and hanging out with my friends instead of a bunch of white girls," Persia fumed.

"Persia, you know we don't see color in this house," Michelle reminded her. "Besides, you've got plenty of friends at St. Mary's. Sarah and Marty go there too and for as much time as you spend together I thought you guys were close."

"We are close, Mom, but that's because we've lived a block away from each other since forever. I mean my *other* friends."

Michelle twisted her lips. "You mean them little fast girls from Seventh Avenue."

"Mommy, don't act like that. We're from Seventh Avenue too, we just don't live there anymore," Persia shot back.

"Yes, but even when we did live over that way we always carried ourselves to a certain standard and made sure that you grew up with principles, which is more than I can say for your little friends."

"Mom, I know some of the girls from the neighborhood are a little wild, which is why I only really hang out with Karen and Meeka."

Michelle sucked her teeth. "Chile, please! Karen has been a fast ass since she came into the world and don't even get me started on that Meeka. Didn't I hear recently that she was tied up in some kind of murder?"

"That is not true. Meeka didn't do anything, but she knew the dude who did, which is why they questioned her," Persia defended.

"Still, I don't know if those are the type of girls I want you hanging around. They're a bad influence."

"Only weak-minded people are influenced by the actions of others, isn't that what you've always taught me?" Persia reminded her. "C'mon, Mom, you know me better than that. Just because my friends are doing something doesn't mean I'll do it. Look at April from down the street. Her parents had to check her into rehab because she was doing hardcore drugs, but me, Sarah, and Marty never tried it and we all hung out together. I have my own mind, Mom, and you're going to have to learn to trust me to make smart decisions."

"I know, baby. It's just hard for me to let you grow up and grow out because of everything we've been through," Michelle admitted.

Persia crawled to her knees on the bed and draped her arms around Michelle's neck. "I know, Mommy, but I promise I'll stay focused on school and avoid things I have no business being a part of." She kissed her on the cheek. "Now get out so I can get dressed. I don't wanna be late for school."

"Girl, cut it out. It ain't like I've never seen your goodies before." Michelle laughed.

"Mother, I am seventeen now, which means that I don't have goodies anymore, I have woman parts," Persia said dramatically.

"You're a riot, Persia. Now hurry and get dressed so you can come down and eat breakfast." Michelle left her daughter to her privacy.

Persia hopped out of bed and went into her private bathroom get her day started. After brushing her teeth and showering she came out wrapped in towel. She was standing with one foot on the stool to her vanity table, applying lotion to her smooth brown skin when she happened to catch a glimpse of herself in the mirror. She dropped the towel and admired her body. Persia had always had a nice shape, but never much to fill it out until over the past summer when she had suddenly gotten thick in all the right places. It didn't go unnoticed by the boys in her old neighborhood either. All of her the girls in her crew were pretty, but there was something about Persia that always made her the first choice whenever they met guys. Persia didn't understand it back then, but later in life she would realize that it was her innocence that made her stand out. Karen and Meeka stunk of the streets, and Persia didn't have that with her. This quality, coupled with being naturally beautiful, made her loved by some and hated by others.

After rubbing herself down with lotion she slipped on a pair of black fitted jeans and grey Air Max with a grey sweater that showed off her shape. She didn't really do makeup, but she hit her eyelids with a soft shadow and applied a coat of gloss to her lips. Rolling her hair into a tight bun, she was ready to face the world.

By the time Persia made it downstairs Michelle and Richard were already halfway through breakfast. Richard was Michelle's husband and Persia's stepfather. He was an older man, but still handsome and very fit for his age. Richard spent countless hours at the gym. Richard and Michelle had known each other for years, with him being a friend of one of her uncle's. They had always flirted with each other, but never took it beyond that because of the age difference between them, and when Michelle did become of age, she was already with Face. They happened to bump into each other one day, two years into Face's sentence, and exchanged numbers. They had started out as friends but over time their friendship grew into a marriage. Persia was initially resentful of her mother and Richard's relationship, because she felt like she was being disloyal to her father, but as she got older she began to get a better understanding of their circumstances. Richard was only filling the void in her mother's soul that her father had left. She couldn't fault her mother for wanting to live, so she learned to accept Richard. He was a boring square, nothing like kinds of men Persia heard her mother was known to date, but he was good to them. Richard had been in Persia's life since she was seven and though she wasn't his biological child he still treated her as if she was, without ever once acting like he was trying to take her real dad's place.

"Hey, sweetie, how did you sleep?" Richard asked, without looking up from the newspaper he had his nose buried in.

"Like a baby," Persia lied and busied herself rummaging through the fridge. She came out with an apple and a bottle of water.

"Girl, put that fruit back and stop acting like you don't see these grits and eggs on the table." Michelle pointed to the plate she had made for Persia.

"Mom, you know if I eat that stuff it'll all go to my hips and my butt will end up as big as yours," Persia teased her.

"Baby girl, I don't get any complaints about this big ol' booty." Michelle slapped herself on the ass.

"I sure don't have any," Richard chimed in.

Persia shook her head. "Y'all are so corny. Anyway, I'm about to get out of here so I can catch this bus to the train station." She grabbed her knapsack from the banister where she'd left it the day before and headed for the door.

"Hold up, Persia. I'm about to head out so I can drop you off at the Queens Plaza," Richard

offered. He sipped down the last of his coffee and
dabbed his goatee with a napkin.

"You don't have to go through the trouble,
Rich. I'm okay with taking the bus," Persia blurted
out almost too quickly. She had things to do and
didn't want him all in her business and reporting
back to her mother. Aside from her being up to no
good, she hated spending time alone with Richard
because it was always so awkward. Outside of her
mother they had nothing in common.

"Nonsense; besides we don't get to spend
any quality time anymore without your mother
over-talking us." He smirked.

"Y'all better stop talking about me like I'm not
sitting here, before the only thing cooked in this
house for the next week is butter sandwiches,"
Michelle threatened. Whenever she sensed tension in the house she would interject and try to
make everybody laugh.

Persia picked up on what her mother was
trying to do. "Okay," she reluctantly agreed to
ride with Richard.

Persia occupied herself looking out the window and tried to drown out the news station that
Richard insisted on listening to every morning.
Her mind was in a daze thinking about hooking
up with her friends in the city, when Rich tapped
her on the leg.

"Did you hear me talking to you?" Richard asked.

"No, I'm sorry. What did you say?"

"I was asking how you liked the new school so far?" he repeated.

"I'm loving it. It's a welcome change from St. Mary's and that dry routine," she said.

"I can totally understand that. I went to Cardinal Hayes back in my day, so I know what it's like. You making any new friends?" Richard asked.

"Don't need new friends when I got my old ones."

"I know Karen and Meeka are your girls, but don't be afraid to expand your circle and connect with other likeminded people. Growth is good, especially for a girl your age." Richard continued to talk, but Persia tuned him out. She knew he meant well, but Richard's speeches were like nails on a chalkboard. Before she knew it they were pulling up at Queens Plaza.

"Thanks for the ride, Rich." Persia collected her knapsack and prepared to make her escape.

"No problem. How are your pockets looking?"

She shrugged. "I have a few dollars on me."

Richard pulled out his wallet and handed her a twenty. "Here, add that to whatever you already have."

"Thanks . . . again," she said and got out of the car.

Richard sat there for a while and watched as Persia jogged across the street and disappeared into the train station, before pulling back into traffic.

Persia waited until she thought Richard was gone and came back out of the train station. She was careful to watch for his car as she hustled across the street to the newsstand. Sitting within the stand, listening to a Walkman and reading a magazine, was the son of the owner, Hamid. Persia had come to know him over the past few weeks from stopping to get magazines and other necessary goodies for her commute to school.

"Hi, Hamid," Persia greeted him.

Hamid looked up and when he saw Persia, he smiled and removed his headphones. "What's up, pretty lady," he greeted her.

"Nothing much. I need to grab a few things for my trip to the city," she told him.

"Of course, you know I've got whatever you need." Hamid got up from the stool he was sitting on and grabbed several magazines, which he handed to Persia to check out. "I got the new *Source, Don Diva,* and that hair magazine came in that you were asking about."

"Cool. I'll take the hair magazine and the *Don Diva,* but I need something else from you, too." Persia gave him a knowing look.

Hamid winked. "I got you, baby." He leaned over the candy rack and looked up and down the street cautiously before reaching behind the potato chip rack and pulling out a pencil case. She smelled the weed before he pulled it out. "I got that Hydro shit that all the project kids are going crazy over." He discretely handed her a bag of weed.

Persia sniffed the bag and frowned. "Damn, this weed smells like dog shit."

"That's how you know it's good. That's a twenty sack, but since you're so pretty I'll give it to you for ten dollars and I'll only charge you for one of the magazines. "

Persia looked hesitant. "Can I owe you for the weed? I'm kind of short on cash today," she lied.

"Persia, you know I fuck with you, but I don't do consignment. I need cash for my stash." He rapped like it was a song.

"Don't be like that, Hamid. You know I'm good for it. I'll hit you back as soon as I get my allowance at the end of the week," she said sweetly.

Hamid leaned on his elbows and looked at Persia. "I don't understand how you live in that big house, and both of your parents drive nice cars, but you're always screaming broke."

"Because that's their money, not mine. Look, if I have to beg you for it then I don't even want it." Persia rolled her eyes at him. She extended her hand like she was about to give the weed back to him.

Hamid didn't reach for the weed. "I'll tell you what; I'll let you have the weed if you promise to go out with me."

"You know my parents don't allow me to date," Persia half lied. Michelle was okay with her going out with boys, as long as she got to meet them first so she could ask a million questions. Persia didn't mind bringing the good boys from her neighborhood around her, but she kept the hustlers hidden.

"Bullshit, I saw you in the sandwich shop the other night with that dusty-ass dude from the projects. You want something from me and I want something from you." Hamid looked her up and down hungrily.

"A'ight, Hamid. I'll go on one date with you, but don't think you're getting no ass for a twenty dollar bag of weed," Persia said, rolling her neck.

Hamid laughed because it was like Persia could read his mind. "A'ight, pretty lady. Just one date, and no funny business. So let me get your number and I'll call you later on so we can make the arrangements."

"I can't right now, I'm late for school." Persia looked down at her watch. "I'll catch you later though. Thanks again." She waved and jogged back across the street to the train station.

Hamid called after her, but Persia didn't even turn around. He knew she had just run game on him, but he would see her again. "Slick bitch didn't even pay me for the magazine."

Persia had just made it onto the platform as the train was pulling into the station. Slipping through the crowd of passengers getting on and off the train, she grabbed the double seat near the conductor booth. Just to make sure nobody tried to sit in the next seat and crowd her, she threw her knapsack on it.

It was shady for her to game Hamid out of the weed, but he had been trying to game her out of her pants for weeks so she had just given him a dose of his own medicine. Her friend Karen had once tried to convince her to date him so they could get free weed and snacks, but Persia wasn't with it. Hamid was nice enough, but he was only a paperboy. One thing she had learned from her mother was never to bother with a man who wasn't financially well off. If he couldn't do anything for himself he couldn't do anything for her.

Thinking of her mother made her feel guilty. She thought Persia was on her way to school, but Martin Luther King Jr. High School wouldn't see her that day; she was going to Harlem to meet up with her girls, Karen, Meeka, and Ty. They had declared it an unofficial holiday. She loved hanging out in Harlem, but her mother had forbidden her, so she had to sneak anytime she wanted to see her girls outside of school. It never made sense to her why her mother was so adamant about her not hanging out in Harlem, especially since that's where they were from. She chalked it up to her mother being paranoid of someone trying to retaliate against her for the boy her father had killed twelve years prior. Persia knew her mother meant well, but she was seventeen years old and almost grown.

Persia settled back in her seat and cupped her hands to her nose, inhaling deeply the smell of the exotic weed and thinking about what they were going to get into when she got uptown. It was going to be a good day . . . at least for her it was.

CHAPTER 5

Li'l Monk awoke to the sounds of rap music coming from the small radio mounted on his windowsill. Over the music the disc jockey announced that the weather was sixty-eight and chilly and the time was a quarter to nine, which meant he was late for school. It was all good, because Li'l Monk wasn't sure if he felt like going that day anyway. He and school hadn't really seen eye to eye since his most recent release from juvenile detention, but he made sure he attended enough so that his probation officer didn't violate him. If nothing else, his many brushes with the law had taught him how to work around it.

He rolled off the mattress on the floor that served as his bed and stretched his long arms, twisting right to left to work the kinks out of his back. He ran his hands over the thick cornrows on his head and tried to remember the last time he'd had his hair braided. When he got his hands on a few dollars he would have one of the neighborhood hood rats tighten him up. After giving up thanks to God for letting him see another day, Li'l Monk began his morning calisthenics, 200 quick push-ups and one hundred sit-ups. Li'l Monk wasn't big on fitness, but he was big on survival. Every day before he left the house his mind and body had to be right. The world was full of predators and only the strong survived. It was the one lesson his father, Monk, had taught him, which he applied to his everyday life.

After his light workout, Li'l Monk stood in front of the mirror and looked himself over. He was only eighteen years old, but was already six feet tall, and weighed about 215 pounds, give or take. A few whiskers sprouted from his chin, but he was a long way away from having anything that resembled a beard. Li'l Monk had the face of a baby, but the eyes of a man twice his age. In his short time on earth he had seen both sunshine and rain, but the last few years had been mostly rain.

After dressing in a white thermal shirt, black jeans, and black steel-toed boots, Li'l Monk was ready to hit the turf. He walked to his father's bedroom, and listened before carefully easing the door open. His father's bed was empty and unmade, and the room was in disarray, but that was nothing new. His father was rarely home, unless it was to sleep it off when he finally crashed from his constant street running. Since "the day," as they called it, Li'l Monk had pretty much been raising himself.

When he entered the kitchen he was greeted by piles of dirty dishes, and roaches playing freeze tag on the counter. Li'l Monk grabbed a box of cereal, peeking inside with one eye and shaking it to make sure there weren't any critters living in it. He popped open the fridge for some milk. The inside of the refrigerator was so empty that he could hear an echo. There was nothing in it but a half-empty forty-ounce bottle of St. Ides, an old cheeseburger that looked like it was growing fur, and a container of milk. When he went to pour the milk over his cereal, it came out in thick clumps, obviously spoiled.

"Fuck." Li'l Monk tossed the carton in the sink. He was starving, but it would have to wait until he hustled up some money for a meal. Tightening up his belt, he left the apartment and hit the streets.

The sun was shining outside, but the air had a chill to it. It wasn't quite cold, but you could tell winter would come early that year. With his hands shoved into his pockets, he walked up to the Avenue to see who was out and what was going on. Standing in the doorway of the Chinese restaurant was Li'l Monk's friend, Charlie. He had on an oversized hoodie and dark sunglasses. From the way Charlie was looking up and down the Avenue suspiciously, Li'l Monk knew he was up to no good.

"Fuck you doing out here on some James Bond shit and what's with the glasses?" Li'l Monk asked before giving his friend dap.

"Shit, I'm just trying to make the best out of a bad situation. I know you heard what happened?" Charlie asked.

"Nah, I'm just coming out. What went down?" Li'l Monk asked.

"Fam, it was popping out here!" Charlie said excitedly. He went on to tell Li'l Monk the story about how the dudes had come through and robbed one of Pharaoh's drug houses. "They took the work and the money so everything is shut down until somebody comes through with another package."

"So what you doing standing around like you're waiting for it to rain?" Li'l Monk asked.

"Trying to get in where I fit in." Charlie opened his hand and showed Li'l Monk the two baggies filled with white chips.

Li'l Monk looked around suspiciously, as if the police might've been watching them at that moment. "I thought you said the stick up kids took all the crack off the block?"

"This ain't crack, it's a dummy," Charlie said, grinning stupidly. A dummy was counterfeit crack. Most times it was made out of soap chips, so at a glance it looked real and by the time the fiend realizes you played them, you were long gone with their money. The grin was wiped from his face when Li'l Monk slapped the fake crack out of his hand. "Fuck is you doing?"

"Trying to keep you from getting murdered out here, dumb ass." Li'l Monk shoved him inside the Chinese restaurant. "I swear it seems like you get stupider by the day, Charlie."

"Li'l Monk, I don't know why you acting like that. Me and you have slung dummies plenty of times when we were hard up for cash. I don't see why you're all upset over it now." Charlie didn't see what the big deal was.

"Yeah, we have sold burn bags together, but never on the same block where we rest our heads. What do you think would've happened if somebody had caught you out here wrong and told Ramses?" Li'l Monk asked him.

A worried expression spread across Charlie's face. Ramses was Pharaoh's right hand and his voice on the streets. He was a man quick to violence and wasn't known to give passes when people offended him.

"Ramses would've sent Chucky or Benny looking for you and ensured that your mother couldn't give you an open-casket funeral," Li'l Monk continued. "Only a fool shits where he lives, Charlie."

"I hear you, Li'l Monk." Charlie adjusted his sunglasses.

"And what is it with you and those fucking shades, you high or something?" Li'l Monk snatched Charlie's sunglasses off before he could stop him. "What the fuck happened to your eye?"

"Nothing, man. Me and Burger were just horsing around. It was an accident." Charlie tried to downplay it.

Li'l Monk tilted Charlie's head up so he could get a better look. "What happened to your eye looks deliberate as hell from where I'm standing."

"Li'l Monk, you're acting like he kicked my ass or something. He was just fucking around and hit me a little too hard, that's all. You know Burger plays rough," Charlie said. Burger was one of the kids who hustled on their block, so he considered himself a tough guy. Li'l Monk never liked him because he saw Burger as a bully.

"I don't give a fuck how he plays. If a man puts his hands on you, you put yours back on him! Even if it means getting your ass kicked in the process, at least you fought," Li'l Monk snarled. Charlie was his best friend in the whole world, and he hated talking to him like that, but Charlie didn't understand the seriousness of the situation. In the world they lived in, the strong survived and the weak were food. Food attracted predators, predators Li'l Monk would have to help him fight off.

"I ain't no sucker, Li'l Monk," Charlie said.

"Then show me right when you see this pussy!" The more Li'l Monk talked the angrier he got.

"Li'l Monk, it ain't that serious," Charlie said. He would've much rather have left it alone.

"Charlie, there ain't gonna be no weak links in this chain. You're either gonna take this nigga's head off or I'm gonna take your head off," Li'l Monk told him in a tone that said there would be no more debate about it.

Before the conversation could get any deeper, the door to the Chinese restaurant opened and a man came. "Give me four wings fried hard, Lin!" he shouted to the young Chinese girl who was sitting behind the bulletproof glass. He was decked out in a dusty army jacket and ashy black jeans. They nappy wool hat that sat cocked on his head blended almost perfectly with the untamed afro he sported beneath it.

"No, no, no. You still owe for the last order. No wings for you, Neighborhood!" Lin shouted back.

"Ain't this some shit." Neighborhood hiked his jeans up over his bony hips. He was teetering left and right and his eyes were glassy. "Lin, I been on this block since long before your daddy opened this cat kitchen. How many five dollar bills I put in yours or your brother's and sister's hands when I was getting it? I broke the yellow kids off same as I did the black and browns, and you gonna treat me like a crab over some yard bird?"

Lin gave in. "All right, Neighborhood. I'll give you an order of wings, but the next time you have to come with money or I have to turn you away, okay?"

"That's what I'm talking about, Lin. Look out for your Uncle Neighborhood." He smiled broadly, showing off discolored and rotting teeth. When he spied Charlie standing in the corner his smile faded. "Damn, who got you out here looking like Petey the Dog from *The Little Rascals?*"

"I got your little rascal right there, mutha-fucka." Charlie stepped forward, but Li'l Monk's hand on his chest stopped him.

"Chill out, Charlie," Li'l Monk told him. "Why you gotta fuck with my man every time you see him?" he asked Neighborhood. It seemed like he always went out of his way to set Charlie off.

"Tell him to ask his mama why I always fuck with him," Neighborhood said with a mischievous grin. He plucked a half-smoked cigarette from behind his ear and placed it in his mouth. "Let me get a light, young blood."

"Hey, no smoking in here. Go outside!" Lin shouted from behind the glass. "You got it, baby," Neighborhood replied. "Walk with me outside." Neighborhood stepped out of the Chinese restaurant, followed by Li'l Monk and a reluctant Charlie. "I swear these damn chinks kill me," he continued. "They set up shop in black neighborhoods, make their fortunes of black dollars, then act like they're better than black people."

"They are," Li'l Monk said flatly.

"What the fuck are you, some kind of race traitor?" Charlie asked, looking at Li'l Monk suspiciously.

"No, I'm a realist," Li'l Monk replied. "Look at these stores on the strip. The Arabs own the deli on the corner, the Hispanics own the restaurant up the street, and the Africans own the electronic store. Shit, even the Mexicans are doing their thing with the supermarket, but what do we own in our own neighborhood? Not a damn thing. Niggers are too busy trying to kill each other and tear shit up to worry about ownership in our own communities. Even when we get our hands on a few dollars, we'd rather spend it with someone else."

"Damn, that's deep, Li'l Monk," Neighborhood said.

Li'l Monk shook his head. "Nah, it ain't deep. It's sad."

"So what you two jokers getting into? If you're looking for a vic, them boys from up the way already beat you to it," Neighborhood told them, speaking of the earlier robbery.

"I heard already. Say, have you seen my dad today?" Li'l Monk asked. His father wasn't good for much those days, but if he was lucky, he could catch him early and bum a few dollars for a meal before he fucked up whatever money he had.

"I seen him about seven o'clock this morning with that thirsty look in his eyes," Neighborhood recalled.

"That must mean he's broke and out here trying to come up," Li'l Monk said in a disappointed tone. It would be left to him to come up with a way to eat for the day.

"Man, I remember back in the days your daddy and Face were getting big money out here on the streets," Neighborhood reminisced.

"Too bad I can't eat a memory," Li'l Monk said. He didn't know who he resented more: the man his father used to be or the man he had become. When Face went to prison, Monk started dancing on the edge, but losing Charlene had pushed him over it.

"I'm about to go get my chicken wings before Lin changes her mind. Y'all two gonna be out here for a while?" Neighborhood asked.

Li'l Monk looked over at Charlie and his bruised eye. "Nah, we got something we need to take care of right quick."

CHAPTER 6

It seemed like it had taken Persia forever to
get to Harlem. She came out of the train station
near the park and walked the few short blocks to
Seventh Avenue, where she was supposed to be
meeting her girls in front of Karen's building.

There was a cluster of young boys hanging out
in front of the store on the corner. As soon as
they saw Persia they started in with the catcalls
and whistles trying to get her attention. Persia
acted like she didn't hear them and sped up.
Someone grabbed her arm from behind, and
pulled her back. He was a beefy young man who
wore his hair in a box-shaped afro. Persia had
seen him at her school, but she didn't know him.

"Excuse you." Persia jerked away.

"Chill, shorty, I ain't trying to hurt you. I was
just trying to get your attention," Burger said in
his smoothest voice.

"There are better ways to get a lady's attention
than grabbing her like a mugger," Persia told
him.

"I'm more of the hands-on type," Burger told her. "Yo, I be seeing you around my school with them hood rats from Seventh. Ain't your name Princess or something?"

"It's Persia," she corrected him. "And those hood rats, as you called them, are my friends."

"Ma, you know you're way too classy to be hanging around those chicks. You need to kick it with me, so I can show you how the other half lives," Burger said confidently.

"Thanks for the offer, but I'll pass," Persia told him and turned to leave, but Burger blocked her path.

"Yo, all I'm trying to do is get to know you," Burger told her.

"I said I'm good, now can you get out of my way so I can get to where I need to be?" Persia adjusted her bag.

Burger's boys had begun to laugh, and bruised his ego. "Bitch, you think you all that because you got a Louie bag? This is my fucking block, I'll snatch that muthafucka off your shoulder."

Moving as fast as lightning, Persia's hand dipped in her bag and came back out holding a small canister of pepper spray. "Nigga you touch me or anything that belongs to me and watch what happens!"

"What y'all over there doing to that girl?" Neighborhood came around the corner. He had a half-eaten chicken wing in his hand and his lips were covered in grease.

"Ain't nothing. I'm just trying to explain to this snooty bitch how things work in the hood," Burger said venomously.

Persia placed her thumb on the trigger of the pepper spray. "Let the word 'bitch' come out of your mouth one more time and I promise you'll be blinder than Ray Charles and Stevie Wonder."

"Easy, now." Neighborhood placed himself between them. "Burger, I don't think Face would take kindly to you out here talking crazy to his baby girl."

The change in Burger's facial expression said that the name rang a bell in his head. Though Face had been in prison for many years, he was still a legend in the streets and there were a great many people who still had love for him. "You got that, shorty." Burger raised his hands in surrender and began backing away slowly. "If I were you, I'd be careful while I was out here. These streets are dangerous and not everyone is gonna care who your father is."

Persia kept her eyes on Burger until he disappeared around the corner with his friends. "Thanks," she said to Neighborhood.

"No thanks needed. Your daddy was like family to me. You probably don't remember me, but I've known you since you were born. Ask Michelle about Neighborhood," he said proudly.

Persia recalled the name from back when she was a kid, but the man she remembered looked nothing like the man she was speaking to that day.

"How is Face holding up?" Neighborhood asked.

"He's good, he wrote me a few weeks ago," Persia told him.

"Glad to hear it. The next time you speak to Face, tell him that Neighborhood sends his love."

"Will do," Persia agreed. "Thanks again." She waved and walked across the street to Karen's building. Karen and the others weren't in front of the building, so Persia rang the bell to Karen's apartment.

"Who is it?" a hostile voice came through the speaker mounted on the wall.

"Ah, it's Persia. Is Karen at home?"

A few seconds passed then the door buzzed, allowing Persia to enter. Karen lived in a tenement building that didn't have elevators, so Persia had to walk up to the three flights of steps to her apartment. She was just about to knock on the door when it swung open and Karen's

Uncle Scooter came walking out. Scooter was in his early thirties, but years of running the streets and drug abuse made him look like he was pushing fifty. It was hard to believe that at one time he had been getting money as a part of her father's crew.

"'Sup, Persia?" Scooter greeted her.

"Nothing much, Scooter. Is Karen home?" she asked.

"Yeah, she's in the back room."

"Thanks." Persia stepped around him to enter the apartment.

"Persia," he called after her. "Let me borrow a few dollars until later on."

"Sorry, I'm broke, Scooter," she lied.

Scooter twisted his lips as if he didn't believe her, but he didn't press it. "A'ight," he said, and descended the steps.

Persia walked down the long hallway, following the thump of music and the stench of weed to Karen's bedroom. On her door was a poster of the Harlem rap group The Diplomats. Persia knocked, but she doubted that they could hear her over the music, so she invited herself in.

Karen was lying across the bed, thumbing through a magazine. She had grown into a beautiful dark-skinned girl with hips and ass for days, which she flaunted every chance she got by buying her jeans one size too small.

"Hey, Persia," Ty greeted her from the spot on the floor where she was sitting, fumbling with Karen's portable CD player. She was the newest addition to their crew and some would say the least attractive. It wasn't that Ty didn't have the potential to be decent, but she came from a dirt-poor family so her gear was never quite up to par and her hair was always in a ponytail.

"Damn, do you think it took you long enough?" Meeka asked in her signature deep voice. Meeka was a short, light-skinned girl who wasn't gorgeous but cute, and cleaned up very nicely when she wanted to. As usual she was dressed in tight jeans and Timberlands, which she wore untied. She was the resident thug of their crew, and had a reputation in the hood as an ass-whipping specialist.

"My stepfather wanted to have one of those talks this morning." Persia said as if Richard was on her last nerve. She always played the love/hate role around her friends when it came to her mother's husband.

"Your mom still married to that white dude?" Meeka asked.

"My stepfather isn't white, he's black. Who told you some dumb shit like that?" Persia asked.

"I always hear Karen talking about how your mom married some peckerwood so I always assumed he was a white guy," Meeka said honestly.

Persia turned to Karen. "Your two-faced ass is always talking about somebody."

"Persia, you know that nigga act white as hell." Karen laughed.

"Damn, Persia. Most bitches ain't got no daddy, but you got two daddies. I'd say you're doing better than most," Ty said.

"I only have one father. Rich is just the dude my mother married," Persia said sternly.

"Fuck all that *Maury* 'is or ain't the pappy' shit. Did you get the weed?" Karen asked.

"You know I did." Persia tossed the sack she'd gotten from Hamid on the bed.

Karen smelled the bag. "Damn, this is some good shit."

"Then stop wiping your nose with it and roll up. I'm trying to get high," Meeka said.

"You mean higher. I'm already on the moon from the last L we smoked. Y'all trying to get too high," Ty added.

"Ain't no such thing as too high," Karen told her.

When Karen's room door swung open unexpectedly, all the girls jumped as if the police were about to rush it, but it was only Karen's mother, Sissy. She looked like an older version of Karen, only her body wasn't as tight. Back in the days Sissy was the hottest thing smoking on the block, and even though she was getting on in years, she could still give some women half her age a run for their money.

"Damn, don't you know how to knock?" Karen asked with an attitude.

"As long as I pay the rent in this bitch, I ain't gotta knock," Sissy told her. "Why don't you open a window? You got the whole house smelling like Jamaica."

Rolling her eyes, Karen got off the bed and cracked the window, letting the morning breeze in.

"How are you, Ms. Sissy?" Persia asked.

"Better than most," Sissy said with the hint of an attitude. She never really cared for Persia. It wasn't anything Persia had done to her directly, but Sissy always felt like Michelle had stolen Face from her, which was totally untrue. Sissy was Face's jump off when the mood struck him, but Michelle was his main lady. "What you doing down in here in the slums?"

"Nothing, just came to check Karen," Persia said.

"All of y'all delinquent asses need to be in school," Sissy said.

"Is there anything else I can help you with?" Karen asked with an attitude.

"Yeah, give me a cigarette," Sissy demanded.

"I don't have none," Karen told her.

"Then go to the store and get some," Sissy shot back.

Karen sucked her teeth.

"Suck your teeth one more time and I'm gonna make you swallow them," Sissy warned. "And don't bring me no shorts either; you know I only smoke one hundreds."

"Come on, y'all, we gotta get some White Owls anyway," Karen told her friends, and led them out of the apartment.

"That bitch gets on my last nerves," Karen said once they were outside.

"Ms. Sissy is a trip." Meeka laughed. She always found the arguments between Karen and her mother hilarious.

"I wish she would trip down a flight of damn stairs," Karen said seriously.

"Karen, you shouldn't say that. She's still your mother," Persia said.

Karen rolled her eyes. "Miss me with that shit, Persia. That broad don't love me and I ain't too fond of her. We can't all be blessed to have Betty Crocker as mothers. Just forget about it. Let's go to the store." She stepped off the stoop.

As they were walking down the block, Karen's brother Charlie and someone who looked very familiar to Persia were coming up the block. She had to do a double take when she looked into those big brown eyes and shy smile. It had been years since she'd last seen him, but she'd know her childhood nemesis anywhere.

CHAPTER 7

"Princess P?" Li'l Monk had to blink to make sure his eyes weren't playing tricks on him.

"Li'l Monk? Oh my God." Persia leapt into his arms and hugged him around his thick neck. "Well, I don't know if I can call you li'l anything anymore." She looked him up and down. Li'l Monk had grown quite a bit since Persia had last seen him.

"What you doing on the block instead of in school?" Li'l Monk asked her.

"Nothing, just chilling with my girls." She motioned toward her friends.

Li'l Monk nodded at them in greeting. "Don't get caught up out here following trends."

"Please, I've got my own mind." Persia waved him off. "But forget all that, how have you been? I haven't seen you since . . ." Persia's words trailed off.

The last time he and Persia had seen each other was at his mother's funeral. A few years go

Charlene was gunned down when two men tried to rob her boutique. The police never caught the robbers, but word on the streets was that Li'l Monk's father, Monk, did. For what the men did to the love of his life he made them suffer in unspeakable ways before having Li'l Monk finish them off. Li'l Monk had always thought revenge on the men who killed his mother would make him feel better, but it only made things worse. It left a black mark on his soul that he now wore like dead weight.

"I'm sorry, Li'l Monk," Persia said.

"It's cool," Li'l Monk said as if it were nothing. In truth, he cried every morning over the loss of his mother. It was a wound that would never heal.

"How's my uncle, Big Monk?" Persia changed the subject.

"My dad is still around and doing the same shit he's always done, running the streets," Li'l Monk told her.

"Tell him I miss him and wanna see him. Maybe you guys can come to the house one of these days and have dinner?" Persia suggested.

Li'l Monk laughed. "You know good and well that for as long as your stepdaddy is living in that house, my dad ain't gonna cross that threshold."

"He's still on that?" Persia asked, surprised. Monk had never been able to come to grips with how Michelle was living in his best friend's house, with a new man, while Face was rotting in prison for protecting their family. For killing Tim he had been given twenty-five years to life. Michelle offered to wait, but Face knew it'd be selfish on his part to steal her youth like that, so he let her go. He had even given her his blessings when she told him she was thinking about dating again, but Monk never accepted it. He called Richard's presence disrespectful to his friend's legacy and the only reason he hadn't killed him yet was because Face made him give his word that he wouldn't.

"You know how my dad is about loyalty," Li'l Monk said.

"Well, if he won't come to the house, maybe we could all get together for dinner at a restaurant," Persia suggested.

A look crossed Monk's face. "We'll see, Persia."

"Damn, Li'l Monk the only person you see? Give a nigga some love." Charlie spread his arms for a hug.

"How you doing, Charlie?" Persia hugged him.

"Better now," Charlie said, letting his hand graze her ass.

Li'l Monk caught what Charlie did, and wasn't happy about it. "Damn, don't smother her."

"Don't hate on me, 'cause you a big, ugly nigga and I'm pretty," Charlie said jokingly, but Li'l Monk didn't find it funny.

"You got a slick mouth, Charlie, and that's why you're sporting that shiner now," Li'l Monk said with a chill to his voice.

"Fuck you, Li'l Monk!" Charlie spat.

"No, fuck that nigga who stole on you!" Li'l Monk fired back. He was ready to stomp Charlie out for trying to play tough in front of the girls, but he had to catch himself. He didn't want to come across as a goon in front of Persia.

"I see you're still walking around looking like Rocky," Karen said to Charlie.

"Fuck you, tramp!" Charlie spat back.

"Your daddy's a fucking tramp, nigga." He and Karen had the same mother, but different fathers, which explained why one was light and the other dark. The two of them always argued like they hated each other. "Instead of talking crazy to me, you need to talk crazy to Burger for him dotting your eye!"

"We're looking for Burger right now. We wanna have a chat with him," Li'l Monk said with a deadly edge to his voice.

At the mention of Burger's name, Persia thought about how he had tried to play her earlier and decided to play the devil's advocate. "I just saw him on the corner a few minutes ago."

Li'l Monk's face darkened and became a war mask. "Good looking out." He began marching to the corner where Burger and his boys were standing. Charlie shot Persia a dirty look before falling in line behind Li'l Monk.

Karen shook her head, watching her brother and Li'l Monk like she was seeing her loved ones off to war. "That was some cold-blooded shit, Persia." She walked off. Meeka followed her.

"What did I do?" Persia asked innocently, as if she didn't understand what she had just set in motion.

"Probably got that boy killed," Ty told her and followed the other two girls.

Persia stood there for a few seconds, looking in the direction that Li'l Monk and Charlie had gone in to confront Burger. She hoped that his fat ass got everything he was asking for and then some. Smiling devilishly she walked down the block to join her friends.

Persia was almost at the corner when she heard a car horn. When Persia turned and saw the heavily tinted red BMW coasting next to her, she immediately froze. Her heart beat rapidly in her chest and her breath got short like she was having a panic attack. Flashes of the broken memories she had of the day her father was taken away ran through her mind and she felt dizzy like she was on the verge of having a panic attack. Slowly the window rolled down and Persia heard, "Pardon me, love. Can I talk to you for a second?"

When she saw the handsome young man smiling at her from behind the wheel, and not a gun, she breathed a sigh of relief. Persia was always leery of cars where she couldn't see who was in them. The therapist had told her the reaction it caused in Persia was a result of the trauma from witnessing the murder of the man in the car as a child, and encouraged her to try to let it go. That was easy for the therapist to say, because she hadn't been there. She didn't see the blood oozing from the corpse onto the sidewalk at her feet. Her father hadn't been taken away in shackles while she screamed for him not to go.

"What's the matter, you ain't got no tongue?" the driver called to her.

Normally she wouldn't give a dude trying to kick it to her out the window the time of day, but she was so happy he wasn't a killer that she decided to spare him a minute. "Yeah, I got a tongue, but a real man doesn't try to get with a lady through the window of a moving car," Persia shot back.

The kid behind the wheel said something to the older man in the passenger seat, before throwing the car in park and getting out. Persia watched him as he stepped confidently onto the curb. He was definitely easy on the eyes, brown skinned, with soft lips. He was taller than she'd expected, close to six feet, and had a clean-shaven face. A baggy red Ralph Lauren sweater with a teddy bear embroidered on the front hung loosely on him. His blue jeans looked new, and were tucked neatly behind the tongue of his red Jordans.

Persia folded her arms and gave him a disinterested look. "What can I do for you?"

"You can start by telling me your name," he said.

"Persia," she told him.

He let the name roll around in his head. "It suits you." He nodded in approval. "I'm Chucky." He extended his hand.

When Persia shook his hand, something passed between him. She wasn't sure what it was, but it made the hairs on her arms stand up. "Nice to meet you, Chucky." She withdrew her hand.

"So, what's a flower like you doing out here among the weeds?" Chucky asked.

"Kicking it with my homegirls," she said.

"Well, if all of your homegirls are as fine as you, y'all might cause a riot by walking down the Avenue. Why don't you hop in the whip and I can take you wherever you wanna go?" Chucky offered.

"And what makes you think I hop into cars with strange men? You got the wrong one." Persia turned to walk away, but Chucky stopped her.

"My bad, sis. I didn't mean any disrespect. I just think it's a crying shame your feet should have to ever touch the gound."

Persia blushed. "Listen to you spitting game."

"Games are for kids and athletes, and I'm neither. I'm just a man who understands that to get what we want in life, we have to pursue it," Chucky said.

"So, are you pursing me?" she asked.

He chuckled. "Nah, it ain't that serious. I'm just trying to get to know you and if a casual friendship leads to something more, that's a bridge we'll cross when we come to it."

"So, I guess this is the part where you ask for my number?" Persia asked.

"No, it's the part where I give you my number, and hope you make your next move your best move." He handed her a white business card with his name and number on it.

Persia looked down at the card. It was the first time a man had ever given her a business card. "Okay, maybe I'll call you."

"Shorty, you and I both know you're going to use that number, the question is simply when."

"You're a presumptuous one, aren't you, Chucky?" Persia looked him up and down, smirking.

"Nah, just confident."

"Chucky, we got a situation. Let's bust a move," the older man who was sitting in the passenger seat called out the window.

"I gotta go, Persia, but I expect to hear from you sooner rather than later," Chucky told her before heading back to his car. Giving her a last-minute look, he threw the car into gear and peeled off down the block like he was on his way to a fire.

Persia watched Chucky's BMW bend the corner and shook her head. Chucky was definitely a different breed of dude than she was used to dealing with, but the fact that he was different was what had Persia so intrigued. He was cocky without being arrogant, and unmistakably Harlem, just like her dad had been. Persia wasn't sure whether she was going to call Chucky, but she slipped the number in her pocket just in case.

"Damn, we leave you alone for five minutes and your hot ass is out here trying to throw it at one of the biggest fish in the pond," Meeka said, walking up on Persia. Ty followed her, with Karen bringing up the rear, scowling.

"Ain't nobody trying to throw nothing. That's just some dude who was trying to kick game," Persia said as if it were nothing.

"Yeah, Chucky has got a lot of game," Karen said.

"You guys know him?" Persia asked.

"Everybody knows Chucky. He's a part of Pharaoh's crew, and Ramses's protégé. That pretty-ass nigga is piping some of everything out north of 110th Street," Meeka filled her in.

"Well, if he's slinging dick like that, I won't be calling him," Persia said. Her mother had always told her to beware of loose men.

"Shit, if you ain't gonna call him you can slide me the number. Chucky is getting long paper out here in these streets," Ty said.

"He's a drug dealer?" Persia asked.

"Nah, Chucky is what you call a hustler, because he gets money a few different ways," Meeka said.

"Wow, he seemed so nice and well-spoken. I would've never thought he was out there like that." Persia was surprised. She wasn't naïve enough to think that Chucky wasn't into something, being so young and driving an expensive car, but she didn't know he had rank.

"That's Chucky's gift, he's a wolf in sheep's clothing," Ty said.

"Well, that's one wolf that can bite me whenever he wants, wherever he wants," Meeka declared.

"Y'all out here riding dick like he's famous. Chucky ain't nobody, but another nigga getting money on the strip. Fuck that nigga, let's go back to my house so we can smoke." Karen stormed up the block, back toward her building.

"What the hell is her problem?" Persia couldn't understand why Karen was suddenly so sour.

"She'll get over it. Let's catch up with her before this thirsty bitch smokes all the weed without us." Meeka followed Karen.

"Did I do something wrong?" Persia asked Ty.

"It ain't got nothing to do with you, Persia. Karen and Chucky used to fuck around back in the days, but she was more into him that he was into her and it went sour," Ty whispered as if Karen would hear her from halfway up the block. "Look, just forget about it and let's go smoke." She walked off.

Persia and Ty caught up with the girls in front of Karen's building. Karen and Meeka had been talking about something, but they changed the subject when Persia and Ty joined them. Persia felt the tension and was about to address it when they heard a gunshot. Meeka, Karen, and Ty hit the floor, but Persia stood there like a deer frozen in headlights. A few seconds later, a rush of people came running down the block. Karen stopped one of the passing young men and asked him what had happened.

"Somebody got killed!" he told her and kept going.

"Damn, it stay jumping in the hood," Meeka said, brushing the dirt off the knees of her jeans.

"Let's go smoke in the house. The block is about to be hot." Karen took out her keys to unlock the lobby door.

"You think it was somebody we know who got hit?" Ty asked.

It wasn't until then that Karen thought about her brother Charlie and froze in her tracks.

CHAPTER 8

"You ready to handle your business, Charlie?" Li'l Monk asked him.

Charlie looked over at Burger and his friends, who were posted in front of the corner store. Standing among the other teens, Burger looked like a full-grown adult. "There are more of them than us, Li'l Monk. Maybe we should just wait until we catch him by himself," Charlie suggested.

Li'l Monk turned his dark eyes back to Charlie and rolled his broad shoulders. "Somebody gonna bleed today, Charlie. Is it gonna be you or him?"

Charlie weighed his options. Either way it went, he was going to end up getting his ass kicked, it was just a question of who would hurt him worse, Burger or Li'l Monk. "Fuck it." He started toward his enemy.

Burger spotted Charlie and stood to meet him. "What up, Charlie? Why ya lips all twisted like you been eating lemons?"

"I don't appreciate what you did to my eye, Burger," Charlie told him.

Burger looked at Charlie's black eye like he had just noticed it. "Oh, did I do that when I socked you? I'll tell you what." He pulled a few crumpled bills from his pocket and extended one to Charlie. "Take this and buy yourself a steak to put on it." He laughed as if he just told the funniest joke in the world.

Charlie looked back at Li'l Monk, who was watching him like a hawk and shaking his head in disappointment. A small crowd had started to gather, anticipating violence. If he went out like a sucker, the blabbermouths in the neighborhood would surely put his business in the streets and what little reputation he did have in the hood would be shot. With nothing else to lose, Charlie decided to put his balls on the table, and swung at Burger with everything he had.

Burger looked as if he had just been slapped by a woman, instead of punched by a young man. He smiled before giving Charlie a vicious blow to the gut that sent him spilling to the ground. Within a heartbeat, Burger and his boys swarmed on Charlie.

Li'l Monk moved as silently and as swift as the wind when he struck. The first of the boys, who was with Burger, didn't see it coming, but he felt his jaw shatter when Li'l Monk's massive fist connected with his chin. He went down in a heap and Li'l Monk moved to the next target. The second kid managed to put up a weak defense, but Li'l Monk's heavy fist broke through it and connected with his forehead. His body wobbled once before falling on the ground next to his friend. When Li'l Monk turned to the third kid, he threw his hands up in surrender and ran. This left Li'l Monk and Burger.

The two young men stalked each other, snarling like two pit bulls, in their strange war ritual. Burger was a tough guy, but so was Li'l Monk, and there wasn't enough room on the hill for both of them. Burger lost his patience first and lunged at Li'l Monk. Li'l Monk twisted to one side, avoiding Burger's flailing fists, and kneeing him in the stomach. Instead of going down, as Li'l Monk had predicted, Burger grabbed his leg and started trying to lift him off his feet. Li'l Monk was strong, but so was Burger. He knew if he let Burger get him off the ground, the fight would be over. Li'l Monk drew his fists back and started firing them into Burger's exposed face like jackhammers. Burger ate the first few punches, but eventually he ended up down on one knee and at Li'l Monk's mercy.

By now a crowd had formed, watching the two combatants go at it. More than a few of them cheered for Li'l Monk to kick Burger's ass, as they had been victims of his bullying. Li'l Monk rained blow after blow on Burger's face, long after he had stopped fighting.

"Stop it; you're going to kill him!" someone yelled, but Li'l Monk was too far gone in his rage to hear them or care.

Li'l Monk dragged Burger roughly to his feet and wrapped his massive hand around Burger's neck. "I want my face to be the last thing you see before you leave this world."

Li'l Monk would've surely killed Burger right there in front of all those witnesses and spent the rest of his days in prison, had it not been for someone firing a gun directly behind him.

"First one was in the air, but the next one is all yours," Chucky told Li'l Monk, pointing a smoking gun at him.

He raised his hands in surrender and slowly backed away from Burger's unconscious body. "You got it."

"Chucky, put that away before you get us locked up." Ramses tapped him on the shoulder as he stepped onto the curb. Ramses was the older dude who had been sitting in the passenger seat of Chucky's BMW. He was in his mid to late thirties with premature grey hairs that peppered the top of his neat fade. Decorating his ears, wrists, and fingers were diamonds of all colors. Around his neck he wore a chain that was as thick as a garden hose with a medallion on it that was easily the size of a dinner plate, and flooded with diamonds. Ramses had a thing for jewelry. Wearing all that shine was excessive and foolish in the poor neighborhood, but Ramses never worried about being robbed. Only a fool would try to take something from anyone connected to Pharaoh. "Fuck is going on out here?" he asked Burger, who was just getting back to his feet. His face was bruised, and the left side of his jaw had swollen to twice the size of his right. "What a fucking embarrassment you are."

"That dude snuck me, Ramses!" Burger said through his split and bloody lips.

"You lying muthafucka." Li'l Monk stalked toward him, but a look from Ramses froze him.

"Burger, I don't wanna hear nothing else that you've got to say out of your bloody-ass mouth. You're supposed to be out here getting money and instead you're getting clowned." Ramses scolded him like a child. "First you get robbed and then you get beat up. And where the fuck is

Benny? He's supposed be out here maintaining order."

"I haven't seen him since earlier. He slid off with some bitch," Burger told him.

Ramses shook his head. "He's supposed to be minding my ice cream shop, but he's off in some pussy? It's no wonder muthafuckas think they can take my shit and beat up my workers. I want to know where the fuck Benny is, ASAP!"

"I'm on it." Chucky whipped out his cell phone. He called Benny's phone three times, but it kept going to voice mail. Chucky shrugged, letting Ramses know that he couldn't reach him.

"That nigga better either be dead or in jail, because I promise you if he's not he's going to wish that he was," Ramses said. "And you," he addressed Li'l Monk. "Do you know who the fuck I am?"

Li'l Monk nodded. He was still angry and didn't trust his mouth enough to speak.

"If you know who I am then you know the penalty for fucking with a member of my team. Either you're a dumb little shit or you just don't respect my authority, which is it?"

Li'l Monk knew that his next words could mean the difference between life and death, so he chose them very wisely before he spoke. "I respect you, Ramses, because I know you're a real nigga, but I can't respect no bully." He cast a glance at Burger. "Burger whipped my li'l man out, because he knew he wouldn't fight back, so I whipped Burger out. I got no patience for cowards." He spat on the ground for emphasis.

Ramses measured his response. "I can't say you're the smartest young dude I've ever come across, but you're honest and loyal. Those are two qualities that are hard to come by in this game. You get to keep your life, shorty."

"Fuck all that, this nigga stole on me and I gotta get mine back. Let me get your pistol, Chucky!" Burger demanded.

Ramses whirled on Burger and slapped him so hard that he spun around twice before collapsing against a parked car. "I've had just about enough of that fake tough shit coming out of your mouth. You talking like you didn't just get put on your back in front of the whole hood. Y'all are supposed to be out here representing the crew, but instead you're looking like a bunch of pussies. I don't need bitches on my team, I need soldiers!" He turned back to Li'l Monk. "What about you? Are you a bitch too or are you a soldier?"

The question caught Li'l Monk off-guard, so he answered without thinking. "Neither one. I'm a gladiator."

Ramses laughed. "From the beating you put on my boys, I'd say so. So what's up, you want a job, gladiator?"

"Doing what?" Li'l Monk asked suspiciously.

"Making sure that the kind of shit that happened today doesn't happen again," Ramses told him. "You're a tough little bastard, and I might have a use for you. To start out I'll give you one hundred dollars per night to hold my young boys down and make sure nobody else comes through here handing out random ass whippings. You think you can do that?"

"Yeah, I can do that," Li'l Monk told him.

"You better hope so, because from here on out, you're gonna be the first line of defense on this strip. Keep my money straight and my people's safe. If not you're gonna have to answer to me. You fuck up and you're fired, and I ain't talking about retirement." He made his fingers into the shape of a gun, so that Li'l Monk understood his meaning. Ramses pulled a large roll of money from his pocket and peeled off five twenties, which he handed to Li'l Monk. "Consider this an advance against your first bit of bread."

"Thanks," Li'l Monk said, trying not to sound too excited over the money. In all truthfulness, he was so hungry that he felt if he didn't eat soon he'd likely pass out.

"There's plenty more where that came from, shorty." Ramses gave him dap. "By the way, what's your name?"

"They call me Li'l Monk."

Ramses looked over at Chucky whose face was now twisted and angry. He was about to open his mouth and say something, but Ramses motioned for him to be silent. "You Monk's kid?"

Li'l Monk lowered his head in shame. "Yeah."

"No need to be ashamed, kid. Your pops was a real piece of work back in the days," Ramses told him.

"Now he's just washed up," Chucky said cruelly. He made it no secret that he didn't care for Li'l Monk's father.

Li'l Monk's eyes flashed rage and for a minute he thought about trying Chucky, but he wasn't stupid enough to bring his bare hands to a gun fight. Monk had done a lot of foul things to people over the years and there could've been any number of reasons that Chucky didn't like Monk, but Li'l Monk still wasn't comfortable with anyone disrespecting his father in front of him.

"Pay Chucky no mind," Ramses said, picking up on Li'l Monk's anger. "Old grudges got no place with new money and that's what we're about to get, some new money. If you're anything like your old man used to be, I'm sure you'll fit right in. Just make sure you're on time for your shift tonight."

"Okay, I'll see you later," Li'l Monk told him.

"No, you won't. This is likely the last conversation we'll ever have until I'm sure of how you're built. Benny should have reappeared by tonight and you'll report directly to him," Ramses told him, walking back toward the car.

About then Persia, Karen, Meeka, and Ty arrived on the scene. After what the kid said about someone getting killed, they put two and two together and expected the worst when they arrived on the corner. Thankfully, the boy's words were untrue and nobody had died.

Persia saw Li'l Monk exchange a few last minute words with the man who had been riding with Chucky, before they both climbed back into the BMW and left. She wondered what they had been talking about, but didn't want to come across as nosey by asking.

Charlie was leaning against a car, bruised, dirty, and looking like he just taken a serious ass whipping. When he saw his sister and her friends coming, he tried to straighten himself up. His signature cocky smile was plastered across his lips, but his face looked like he was having trouble controlling his bowels.

"We heard somebody got killed and thought it was one of y'all," Ty said.

"You know real niggas don't die," Charlie boasted, but his body language said different. His hands shook violently as he tried to light the cigarette pinched between his lips. Normally Karen would've given him grief about it, but she didn't say a word. She simply lit his cigarette for him. Their family wasn't big on showing each other affection, so that was her way of letting him know that she was happy that he was alive.

Li'l Monk ambled up, looking like he had been through the wringer. His shirt was filthy, and his knuckles bloody and beginning to swell. Now that his adrenaline had worn off from the fight, he began to feel the aches and pains from the brawl.

"What the hell happened?" Meeka asked the question everyone wanted to know the answer to. All eyes turned to Li'l Monk, wanting an accurate recounting of the story.

Li'l Monk looked from the bills in his hand to the girls and smiled. "I just got my first job. Let's get a bottle and celebrate. It's on me."

CHAPTER 9

"How many times do I have to tell you about being so quick to pull that burner in public?" Ramses asked Chucky once they were away from the block.

"You're lucky I didn't blow that little mutha-fucka's head off," Chucky spat.

"For as tough as that little dude seems, he might've eaten the bullet," Ramses joked. "I see a lot of his old man in him."

"That's even more of a reason why you should've let me blast him! His daddy ain't shit and he's gonna grow up to be less than shit," Chucky spat. "I think you giving that kid a job is a mistake that's gonna come back to bite you on the ass."

"Then it's a good thing I'm not paying you to think," Ramses replied. "In your mind, Li'l Monk is guilty by association, so you aren't seeing the bigger picture. Real niggas are becoming an en-dangered species in this game, so when you find them that young with that much heart, you don't turn them away, you put them on the payroll. With the proper guidance, in five years that kid is going to be a fucking animal on these streets."

"Whatever, man. I still say it's a bad idea to do business with that sneaky little nigga. For all we know it could've been him and those creeps he runs with who have been hitting our spots," Chucky said.

"I seriously doubt that. I know he's got sticky fingers, because I've seen him out here up to no good, but that's mostly preying on delivery men and tourists who make the mistake of getting lost on the wrong side of town. He's a petty thief, and it wasn't no petty thief who's been running in our spots and taking our shit. They had balls and a helping hand."

Ramses's last remark made Chucky tense. "Nah, man. All of our guys are solid. I think it's just some dudes who got lucky."

"If it had happened once, I'd go with luck, but happening three times in a week? That's a little more than luck. Seems like they know which spots to hit and when to hit them. There's some funny shit going on. Speaking of funny shit, you got any idea what rock Benny is hiding under?"

Chucky shrugged. "Your guess is as good as mine. I do remember him telling me about a new chick he met, so he's probably breaking her in," he lied.

"While we're on the subject of new chicks, what's up with you and that little girl you've been hounding after?" Ramses asked.

"Shit, that's what I'm trying to find out. I'm digging that little fine bitch," Chucky told him.

"Yeah, she's fine as hell, but she's also a problem waiting to happen. She's a baby. That girl can't be no more than sixteen or seventeen," Ramses said.

"Age ain't nothing but a number," Chucky sang.

"Chucky, let me give you some advice. This ain't some young hood rat whose parents aren't paying enough attention to know their kid is fucking a grown man. The law is gonna be on you like white on rice. Stop being so reckless and use your head," Ramses told him.

"A'ight, man," Chucky reluctantly agreed. Ramses was stressing that Persia's age was the reason he didn't want Chucky seeing her, but Chucky wasn't a fool. Ramses had a short memory, but Chucky did not. Regardless of what Ramses said, Chucky planned to go forward with his plans with Persia. Chucky reached in the ashtray and pulled out a half-smoked blunt. No sooner than he placed it between his lips and went to light it, Ramses plucked it out of his mouth. "What the fuck?"

"Didn't I just tell you about being reckless?" Ramses snapped. He rolled down the window and tossed it out.

"That was hydro!" Chucky complained.

"Foolish young nigga, that was time! What do you think would happen if the police pull us over for some stupid shit like weed and find these guns in the car? I ain't never been to jail a day in my life and don't plan on going, especially because of some simple-minded nigga with a petty drug habit."

"You got it, Ramses," Chucky conceded. For the rest of the ride to Ramses's destination, Chucky didn't say anything. He just sat and stewed, waiting for Ramses to get his ass out of the car.

"Don't forget to be on point when the young boy's shift starts in case Benny isn't back," Ramses told him as he was getting out.

"I got you."

"And remember what I said about being reckless. You hear me?"

"Yeah, I hear you, Ramses," Chucky said, letting it go in one ear and come out the other. Chucky couldn't wait for Ramses to leave so he could peel off. He waited until he got a few blocks away and retrieved another rolled-up blunt. He had been holding that particular blunt until he was alone, so he could savor it.

Chucky drove slow, smoking and bobbing to the music in his head. He'd only taken a few pulls and was already halfway to fried. Ahead the light had just turned yellow, so Chucky stepped on the gas, hoping to catch it, but ended up floating right through a red light. Immediately after, he saw the flashing blue and red lights of the police car behind him.

"You fucking jinx," Chucky cursed, thinking of his conversation with Ramses. He scrambled to roll all the windows down and try to air the car out. As he was pulling over, he quickly put the blunt out in the ashtray then tossed it in his mouth and ate it. It damn near choked him going down, but it beat the alternative. By the time the cop reached the driver's side window, he already had his license and registration in his hand. When looked up to give the officer his information, all the color drained from Chucky's face. Of all the people he wanted to see, he wasn't one of them.

"What's up, Chucky?" Narcotics Detective Wolf James greeted him with a gold-grilled smile. "You ain't been returning my phone calls."

CHAPTER 10

It was past ten o'clock at night when Persia finally made it home, much later than she usually got in from school. Normally she would've called if she was going to be that late, but they had been having so much fun that time had gotten away from her. Li'l Monk bought a big bottle of E&J Brandy and two dime bags of chocolate from the dread. The girls descended on the free weed and liquor like vultures. Li'l Monk had barely gotten more than one cup from the bottle he'd bought, but he didn't seem to mind. He was enjoying himself just watching everybody else have a good time on his dime.

Persia had never been a big drinker, but it seemed like every time she turned around someone was refilling her cup. When she'd tried to quit, the girls teased her by calling her a lightweight, so Persia drank more. By the time she headed back to the train station, she could barely walk a straight line. She'd even nodded off on the train and missed her stop, which also contributed to her lateness.

Sticking her key in the door, Persia prayed to the teenage-mischief gods that her parents would be asleep. As quietly as she could, she eased the door open and slipped inside the house. The living room was dark and quiet, which she took as a good sign. Moving as quietly as a cat burglar, Persia began creeping up the carpeted stairs to her bedroom. She had almost made it to the top when she heard her mother's voice.

"Persia Chandler, you bring your tail down here this instant!"

Sighing heavily Persia went back downstairs to face the music. She found her mother and Richard in the kitchen, both wide awake. Her mother sat at the kitchen island, scowling at her, while Richard was at the breakfast table on his laptop. He spared her a glance and a disappointed look, before going back to whatever he was doing.

"Hey, y'all." Persia finger waved.

"You're just bringing your ass in the house and that's all you've got to say?" Michelle asked.

"Sorry, I guess. The time got away from me," Persia said in a measured tone. She was concentrating on keeping her words from slurring.

"That's obvious, considering you got out of school hours ago. Where were you?" Michelle asked.

"Just out with some friends," Persia said.

"Which friends? I called Sarah's and Marty's houses and neither of them has seen you today," Michelle informed her.

Persia was normally quick on her feet when it came to lying, but the liquor and weed had her brain moving slow so she told the truth. "Karen and them."

Michelle shook her head. "Now how did I know that?" she asked sarcastically. "Persia, I don't I know why you're so fascinated with these street girls."

"They're not street girls they're my friends," Persia defended them.

"Yes, your friends who are always up to no good," Michelle countered. "Now where were you girls that kept you out until this hour on a school night?"

Persia didn't answer.

"Persia, if I have to repeat myself we're going to have a problem," Michelle warned her.

"Okay, okay, we were in Harlem," Persia admitted.

Michelle was on her feet and standing in front of Persia so swiftly that it even surprised

Richard. "What did I tell you about staying out of Harlem?"

"Mom, I wasn't standing around on the corner, I was at Karen's house the whole time," Persia lied.

"I don't give a damn whose house you were at, I told you to stay your hardheaded ass out of Harlem! Do you know what kind of shit goes on up there? It's dangerous!"

"You're acting as if I don't know how to handle myself. I know how to avoid trouble," Persia said. She had lived a very sheltered life, but her mother and father made sure that she had street smarts from an early age.

"Persia, what you're not getting is that sometimes trouble comes to find you and that's what I'm trying to avoid," Michelle explained.

"I'm a big girl, Mom," Persia insisted.

"A big girl who is walking around viewing the world through rose-colored glasses. The ghetto is full of predators whose favorite delicacies are naïve young girls. I know that Karen and the others are your friends, but you're moving at two different speeds. Those girls are fast and loose, and I raised you better than that. The last thing you need is to get wrapped up in their foolishness and end up somebody's baby mama or the showpiece of a drug dealer."

"You mean like you were?" Persia asked coldly. She wasn't sure what had made her say it, but it was too late to take it back.

Michelle took a step back. "Excuse you?"

"Mom, I don't know why everyone walks on eggshells around me like I don't know who my father was and where we come from," Persia said heatedly. It was like the more she talked the angrier the liquor was making her.

"Okay, how about we all just calm down for a second," Richard interjected. He saw the direction the argument was going in and it wasn't going to be pretty.

"No, I don't need to calm down. It's about time we had some truth in this house of lies," Persia continued.

Michelle closed her eyes and took deep breaths to calm herself. "Persia, I can tell you've been drinking, because I can smell it on you, so I'm going to act like we didn't have this conversation. If I were you, I'd go to my room and sleep it off."

The alcohol had her feeling bold, so Persia kept going. "I'm not drunk, Mom, I'm buzzed, so I can't blame it on the alcohol. You just wanna shut me up because I struck a nerve. That's the problem with this family now; everybody would rather sweep things under the rug instead of addressing them. I'm not some silly kid who still thinks Daddy worked construction; he was a drug dealer and a killer."

"Persia, you need to watch your mouth. You don't know the whole story, so you can't speak on it," Michelle said. She felt her anger rising.

Persia folded her arms and looked her mother up and down defiantly. "No, I might not know the whole story, but I know the gist of it, Mother. You thumb your nose at street people like we're better than them, but it was a street nigga and street money that bought this house you and your new husband live so comfortably in!"

What happened next was hazy for Persia. She just remembered waking up on the floor near the refrigerator, watching Richard restraining her mother.

"Calm down, sweetie," Richard was telling Michelle, while doing his best to keep her from jumping on Persia.

"How dare she speak to me like that?" Michelle raged.

"I can't believe you hit me," Persia said, picking herself up off the floor. It was the first time she could ever remember her mother raising her hand to her.

Michelle had tears in her eyes when she spoke. "You're lucky I didn't kill you! Little girl, you have no idea the sacrifices your father and I made to ensure you didn't end up some fucking gutter trash, not knowing where your next meal was coming from. You think your father is sitting in prison now because he wants to be? Everything Face ever did on them streets was so that we could live a cut above the rest of these muthafuckas you're so damn loyal to! The next time you try to read me, you better damn sure have your facts straight."

With tears in her eyes, Persia ran from the kitchen and upstairs to her bedroom. She slammed the door behind her with so much force, the picture of her and her mother at her sixth-grade graduation fell off her nightstand. She picked the small frame up and saw that the glass was cracked down the middle, between them. It was broken, just like Persia felt like their relationship was.

Persia threw herself across the bed, still fully dressed, and buried her face in the pillow. She normally would've jumped in the shower before bed, but that night she didn't have the energy. Persia felt spent after the argument with Michelle. The things she had said to her mother in the kitchen were things she was already feeling and always wanted to address at some point, but the liquor made her delivery cruel and ill-timed.

The argument made Persia think of her father and how much she missed him. She had been very young when he first went away, but she remembered him vividly. When Face was on the streets she spent more time with him than her mother. Even in prison he remained a fixture in her life. Persia had visited him a few times, but after the first few years Face had put a stop to the visits. Persia was getting older and at an age where kids were like sponges. Prison visits weren't something he wanted ingrained in his baby girl's character. Still, they kept their bond strong through pictures and nightly phone calls, but Persia still sometimes felt the emptiness of him not being there. She vowed that on her eighteenth birthday, when she would finally be old enough to make the trip on her own, she would go visit her father. He was the one man who had always made her smile.

Persia began taking her clothes off and preparing for bed. As she was pulling her legs out of her pants, the business card with the phone number on it fell out. She picked it up and thought back to her adventure in Harlem that day, and the handsome young man with the pretty car. Initially she hadn't planned on calling him because her conscience started eating at her and she felt like she'd be stepping on Karen's toes, but she was half drunk and feeling rebellious. She was too stressed to sleep, so she grabbed her bedroom phone from the nightstand and dialed the number.

As the phone rang, Persia started getting nervous and thought about hanging up. How would it look on her, calling a strange man at that hour of the night with nothing to talk about? Before she could come to her senses and hang up the phone, his voice came on the line.

CHAPTER 11

After a few hours of smoking and drinking with Karen and her crew, Li'l Monk barely had time to grab something to eat and change his clothes before his first night on the job started. He should've gone home and taken a nap, especially since he was going to be out all night, but spending time with Persia made the fatigue he was feeling worth it.

Of all the people Li'l Monk expected to bump into, Persia Chandler wasn't one of them. According to Charlie, Persia crept through that way every so often, but they'd never bumped heads because Li'l Monk spent so much time incarcerated. It was a shame that at eighteen, Li'l Monk had spent nearly as much time in juvenile facilities as he did in school. They had labeled Li'l Monk a bad seed, but it wasn't that. He was just a kid who had made some poor decisions in the name of survival.

Adjusting the black hoodie that he had changed into, Li'l Monk stepped out into the night air. The temperature had dropped and the breeze picked up, but it felt good on his face. It helped to clear his head. He made hurried steps down the street, wanting to be early for his first night of work. As he passed the shadowy doorway of a building, he felt the hairs on the back of his neck stand up. Reflexively, Li'l Monk threw up his defenses, peering into to the darkness.

"That's my boy, always on point," a voice said from the shadows. From the recesses of the doorway stepped a man wearing a black army jacket and black sweatshirt beneath. His bearded face was ashy and his cheeks looked a bit drawn, but he still had the most intimidating scowl Li'l Monk had ever seen on a man. Dark eyes seemed to look everywhere at once, constantly scanning the faces of everyone who passed. For a man like him, his list of enemies was a long one and death could come at any time.

"What you doing out here, Dad?" Li'l Monk greeted his father. He was hoping to avoid him for the rest of the day.

Monk opened his jacket and showed his son the sawed-off shotgun under his arm. "Hunting. Where're you going, dressed like you're about to pull a lick?" Monk asked.

"Just down the block," Li'l Monk told him.

Monk looked at him suspiciously. "Down the block for what?"

"Nothing," Li'l Monk lied.

Without warning, Monk punched Li'l Monk in the chest. "What I tell you about lying to me, boy? You should know by now that I don't ask questions unless I already know the answer to them. You think I didn't hear that you're down with Ramses and them now?"

"I ain't down with nobody. Ramses is paying me to make sure nobody comes and fucks with his boys while they're hustling. I don't sell drugs for him," Li'l Monk told him, while rubbing his chest. His father had lost weight, but his punches still felt like being hit with bricks.

"Always starts out like that, a little at a time until you're sitting at the table and they won't let you get up," Monk told his son, reflecting on how he had graduated from one extreme to the other.

"It ain't that serious for me, Dad. Ramses is just putting a few dollars in my pocket, that's all," Li'l Monk told him.

"More like putting a yoke around your neck. Ramses, Pharoah . . . them niggas are vampires. They'll bleed your soul from you and put you on the dark road with your old man. Like father like son, huh?" Monk snickered.

"Not in this lifetime," Li'l Monk told him.

"That's what they all say. Son, money is sweeter than the hole of any bitch you'll ever lie with. Once you get a little taste of it, you're gonna be turned out and willing to do anything and everything to get more of it." Monk smiled, thinking of better days.

"Kinda like you out here chasing that shit?" Li'l Monk asked. At one time his father had been a man of respect on the streets Li'l Monk could be proud of, but after Charlene died Monk let the drugs take control and it was all downhill from there.

The smile faded from Monk's face and the scowl was back. "You trying to get cute with me, li'l nigga? I don't care how big you've grown, I'll still fuck you up. You're a tough nut because I raised you that way. I taught you how to survive on these streets, and it's my blood coursing through your veins and pumping into that steel heart in your chest. I can smoke a million rocks and niggas out here will still respect my gangsta. Wanna know why? Because they know I don't give a fuck about life or death, mine or theirs. I do what the fuck I do, but I ain't out here sucking no dick or begging for a hit. I take mine like a real goon, not some li'l snot-nosed-ass kid playing bodyguard to some pussies who can't hold their own weight."

"You got it, Dad," Li'l Monk conceded. Getting into a fight with his father would only make him late. "Can I go now?"

"Yeah, run yo' ass along to punch the clock, and make sure you bring some food in the house whenever you come in," Monk dismissed him.

"A'ight." Li'l Monk turned to leave, but Monk stopped him.

"What you packing?" Monk asked.

"I ain't packing nothing," Li'l Monk said.

Monk shook his head sadly. "Boy, how the hell are you supposed to defend your territory if niggas run up and you ain't got no heat?"

Needing a gun wasn't something Li'l Monk had taken into consideration when he had accepted the position. He hoped that he could borrow one from Chucky or one of the guys until he was able to save up enough money to buy his own.

Monk looked around to make sure no one was watching before reaching into his jacket and producing a long Desert Eagle. "Take this." He handed the gun to Li'l Monk. "The safety doesn't work, so you don't have to worry about taking it off if you gotta put a nigga's head to bed."

"Thanks, Dad," Li'l Monk said, tucking the gun in his pants, and covering the handle with his hoodie.

"You really wanna thank me then make this worker position you got a temporary one. I can't say I agree with what you're doing, but I can condemn you for it either because I ain't never showed you no better. All I can do is tell you that if you're gonna play, play all the way. Get your money, but never forget that the men in this family don't take other niggas' packages, we hand them out. We're born to be bosses," Monk told him and left.

Long after Monk had vanished around the corner, Li'l Monk could still hear his words in his ears. *We're born to be bosses.* And with that thought etched into his mind, he went off to start his shift.

Li'l Monk arrived fifteen minutes early and found Chucky on the block already waiting for him. He was leaning against the car talking to some kid who Li'l Monk had never seen before. He was light skinned, slim, and looked to be about the same age as Li'l Monk. His hair was dusty brown, and twisted up into locks that hung to his shoulders. Chucky and the kid were engrossed in a deep conversation, but when they saw Li'l Monk it abruptly stopped.

"You're late," Chucky said with an attitude.

"Nah, I'm actually here early. Ramses said—"

"Whatever, man. Let me introduce you to the kid you'll be working with." Chucky waved the kid with the dreads over to join in the conversation. "Li'l Monk, this is Omega." He made the introductions. "Omega will be running the show tonight, but I'll be around if y'all run into something he can't handle."

"What happened to Benny?" Li'l Monk asked curiously.

"Your job is to watch Omega's back, not ask questions," Chucky said sharply. He was having a rough day and didn't feel like answering a bunch of questions. All he wanted to do was go somewhere, smoke, and figure out his next move.

"Don't worry about it, Chucky. Me and Li'l Monk will be able to handle things just fine," Omega cut in. He gave Li'l Monk a wink, letting him know he had his back. Li'l Monk had only known Omega for a few minutes and he already liked him.

"A'ight." Chucky gave Omega dap, but ignored Li'l Monk. "I'll see y'all in the morning, but if anything jumps call my cell." And with that he left them to it, and disappeared into the building across the street.

"Fuck is that nigga's problem?" Li'l Monk asked Omega, once Chucky was out of earshot.

"Chucky is cool as hell usually. He's just stressed out because nobody can find Benny," Omega said.

"I heard; everybody has been talking about it. You think he's okay?" Li'l Monk asked.

Omega shrugged. "I hope so, but when you play like we play, nothing is a given. That goes double when you're down with Pharaoh."

"I keep hearing about this Pharaoh cat, but I've never seen him. You met him yet?" Li'l Monk asked.

"Nobody meets Pharaoh except Ramses and a select few from his inner circle. I don't even think Chucky has ever met him, and he's been hustling for Ramses for years. They say that he stays tucked away in a big house somewhere with all kinds of trained assassins guarding it and rarely leaves." Omega told Li'l Monk what he'd heard.

"So these niggas just follow him blindly? How does he control the streets if he's never in them?" Li'l Monk asked.

"Through Ramses. He's Pharaoh's eyes, ears, and executioner," Omega said like he was recounting a ghost story.

"I heard Ramses is gangsta with it."

Omega laughed. "Gangsta doesn't even begin to describe a nigga like Ramses. I've seen Ramses do shit to people that made me wanna get off the streets and get a job. That's the most black-hearted nigga I ever met, and you better watch yourself when dealing with him."

"I will," Li'l Monk told him.

"Smart man. Listen, I'll make sure that you know who is who and what's what before the night is over. For right now, let's make a quick circuit of the workers to make sure everybody has got what they need so we can get on this paper."

Li'l Monk accompanied Omega, hitting every corner of the square block they commanded, making sure the pitchers had work, and the money men turned in drug money they were holding on to. Omega wasn't even from the hood, but the people they encountered on the block showed him love. Li'l Monk and Omega were probably about the same age, but hardly in the same weight class.

"Born to be bosses," Li'l Monk said to himself, thinking back on what his father had told him.

"What'd you say?" Omega asked.

"Nothing, just thinking out loud."

***

Chucky used his spare key to get into the apartment. He had a special set of keys that allowed him access to all the stash houses, but only he and the tenant, Yvette, had access to that one. Not even Ramses could enter uninvited.

He found Yvette sitting on the couch in front of the television, holding a cigarette lazily between her fingers. The ash at the tip of it was long overdue to be flicked, but it held fast when she put the cancer stick between her lips and took another pull. The New York Jets jersey she wore did little to hide the fact that she didn't have any panties on beneath it. She turned her dreamy eyes toward Chucky and gave him a goofy smile.

"Looks like you're dancing on a cloud, baby," Chucky said.

"Until a little while ago I was caught up in a beautiful dream, but that dream is starting to fade, and I ain't trying to wake up just yet," she told him. Yvette was what you would call a chippie. She dabbled in cocaine, but it hadn't officially taken over her life yet. The cocaine had made her look slightly older than her thirty-one years, but she still had a nice body and all her teeth. You wouldn't know Yvette fucked around unless someone told you.

"You always cut straight to the chase, and that's what I love about you, Yvette," Chucky said. He dug in his pocket and pulled out a small sandwich bag that had a few grams of cocaine in it, and tossed it on the coffee table.

Yvette eyed the bag and smacked her lips. "Damn, it's that kind of night?"

"I'm still trying to figure it out. For right now, I'm just looking for a quiet place to get my thoughts in order," Chucky told her.

"Do you need me to leave?" she asked.

"Nah, you good." Chucky sat in the recliner across from her. Worry lines were etched all across his face.

"Looks like you've got the weight of the world on your shoulders," Yvette said.

"Sometimes it feels like it," Chucky admitted.

Chucky didn't need her to elaborate to know what she meant. He reached in his pocket and tossed two loose bags of cocaine on the table.

Yvette scooped the bag of coke, a small wooden box from its hiding place under the table, and sat on the floor between Chucky's legs. From the box, she produced a cigar, weed, a mirror, and a stained razor. He watched her as she dumped some of the powder out and began chopping it into fine lines. In a deft motion, she used the same razor to slit the cigar open and dumped the guts into a paper bag. Skillfully, she broke the weed up in the cigar and scooped one of the lines of cocaine up, spreading it over the weed before twisting the blunt closed and sealing it with her spit. What she had just created was known as a Woo or Woola in the hood: weed laced with crack or cocaine. You could hear the crackle of burning cocaine when she lit the blunt and took a deep pull, which she held for several seconds before exhaling.

"Damn, that's some good shit," Yvette mumbled through clenched teeth. The numbness from the coke had spread through her mouth and was affecting her speech. "You want a taste?" She extended the laced blunt to Chucky.

"Not right now, ma," Chucky declined. For as much as he could've used a blast, he was already on edge and it would've only made him more paranoid. Chucky had two huge problems: his missing friend and a greedy cop. Technically the problems were connected, since it was the pressure from Detective Wolf that had put the idea in Chucky's head to try to do the impossible in the name of a dollar.

Chucky was making good money under Ramses, but he was also making side deals. He had a select clientele who could call him direct if they wanted weight, one of whom was a dude from Brooklyn named Wolf. It was never more than a few ounces at a time, but by the time he found out that Wolf was a cop, he had sold him enough cocaine over a period of time to amount to a lot of years in prison. Chucky already had two strikes, so he did what he had to do and rolled. He never told on anyone in his crew, but he'd given up a few random cats he'd met in his travels who the world wouldn't miss. Chucky had done his service, but Wolf wanted more. Chucky had only signed on to trade a bit of information to make the drug charge go away, but Wolf was trying to make him a confidential informant. It was bad enough that Chucky was breaking the code, but making a career out of it was out of the question. Chucky was tired of playing deputy and he needed a way to get Wolf off his back, so he played on his larcenous side. Wolf was a cop, but he was also a gambler and Chucky had heard through the grapevine that he had some serious debts. Chucky offered Wolf $100,000 to get out of his life. Just as he'd hoped, Wolf agreed to take a pay off but he wanted a quarter of million dollars. That was the price for Chucky to purchase his life back.

There was no way that Chucky would be able to come up with that kind of money, but he agreed to it anyway in order to buy himself some time. He had been ducking Wolf for nearly a month before that day he got pulled over. Wolf let him known in no uncertain terms that if he didn't come up with the money sooner rather than later, not only was he going to hang the original cocaine charges on him, but he would make sure word got back to Pharaoh about his extracurricular activities. Chucky was a man on borrowed time.

Then there was Benny and his unexpected disappearing act, which was complicating Chucky's plan to get the money up for Wolf, and his life. Not only was Benny gone without a trace, he vanished with a good chunk of money that belonged to Chucky. It was part of what they had been stacking in the pot, and Chucky needed it now more than ever. It was a prime example of a well-laid plan being shot to shit.

The drug spots getting robbed had ruffled some feathers, but nothing too major. Stash houses got robbed all the time in the hood. Ramses had trusted that Chucky and the street crews would get to the bottom of it, but Benny disappearing around the time Pharaoh got hit for a big shipment sent up a red flag. Things weren't adding up and people were growing suspicious. He knew what was coming next: Pharaoh was going to start cleaning house and bodies were gonna drop. Chucky had to find Benny before Ramses did or run the risk of somebody making him disappear too. Knowing how close Benny and Chucky were, he knew he was on the short list and there would be nothing Ramses or anyone else could do to save him once Pharaoh handed down the decree. He needed to find Benny before Ramses did.

"If you're turning down this sweet candy, you must be more stressed out than you look," Yvette said. Chucky had been so deep in his head that he'd almost forgotten that she was there. "Don't worry about it, baby. I'm about to help you work that stress out." She rolled up a dollar bill and leaned over the mirror, where she snorted one of the remaining lines. When she turned back to Chucky her eyes were glassy and wild. Chucky's dick was limp when she pulled it from his pants, but not for long. Yvette was an expert at using her mouth, and in no time she had him as hard as a rock. "That's what I'm talking about." She licked his shaft. Yvette ran her finger through the cocaine residue and coated Chucky's dick then like magic, made it disappear in her throat.

Yvette's mouth on him took Chucky to a pretty place. She licked him from his balls to the tip of his dick and back down again, making his toes curl in his sneakers. She paused, looking up at him, stroking his dick before putting him back in her mouth. Yvette paused to relight the blunt, and take a toke before getting back to the business at hand. Without looking up, or removing him from her mouth, she tried handing him the blunt again.

Chucky hadn't come up there to get high or get his dick sucked, but since both were conveniently at his disposal he figured, *why not?* He accepted the blunt and took a long drag, letting the numbness invade his lungs and spread through his body. He felt an icy chill run through his limbs and settle in his dick, making it feel like it was getting harder than it already was. Chucky had been a closet cocaine addict for quite some time. He started out snorting a few lines here and there when in the company of females who did coke, then graduating to getting high by himself. The more coke he did, the more he liked it. Soon it was a regular thing. Sometimes he would even ride around in his car, smoking Woos in plain sight. Unless you were in the car with him or close enough to smell it, you'd have assumed it was nothing more than a regular blunt. Chucky had to be careful with his addiction, because Ramses frowned on his people doing harder drugs than weed or alcohol and the punishment was swift and cruel.

Yvette kept sucking Chucky's dick, while he smoked the Woo down to a roach. Yvette's mouth felt good on him, so good that he grabbed her by the back of her head and fucked her in her throat until she gagged. Instead of being upset with him for trying to choke her, she seemed to get more turned on.

"You're trying to kill a bitch with this big black snake, ain't you?" Yvette asked, while stroking him. The Woo had Chucky's jaw so tight that he couldn't even open his mouth to reply, but the way his eyes kept rolling back in his head said he was enjoying himself. "I want you to get just as deep in this pussy as you were in my throat." She got off her knees and straddled his lap. Yvette's pussy was soaking wet. "You feel that, baby?" she whispered in his ear, sliding up and down on his dick slowly. She grabbed him by the back of the neck and switched gears, putting all her weight down so that he was touching her insides, and began swirling her hips. Chucky's face twisted, letting Yvette know he was reaching his climax. Without missing a beat, she hopped off his dick and got back on her knees. "Let me get it, baby. Let mama have that," she demanded, stroking him while rubbing her tongue around the head of his penis. Chucky exploded, painting Yvette's lips and face with his semen.

Chucky sat there, dick still leaking, and breathing heavily. He looked for the blunt, but there was nothing left so he picked up the mirror and finished snorting the cocaine off it. When that was gone he ran his fingers over the mirror before licking the residue from them. When he heard something buzzing, he almost jumped out of skin. Cocaine always made him extremely paranoid. It took a few seconds before he realized the buzzing sound was coming from his pants, which were around his ankles. He fished the phone from his pocket and looked at the caller ID screen. He didn't recognize number and started not to answer it, but he thought that it might've been Benny. "Hello," he hastily answered. To his dismay, it wasn't Benny on the other end, but he welcomed the call just the same. He'd known it was coming, but not this soon. "This was an unexpected call. How ya doing?"

"I've been better. I hope I'm not interrupting anything?" Persia asked on the other end of the line.

Chucky looked down at Yvette, still kneeling, face dripping with cum and staring at him like a lost puppy. "Nah, you weren't interrupting anything at all."

CHAPTER 12

Outside, all was quiet . . . much quieter than Li'l Monk had expected for his first night as a part of Pharaoh's crew. The past few hours had crawled by without too much going on, which was probably a good thing, since he'd have to handle it if anything did pop off. He and Omega passed the time, sitting on the stoop, talking shit and getting to know each other. He learned that Omega was from Brooklyn, and had been on his own since he was fourteen. He never knew his father and his mother died of an overdose. He had been living from pillar to post over the last couple of years, hustling in the Lafayette Gardens Housing Projects until he was recruited by Benny into Pharaoh's organization.

"So, it was Benny who brought you in and not Chucky?" Li'l Monk asked after hearing his tale.

"Chucky is my dog, make no mistake about it, but it was Benny who taught me the ins and outs of the game," Omega confessed.

"So you must be just as worried about him as everybody else."

"Yeah, I'm worried about my big homie, but I can't lose sleep over it. One thing Benny taught me about this game is that whenever you leave the house there's only a fifty percent chance that you'll make it back. Nothing is promised when you're doing dirt. I hope they find him alive and in good health, but if they don't, I'm next in line for this strip, and I'll make sure I ball every night in his memory," Omega told him.

Li'l Monk wasn't sure what to make of the Brooklyn native at first, but the more they talked the more he grew to like him. He was a little surprised how candidly Omega was speaking, but he understood why he was revealing so much so soon. If they were going to be working together, he was laying all his cards on the table early so that there was no misunderstanding between him and Li'l Monk as to what kind of person he was and how he moved. Li'l Monk respected his blunt honesty, and decided that he and Omega would get along.

The lobby door to the building that they were sitting in front of swung open and Li'l Monk was immediately on his feet, gun drawn.

"Hold on, youngster. It's just me!" Neighborhood threw his hands in the air.

"Man, what are you doing skulking around in the middle of the night?" Li'l Monk asked, tucking his gun back in his pants.

"Nigga, I'm a crackhead. That's what we do." Neighborhood flashed his rotten smile. "They got you two running the block all by your lonesome? Where're Benny and Chucky?"

"Chucky is around and there's still no sign of Benny. I'm sure he'll pop up though," Omega said hopefully.

Neighborhood shook his head. "After all this time and still not a word. I doubt it. This shit is starting to smell funny."

"Watch how you talk about my friend, old man," Omega warned.

"I ain't talking about him. I'm just giving you a history lesson. In my years of hustling, anytime a dude who is clocking the kind of bank that Benny was disappears without an explanation, they were either dead or the police had them tucked away somewhere, bleeding information out of them."

"Then Benny must be dead, because he'd never rat!" Omega said heatedly.

"That's the same thing they said about Nicky Barnes." Neighborhood cackled.

That was the final insult. Omega lashed out and landed two punches to Neighborhood's chin, dropping him onto the stoop. Omega swooped in to stop the helpless addict, but Li'l Monk grabbed him.

"Chill out, man," Li'l Monk told Omega.

"Fuck that, this fiend is out of pocket." Omega struggled, but Li'l Monk was bigger and stronger than he was.

"Shut up that noise down there before I call the police!" a woman shouted from a window above them.

"Fuck you, bitch!" Omega shouted back.

"Omega, you're making the block hot and if the police come through here, Ramses is gonna kill both of us. Let's take a walk." Li'l Monk pulled him away from the stoop and down the street.

"I don't like that nigga," Omega said as they were walking.

"Neighborhood is harmless, but sometimes he just doesn't know what to say out of his mouth," Li'l Monk told him.

"Then maybe I should teach him." Omega started to turn back, but Li'l Monk wouldn't let him.

"Leave that shit alone and let's check on Burger and them. They should be finished with the packages you gave them by now," Li'l Monk said. He looked at the corner where Burger was supposed to be, but saw no sign of him. "Where the fuck is he?"

"Knowing that fat fuck, he's probably off getting something to eat. Burger is the only cat I ever met who seems like he's hungry twenty-four-seven."

"Still, wasn't smart of him to leave his corner unattended like that. What if Chucky had come back out and peeped it? It would've looked bad on us." Li'l Monk couldn't help but to rub salt in because he didn't like Burger.

"You're right. Let's go find this nigga before I end up having to smack the shit out of him."

Omega and Li'l Monk walked down the Avenue, toward the chicken shack, where they figured Burger would be. They were passing a building, when something in the lobby caught Li'l Monk's attention. He peered through the glass and saw three men in the dark nook under the stairs. One man faced the wall, and the other two stood behind them, with their backs to the door. It only took Li'l Monk's brain a second to register what he was seeing. Without saying a word, he drew his gun and pressed his back to the side of the building.

"What the fuck are you doing?" Omega asked suspiciously.

Li'l Monk jerked his head toward the lobby door, motioning for Omega to take a peek.

"Oh, shit, they're trying to rob Burger." Omega caught on. He immediately slipped into combat mode, drawing a .380 Li'l Monk didn't even know he was carrying. "Not on my watch."

"I got a plan," Li'l Monk whispered. "Watch the door," he told him before disappearing into the building next door.

Li'l Monk bounded up the stairs to the roof, and it was there that he crossed onto the next building where Burger was being robbed. He kept his gun at his side, out of sight in case he ran into a tenant, but still ready. It'd have been a lie if Li'l Monk had said that he wasn't nervous. His palms were sweating so bad that he prayed that he wouldn't drop the heavy pistol. When he got to the second-floor landing, he stopped and peered over the edge so that he could see down into the lobby. Burger had his hands on the wall, while a dude wearing a stocking cap over his face was patting him down. Another man, wearing dark sunglasses, stood a few feet away, brandishing a gun and looking around nervously.

"Man, I gave you what I had. I ain't hardly sold nothing tonight," he heard Burger whine.

The dude who had been patting Burger down slapped him in the back of the head. "Stop playing with me, fat boy, and set it out before we air you out."

"Man, hurry up and grab whatever this nigga got, before somebody comes through here. We've already been in the building for too long," the one holding the gun said.

Neither of them saw Li'l Monk. He had the drop, but was hesitant. He had fired guns before, but never at a person. Li'l Monk was fearless and would go at it with anyone, but he wasn't sure if he had it in him to kill a man.

"Dear Lord," someone said from behind Li'l Monk. He was so focused on the robbers and his moral dilemma that he didn't see the woman come out of her apartment. She had blown Li'l Monk's cover and all eyes were now on him.

The sounds of gunfire were deafening in the cramped lobby. The dude who had been holding the gun started firing blindly. Li'l Monk tackled the woman to the ground, just as a bullet struck her apartment door. The woman was screaming hysterically and people were coming to their doors to see what was going on.

Li'l Monk felt his stomach lurch, but he had to hold it together for the sake of his own survival. He was not going to die in a tenement hallway. Moving off fear and adrenaline, Li'l Monk scrambled to his feet, and returned fire down the stairs. He didn't hit anyone, but it backed the robbers off.

Burger tried to make a break for it during the chaos, but his sudden movement startled the man with the gun. A slug hit Burger high in the chest and back-flipped him into the mailboxes along the wall.

Seeing Burger's body laid out at an awkward angle reinforced the seriousness of the situation to Li'l Monk. He steadied the gun in both hands and fired high. The top of the gunman's head burst, splattering onto his partner. The man with the stocking cap over his face suddenly decided that the risks were no longer worth the rewards for the caper they had set out on, and bolted for the lobby exit.

Li'l Monk's legs felt like noodles when he descended the last few stairs to the lobby. Just beyond the last step lay his handiwork. He thought he would be repulsed by the sight of a man with a gaping hole in his skull, but he wasn't. He was simply numb. His eyes went to Burger, who was lying on the dirty lobby floor, lifeless eyes staring off into space. He didn't like Burger, but he didn't wish death on him. Seeing a boy who was his age, and caught up in the same struggle that he was, dead before his prime filled Li'l Monk with anger. With a firm grip on his gun, he turned toward the fleeing man.

The man with the stocking cap had almost made it to the lobby exit, when the door swung open and Omega stepped in. His dreads hung loose around his face, and his green eyes cold and

unmoving. With a sneer on his lips, he raised the
.380 and pointed it at the man wearing the stocking cap. "When you get to hell, tell them Omega
sent you." He fired twice into the man's face.

When Li'l Monk approached Omega, he was
watching him intently, waiting for a reaction. Li'l
Monk looked from the corpse at Omega's feet to
the one he'd left at the other end of the hallway.
When he met Omega's gaze an unspoken understanding passed between them. They hadn't
known each other long, but the acts committed
in that hallway would be the tie that bound them.
They would burn together or prosper together.

"They killed Burger," Li'l Monk finally managed to say.

Omega's just nodded. "These are probably the
same dudes who robbed us before." He knelt beside the corpse of the man wearing the stocking
cap, and uncovered his face. When Omega saw
who it was, it hit him like a brick. "Damn," he
sighed.

"You knew him?" Li'l Monk asked.

"Yeah, I knew him." Omega stood. "Let's get
outta here before the police come."

Li'l Monk made no arguments about that.
"Shouldn't we tell Chucky what happened?"

"We will, but Ramses is gonna wanna hear
this first."

PART 3

FRIEND OR FOE

CHAPTER 13

Chucky was awakened by the sounds of banging on the front door. At first he was disoriented and couldn't remember where he was, but when he saw Yvette passed out on the couch across from him, everything came back.

During his freak session with Yvette, Persia had called. Had he been in his right frame of mind instead of coked up, he would've ignored the call, but the drugs put the devil in him. He had plans for Persia, so he might as well start laying the ground work early. From the first time he'd seen her on the block he'd been thinking about pushing up on her, but when he found out who her parents were it changed his whole game plan. Her father had been in prison for years, but his name still rang in the streets and in Chucky's ears.

The Persia he spoke on the phone with was different than the Persia he'd met on the block. She still had a slick mouth, but he also found that she was smart and articulate. Chucky listened, without interrupting, as Persia rattled off about her life and her struggles. He found it hard to believe that her life could be as dismal as she made it sound, considering that she didn't live in the hood and came from a two-parent home, but she made it sound so tragic that it nearly tugged at the strings of his cold heart.

After speaking for almost three hours, Chucky's phone beeped letting him know the battery was going dead. He could've plugged it into the wall charger and continued the conversation, but he'd heard all that he needed to at the moment. Now it was time to process the information. Persia was the total package: brains, beauty, and pedigree. The best part about it was that she was still young enough for Chucky to shape her into whomever he wanted her to be, which was what he intended to do. By the time Chucky was done with her, she would either love him or hate him. Either/or, didn't matter, as long as he got what he wanted.

The banging on the door started again, snapping Chucky out of his daze. He got up from the chair and fixed his pants and grabbed his gun, before going to the door. It was the middle of the night, and those were the hours dudes got caught slipping. "Hold the fuck on," he shouted, as whoever was on the other side continued their pounding. He carefully looked through the peephole, identifying whether it was friend or foe, before undoing the locks and opening the door.

"Do you know how long I've been trying to reach you?" Ramses asked when Chucky finally opened the door.

"I was sleeping and my phone battery was dead," Chucky told him.

"That's inexcusable. You're supposed to be accessible at all times in case someone needs to reach you. That's what being in charge means, or have you forgotten you were supposed to be supervising them young boys last night?"

Chucky had been so caught in his coke high and buttering Persia up that he'd forgotten he was breaking in the new recruits. "Sorry," he said in a low tone. He knew he had fucked up so there was no sense in arguing. "Everything okay with them? Omega didn't fuck up, did he?"

"The young boy has actually proven to be more reliable than certain people who've been with me twice as long, but that's another story. Get your shit and let's take a little ride," Ramses told him.

"What's wrong?" Chucky asked, not liking the tone of Ramses. He had known him long enough to know when something was off.

"I'll be outside waiting for you. And leave the pistol, you won't need where we're going." Ramses turned and walked away.

A ball of ice settled in the pit of Chucky's stomach. Something wasn't kosher. He had been the man knocking on doors too many nights to not know what could be waiting for him. Ramses was his friend and his mentor, but it was the ones closest to you who they sent to end you. Chucky went back into the apartment and jumped in his clothes. He looked at his gun wondering if he should defy Ramses, but figured it wouldn't do him much good anyway if they planned to kill him. Better to do as he was told until he figured out where he stood, and hope he didn't regret the decision.

On his way out the door, he looked over at Yvette, who was still knocked out on the couch, and wondered how the hell she was able to sleep through the banging.

The temperature outside had dropped since Chucky had last been out. It wasn't quite morning yet, but in the distance the sky began to lighten. Ramses was leaning against his Lincoln Navigator flanked by two men Chucky recognized, but didn't see too often, Huck and Boo.

They were older heads, who had been running with Ramses since the eighties. Whenever they came out, somebody disappeared.

"Huck, Boo," Chucky greeted them.

"What up, young blood?" Huck gave him dap. He was brown skinned and wore his hair in a close-cropped afro. As usual he was immaculately dressed in a suit jacket, white shirt, and black shoes polished to a high shine.

In contrast, Boo wore jeans and a sweat shirt. Whereas Huck was a gentleman, Boo was a goon. All he knew was putting in work and didn't care to learn anything else. He looked at Chucky's extended hand, but didn't take it. He simply nodded in greeting. Boo had never been fond of Chucky, though he never said why.

"Jump in, Chucky," Ramses said, climbing in on the passenger side of the Navigator, while Huck got behind the wheel.

Chucky climbed into the back of the SUV, while Boo got in beside him. When the doors closed, Chucky heard the click of the automatic locks. He glanced over his shoulder, to the rear row of the truck, and saw Li'l Monk and Omega. The both of them had worried expressions on their faces. When they pulled out into traffic, Chucky knew there was no turning back.

"Where're we going, Ramses?" Chucky asked.

Ramses made eye contact with Chucky through the rearview. "To bear witness to the Pharaoh's justice."

The whole ride was spent in silence. Not even the radio played. Ramses kept his head forward, whispering to someone on his cell phone. He wouldn't even look back at Chucky, which was a bad sign. Every so often Chucky would glance over his shoulder at Li'l Monk and Omega on the rear row, trying to get a sense of what had happened. Omega wouldn't meet his gaze and Li'l Monk looked confused and nervous. Chucky didn't like it.

Their destination was a condemned house, somewhere in the White Plains section of the Bronx. The house stood three stories tall and looked like it would collapse on itself at the first strong wind that touched it. The Navigator turned into the driveway and pulled to the back of the house. There was a small apartment over the garage. Chucky knew the apartment, because he had been there once. It was the same place he had taken a life to prove his loyalty to Ramses. Those who entered that apartment generally didn't come out.

Huck got out first, giving a quick look around before opening the passenger door for Ramses. Ramses got out, and motioned for Chucky to join him. Chucky was hesitant, but the glare Boo was giving him encouraged him to do as he was told.

Chucky walked with Ramses up the broken stairs to the apartment, while Boo, Huck, and the youngsters followed. He could feel his heart pounding in his chest and had to take short breaths to try to slow it. In his mind he went over every inch of the dirt he'd done in the past few months. It was impossible for them to know. He had been so careful, but Pharaoh had his ways of finding things out. Maybe Wolf didn't believe that he'd come up with the money and decided to give him up? It was too late to worry about it at that point.

Ramses stopped at the top of the stairs and placed his hand on the apartment door, then paused and turned to Chucky. "You know, y'all young boys been with me for a long time, Chucky. When each of you came to me, you had nothing and I gave you something. All I asked in return was loyalty."

"You know I'm loyal to you, Ramses," Chucky assured him.

Ramses raised his eyebrow. "Are you?"

"Of course I am, and if anybody ever says different I'll personally blow their fucking heads off," Chucky declared.

Ramses studied his face, searching for signs of a lie. After a few seconds, he nodded and smiled. "I'm gonna hold you to that," he said, pushing the door open and stepped inside.

The tiny apartment was the only thing on the property that had looked halfway functional. The kitchenette was dressed up to look like a recording studio: a few chairs, a sofa, and equipment that was seldom used. A heavily tinted two-way mirror divided the room, shadowing the recording booth.

"What, you feel like cutting a record or something?" Chucky tried to make a joke, but Ramses didn't laugh.

"We ain't cutting records today, Chucky. We're cutting losses," Ramses said. He turned a switch on the console, and darkened glass came to life, illuminating the recording booth behind it.

When Chucky looked inside the booth his heart sank. The mystery of Benny's disappearance had finally been solved.

CHAPTER 14

Benny had always been the so-called pretty boy of their crew. He was high yellow, with curly hair that he always wore in a close fade, and left wild on top. Women threw themselves at Benny like LL in the nineties, but the man sitting tied to a chair in the recording booth was a far cry from that. Benny was naked, except for his underwear and socks, and covered in bruises. A blindfold covered Benny's eyes, which was probably for the best so he couldn't see what they had done to him. There were slash marks across his chest and thighs, most of which were still fresh and bleeding. They had been working him over for only God knew how long. Chucky didn't know what he was more baffled by: the fact that his best friend was being tortured or who was doing the torturing.

Ahmed Kaplan, known to some as the Butcher, was an older Turkish man, who Chucky had met once when he was riding around with Ramses in Queens. He owned a butcher shop and delicatessen, where Chucky had sat with him and Ramses sat eating cold sandwiches and drinking Raki, while listening to Kaplan tell dirty jokes and debate sports. The man working Benny over seemed nothing like the sweet old dude he'd met at the deli, having traded in his ratty wool sweater for a meat cutter's smock and hatchet. He stalked Benny like game, every so often stopping to bark something at him that Chucky couldn't hear through the soundproof glass.

"Sweet Jesus," was all Chucky could think to say.

"More like the devil." Ramses chuckled. "I forgot, you've never seen the Butcher at work. Before age and hard living kicked in, that muthafucka was an artist with this murder shit. Now he's a tired old man who takes the occasional contract to cover his gambling debts and keep up with the tuition at that private school he hides his bastard kid at. Did you know that he and his wife would be outcasts in their community if word ever got out that he fathered a son with a black junkie broad? They're funny about that kinda shit."

"What the fuck is he in there doing to my boy?" Chucky asked, stalking toward the entrance to the recording booth.

"I wouldn't if I were you," Ramses called, stopping him in his tracks. "Best not disturb the Butcher when he's in his zone. I'd hate for you to accidentally take a whack from that cleaver that was meant for Benny."

"Ramses, what's going on?" Chucky asked nervously.

"Oh, you didn't get the memo? Benny here was planning on branching out on his own, but instead of stepping up like a real nigga and putting his money where his mouth was, he decided he would steal from us to kick start his little operation, but he fucked up when he got greedy and took one bite too many of the same pie."

Chucky shook his head in disbelief. "Benny is one of us. This has got to be some kind of mistake." He faked shock, but he knew Benny was foul, and if Ramses knew it too then there was nothing he could say to save his friend. Still he tried to advocate for him. If for nothing else, so he could say he at least tried.

"Ain't no mistaking it, Benny is as dirty. I told you whoever was hitting our spots had a helping hand. I just never thought it was Benny's hand."

"How did you find out?" Chucky asked, still trying to process everything,

"It was the young boy who put the nail in his coffin." He nodded at Omega.

"You did this?" Chucky looked over at Omega, who turned his eyes to the floor. The shame was apparent. Benny had been good to him and he'd returned the kindness by putting him in harm's way.

"Tell him what you told me," Ramses ordered.

"These dudes moved on us last night after you left," Omega reluctantly began. "Me and Li'l Monk bodied the men who tried to rob us, but Burger got killed."

"So how does that fat muthafucka being dead explain why my homeboy is tied up?" Chucky asked impatiently.

"Shut up and wait for the punch line," Ramses commanded.

"I recognized one of the dude's faces," Omega continued. "I had seen him on the block a few times before . . . with you and Benny."

The room suddenly got quiet, but inside Chucky's mind he heard a name, *Louie*. Louie was a dude who had a baby with Benny's sister. Chucky told himself that Benny couldn't have been dumb enough to use someone who could be traced back to them for the robberies, but the fact that he was tied to a chair said that he was. Chucky felt all the moisture drain from his mouth and his bowels shifted. His eyes instinctively went to Boo, who was watching him from the corner.

His hand rested on the butt of the gun tucked in his jeans. Chucky wished that he'd brought his gun with him. At least then he might have had a chance.

"Finding out it was one of my own trying to pull a fast one made me even more determined to find this shirt bird, so I had Pharaoh call in some favors," Ramses said. "We followed Benny to a crack house in Yonkers, where he had been pushing the shit he stole from us. The dumb muthafucka even still had the birds in the packages with Pharoah's seal on them, so there was no mistaking where the drugs had come from. He had some money, too, but hardly what should've been there considering what he's been licking us for. Knowing Benny he probably tricked it off on bitches."

What Ramses didn't know was that the reason money was missing was because Chucky had it. He and Benny had a collective pot that they put the money in that they made from what they stole. Then there was the money Chucky had been robbing Benny of while they were busy robbing Pharaoh and Ramses. It was greasy on his part, but Chucky needed the money more than Benny and he needed it a lot quicker. It took all of Chucky's resolve not to make a break for the door.

"What's the matter, Chucky? You look like somebody just kicked your dog," Ramses told him.

"Just shocked, that's all." Chucky tried to keep his voice steady.

"I'll bet," Ramses said in a less-than-sincere tone. "So tell me, Chucky, if you were a man in my position, how would you handle this little situation? We all know the penalty for disloyalty, don't we, Chucky?"

Chucky nodded.

"And what is it, Chucky? What's the price a man must pay for being disloyal to the Pharaoh?"

"Death," Chucky said just above a whisper.

"Exactly! Death to the offender and everyone involved!"

Chucky was surprised when Huck and Boo swooped in and grabbed him by the arms. "What the fuck is this?" Chucky struggled.

Ramses drew his gun and pressed it against Chucky's forehead. "Did you know about this nigga plotting to cross us?"

"What? No. Ramses, why would I know anything about that?" Chucky asked in a terrified tone.

"Because you two muthafuckas are thick as thieves; one can't so much as take a crap without the other knowing about it. Chucky, I been around you long enough to know when something ain't right, and you been real off lately. Now, Benny is a good earner, but he ain't got no heart and it took heart to try to pull this shit off. Somebody was in his ear and convinced him that he could get away with it, and I'm thinking that somebody is you. You planted this seed in Benny's mind then stepped back and watched him take all the risks trying to execute it."

Chucky would've fainted had it not been for Huck and Boo holding him up. He had dodged one bullet only to get hit by another. Ramses was so close to the truth that Chucky felt like he would vomit if he opened his mouth to speak, but there was a light at the end of the tunnel. The fact that Ramses had even bothered to question him, instead of flat out killing him, was because he still wasn't totally sure about Chucky's involvement and there was still time to try to worm his way out. He had to say something, anything to save him from the same fate as Benny.

"I haven't been honest with you, Ramses," Chucky admitted.

"I told you this li'l nigga was scum. I say let's take both of these snakes in the back and put 'em to sleep," Boo said.

"Let me finish," Chucky told them. "I'll admit that I knew the packages were coming up short when Benny was left on the block by himself. I thought it might have been one of the workers getting slick and Benny just not catching on, but eventually I learned the truth. Benny's got a coke problem. At first I thought I could help him get cleaned up without you ever finding out, but he was further gone than I thought. By the time I realized just how fucked up in the game he was, Benny had already skated with what belonged to Pharaoh." It was a hastily slapped-together lie, but it was all he had at the moment.

"And why didn't you come to me when you found out Benny was getting high?" Ramses asked. "We might've been able to put this to bed before it got out of hand."

"Everybody knows your rule about hard drugs, Ramses. You hate addicts, and if you'd found out someone you trusted was getting high, you'd have killed him. No matter how bad Benny might've been fucking up, he's still my friend and I didn't want to see him dead."

"Or maybe you kept your mouth shut because you were in cahoots with him," Boo suggested.

"Fuck you," Chucky spat. "I'm the most loyal nigga in this crew, including you. I'm there night in and night out, leaving it all on the court, while you just come off the bench when the coach decides to give you garbage minutes. Why don't you announce your retirement already, and stay the fuck out of my business." He was getting tired of Boo's shit. No matter the dire circumstances he was in, he wouldn't continue to let the older man disrespect him.

"The both of you shut the fuck up!" Ramses barked. "Boo has a point, Chucky. How do I know you ain't just trying to save your own ass?"

"Ramses, I'm willing to do whatever to prove that I'm loyal to you." The minute Chucky said it, he wished that he hadn't. Ramses had baited the hook and he bit it.

"Glad you feel that way." Ramses smirked. "Give it to him, Huck."

Huck drew a big gun from his holster and handed it to Chucky.

"What am I supposed to do with this?" Chucky asked.

"Prove your loyalty," Ramses answered. "You say you weren't down with Benny's plan, prove it by carrying out the death sentence."

"Ramses, Benny fucked up and he's gotta go, I understand that, but you can't expect me to do it. That's been my homeboy since free lunch."

Boo eased up behind Chucky and put his gun to the back of his head. "Nigga, you ain't in no position to be trying to have no moral dilemmas. You should've thought about the fall out when you was keeping Benny's secrets."

Chucky looked to Ramses. "It's like that?"

"I'll put it to you like this: twenty miles outside of the city there are two fresh graves dug in the woods. The number of bodies that goes in them is all up to you," Ramses told him.

Chucky looked from his bound and gagged friend in the booth to the gun in his hand. A part of him wanted to go for it, but his moment of glory was likely to be a short one, being outgunned. Benny hadn't spilled the beans about Chucky's involvement yet, but who was to say that the Butcher wouldn't eventually break him? Benny had become a liability and Chucky knew what he had to do. Taking a deep breath, he stepped into the recording booth.

"Y'all go ahead and start the party. I need to holla at the youngsters for a minute," Ramses told his men, while waving Omega and Li'l Monk over to him. They had been standing in the corner trying their best to be invisible. Omega took the lead, but Li'l Monk followed closely behind him. Ramses glared at them for a few long moments, before speaking. "That work you put in for us hasn't gone unnoticed. You have my thanks, and Pharaoh also sends his gratitude."

"All good, Ramses. You know how I get down when it comes to the team. I'll kill anybody who comes around trying to fuck with us, just like I did that cat in the lobby," Omega boasted.

"You think you're hot shit because you shot a nigga? Any simple fuck with a finger can drop a body. I got a hundred thirsty young wolves who'll kill for me if I tell them to. So don't go thinking you're special."

"I didn't mean it like that. I was just trying to tell you that I'm loyal to the team." Omega tried to clean it up.

"That was the same thing Benny and Chucky told me when I pulled them out of the cold, but look at them now. Loyalty is more than just popping a dude who was trying to kill you; loyalty is murdering somebody you came up with if they're in the way of your movement." He motioned toward Chucky and Benny. "You think you got it in you to murder your right-hand man if he's throwing salt in the game?"

Omega glanced at Li'l Monk, who was watching him for his response. "If I told you yes or no, I'd be lying with either answer. All I can do is speak for myself when I say I'd never put Li'l Monk in that position, and I hope the feeling is mutual. If not, we'll cross that bridge when we come to it."

Ramses nodded, letting him know the answer had met his approval. "Spoken like a young man who wants to succeed in this game. And what about you?" Ramses asked Li'l Monk. "You've seen and done some things tonight that can carry some heavy consequences. There's blood on your hands over something that ain't really got nothing to do with you. I'd respect it if you decided to get out while you could. I might even find it in my heart to hit you with a few stacks for your troubles, provided we never speak of this again."

Li'l Monk weighed the proposition, and thought back to the jewel his dad had dropped on him the night before. "For as much as I could use the easy money, I'd rather the opportunity to make my own way."

Ramses caught his meaning. Li'l Monk wanted in. "This ain't some high school gang, moving nickel bags of weed in high school hallways. You understand the stakes we play for at this level? This is the deep end of the pool."

"Then I guess I'll either swim or drown," Li'l Monk replied.

"So be it." Ramses nodded in approval. "You and Omega will be working together, since you two seem to have chemistry."

"Solid." Omega gave Li'l Monk dap. He liked the kid and was happy to be working with him permanently.

"After the bodies you two left in the lobby, you're probably as hot as firecrackers in the streets, so no more corners. I've got some odd jobs that you can handle to keep yourselves busy and money in your pockets. I want you close to me, so I can oversee your progress."

This was a pleasant surprise. Becoming Ramses's apprentices was a badge of honor; it was how Chucky and Benny had come up so quick. Working closely with Ramses would definitely have its perks, but it would also have its drawbacks. They would have to be on call and at his disposal twenty-four hours per day. When Ramses called they would come or suffer the consequences.

"So, what are we gonna be doing if we're not selling drugs?" Li'l Monk asked. Unlike Omega, he wasn't sure how comfortable he was following Ramses blindly.

"You'll do what I tell you to when I tell you to do it," Ramses answered. "I see potential in you two, and where I fucked up with Chucky and Benny, I'm gonna make right with you. You play your cards right and I'll make you two li'l niggas rich. You fuck up and I'll make you two li'l niggas dead, feel me?"

Omega and Li'l Monk nodded simultaneously.

"Good, then pull up a seat, because your first class in Ramses's school of hard knocks is officially in session." Ramses pointed to the two seats at the console that faced the recording booth. When the youngsters were seated he leaned between them and said, "Today's lesson is loyalty."

It seemed colder inside the booth than it was in the apartment. The Butcher stood off to the side, wiping his blade with a dirty cloth. He gave Chucky a nod in the way of greeting, but didn't speak. Benny looked pitiful and helpless, tied to the chair mumbling incoherently. The Butcher had really done a number on him. For a moment he was hesitant, but Boo's gun poking him in the back edged him forward. Chucky didn't have to look to the two-way mirror to know that Ramses was watching him, because he could feel the heat from his eyes burrowing into his soul. There was no doubt in his mind what would happen to him if he didn't go through with it. He had to do it . . . at least that's what he kept telling himself.

When Huck snatched the blindfold off Benny's eyes, the overhead lights stung them like he was looking into a tiny sun. At first all he could see were shapes moving around him, but after his eyes adjusted his vision cleared. When he saw Chucky standing in front of him, he was like a beacon of hope. Chucky had pulled his ass out of the fire more than once, and if anyone could talk some sense into Ramses, it'd be him, especially considering he was partially to blame.

"Chucky . . . I didn't tell them shit, I swear," was the first thing Benny said.

Chucky glanced over his shoulder to see if Huck or Boo had heard what Benny said. If they had heard him they showed no signs of it. "It's all good, Benny, I already told Ramses how I was covering for you and your drug problem. Everything is all out in the open now."

"*My* drug problem? What the hell are you talking about?" Benny was confused. It was he who had been hiding Chucky's secret, not the other way around. "Chucky, I need you to stop fucking around and go talk to Ramses and get me a pass on this one, man. He listens to you. Don't let me go out like this," he pleaded.

"You put us in a real bad place, Benny," Chucky said, his voice heavy with emotion.

It was then that Benny noticed the gun in Chucky's hand for the first time. The realization of what was about to go down settled in. "Chucky, this is me, your crime partner. We were supposed to take over the world, remember that?"

"Yeah, I remember." Chucky raised the gun. Tears danced in the corners of his eyes and his hand shook.

Benny couldn't believe it. His best friend in the whole world was about to take him from it. If he was going to die then he would do so with dignity. He took a deep breath and stared down the barrel of the gun. To everyone's surprise, including his, Chucky spun and pointed the gun at Boo.

Chucky had come into the recording booth with every intention of killing Benny so that his secret would die with him, but when the moment of truth came he couldn't bring himself to do it. In his head he saw images of him and Benny growing from snot-nosed kids to reckless adults, sharing in good times and bad ones. He thought of Benny's mother, and how she used to make them fried bologna sandwiches and realized he didn't have it in him look her in the eyes and feed her a lie about what had happened to her only son. With that in mind, Chucky turned on their captors.

When Chucky played the scene in his head, he saw himself catching Ramses's men off-guard, taking as many of them with him as he could before he went out in his final blaze of glory. Unfortunately, it didn't go down quite like that. Chucky pulled the trigger, expecting to see Boo's face explode when the bullet hit it, but instead there was only the click of an empty gun. He had been set up.

Once Boo got over the initial shock of what had almost happened, he was enraged. He hit Chucky once in the stomach then again in the side of the head, dropping him to the floor. Chucky tried to get to his feet, but a kick to the ribs sent him back down. Boo began stomping Chucky out, happy for the chance to finally kill the young man, when Ramses stopped the beating.

"Enough!" Ramses shouted, his voice bouncing off the walls of the recording booth. Boo gave Chucky one last kick for good measure before backing off. Ramses extended his hand, but Chucky only looked at it like a frightened rabbit. "It's okay, ain't nobody else gonna lay hands on you. You've passed the test."

Chucky ignored Ramses's hand and got to his feet on his own. "Test? This was a fucking test?" He was livid.

"Calm the fuck down, Chucky. I need to be sure about whether you were involved and this was the only way. The fact that even though Benny is wrong, you were still ready to go out with him because he's your friend shows that there's still some honor left in you. Had you killed him like I told you to, I'd have known you had something to hide, and you would've died next."

Chucky felt lightheaded, but he wasn't sure if it was from the beating or the weight that had been lifted off his shoulders. He leaned his back against the wall and let out a deep sigh.

"I know you're probably pissed, but my way was better than the alternative. Pharaoh told me to have you killed just in case," Ramses told him.

"And what about Benny?" Chucky asked, even though he wasn't sure why.

"Benny is done, he knows Pharaoh's laws and he broke a cardinal one. If I don't take action against Benny, it might be looked at as I'm playing favorites, and that would affect the way the rest of the soldiers look at me. I can't have my authority challenged, not even for a kid I once loved," Ramses told him.

"I understand that and I agree, but you don't have to kill him, Ramses. Let him walk and I'll work off his debt. Whatever Benny owes Pharaoh, I'll wear his weight," Chucky offered. He felt so bad about the fact that he had come within one bad decision of murdering his childhood friend to save his own ass, the least he could do was beg for his life. "I'm not asking you as your lieutenant, I'm asking you as your friend."

The sincerity in Chucky's voice moved Ramses. He had raised both of them up from teenagers and always considered him his adopted sons. "This is the last favor you ever get from me, Chucky. My men won't kill Benny, but he's done in this family and this city."

"I'm on the first thing smoking out of New York and that's on everything I love," Benny assured him.

"Thank you, Ramses," Chucky said.

"Don't thank me just yet. I'm gonna hold you to that promise of working off Benny's debt, plus interest."

"I got you."

"Huck will take you and the youngsters back to the block. Omega will fill you in on what he and I spoke about. Go get yourself cleaned up and get some rest, Chucky. I'll call on you in a few hours," Ramses told him.

"A'ight." Chucky shuffled toward the door with his head low. Between the crash from the cocaine and the fact that he had just narrowly avoided death made him feel wiped out. He needed to lie down.

"Chucky," Benny called after him. "You know for a minute I thought you were really going to kill me." He smirked weakly.

There was no warmth in Chucky's voice when he replied, "I was."

Once Chucky and the others were gone, it left Ramses and Benny in the recording booth. Benny was still tied to the chair, while Ramses leaned against the wall, glaring at him.

"Ramses, I know you're mad at me, but I swear I'm gonna make this right." Benny tried to engage Ramses in small talk, but he wasn't receptive. He remained silent, and just watched. "So, you gonna cut me loose so I can get ghost or what?"

"No, I won't be cutting you loose, but you will be getting ghost," Ramses finally spoke. He pushed off the wall and walked slowly over to Benny.

The door of the recording booth opened and in stepped a man who Benny had never seen. He was tall, and looked scholarly wearing a black suit. One could've almost mistaken him for a lawyer or businessman, but neither profession required the latex gloves he wore on his hands.

"Wait a second, Ramses, you gave Chucky your word that your men wouldn't touch me," Benny reminded him.

"And my word is my bond. This isn't one of my men, he's my benefactor," Ramses told him.

Benny looked up at the man in the suit in wide-eyed shock and when he realized who it was, he shit himself. "*Pharaoh*," he gasped. For all the times he had wondered what the mysterious Pharaoh looked like, now that he had laid eyes on him he wished that he hadn't. He knew what happened to those outside his inner circle who laid eyes on Pharaoh. They never lived to tell about it. "I can make it right."

Pharaoh shook his head. "If only that were true." He drew a straight razor from the inside of his suit jacket. "A cold world breeds hard men, and I'm afraid I just don't see that in you," he told Benny before opening his throat with the razor.

CHAPTER 15

Halfway into third-period English, Persia found that she could barely keep her eyes open. The combination of the joint she'd smoked with Ty before school and burning the midnight oil until the wee hours had her feeling like a zombie. She had stayed on the phone talking to Chucky until almost five a.m. and had to be up for school by six a.m. She could almost feel the bags swelling under her eyes, but they were worth it.

She had initially only planned on talking to him for a few minutes, if that, but she found Chucky to be an interesting character to say the least. He was witty and flattering, hardly what she expected from a street dude. Chucky told her about his life growing up in the hood with no father, and an on-again off-again addict for a mother. He also told Persia how both his bothers had been murdered when he was very young. From the pain in his voice she could tell that it hurt him to talk about it. Chucky opening up like that to her made Persia want to do the same, so she opened up to him about a few things in her life, including her father and seeing a man murdered when she was five years old. It was the first time she had talked to anyone other than her therapist and her mother about it and sharing it with Chucky made her feel like some of the weight she had been carrying was being lifted. She hadn't intended to tell him so much so soon, but Chucky was very easy to talk to. By the time they got done talking, Persia felt like she had known Chucky for years and the birds were chirping outside her window. He promised to call her after school that day, and Persia couldn't help but find herself watching the clock in anticipation.

Talking to Chucky helped Persia take her mind off the nasty argument she'd had with her mother. They had disagreements before, but not to that magnitude. When Persia came down for breakfast that morning, the tension was so thick in the kitchen that you could cut it with a knife. Richard sat in his usual spot, at the table on his laptop, sipping coffee and trying his best to remain invisible. Michelle stood over the sink washing dishes. She didn't even acknowledge Persia other than a halfhearted, "Good morning." She knew she had hurt her mother and wanted to apologize, but felt like it was too soon. She decided that when she got out of school she would talk to her mother and try to make things right.

"Am I keeping you from some other pressing appointment, Ms. Chandler?" Mr. Ages asked. He was giving her the look from over the rim of his glasses. "You've been staring at that clock as if you have somewhere else to be."

"I'm sorry, Mr. Ages," Persia said.

"Sorry isn't going to get you a passing grade in my class, Ms. Chandler." Mr. Ages said her last name in a drawn-out tone. He was about to turn and walk away when his nose twitched. He sniffed the air around Persia. "Ms. Chandler, have you been smoking marijuana?"

All eyes in the class turned to Persia. "Um, no, sir. Some girls were smoking cigarettes in the bathroom and the smell must've gotten in my hair," she lied.

"A likely story. I'll be watching you, Ms. Chandler. With your father being such a highly respected history professor at NYU, I don't think he'd take kindly to hearing that you've fallen in with the slackers," Mr. Ages told her before turning on his heels and walking back to the front of the class.

"Stepfather," Persia mumbled.

Time ticked by at a snail's pace, but finally the end of the period came. Persia was starving and couldn't wait to hook up with her girls and get something to eat from the cafeteria. She saw Karen, Meeka, and Ty lingering outside the door of the classroom, waiting for her, and she motioned to them that she'd be along in a second. Scooping her books hastily into her bag, she headed for the door and had almost made it before Mr. Ages stopped her.

"A word please, Ms. Chandler." He was looking at her over his glasses again.

Persia looked from her friends, who were waving for her to hurry, to the waiting teacher, wondering what he wanted with her. "What's up?" She approached his desk.

"That's what I'm trying to figure out, Ms. Chandler," Mr. Ages said while shuffling some papers on his desk. "I imagine making the transition from an institution like St. Mary's to public school has been quite an experience. How're you adjusting?"

Persia shrugged. "Fine, I guess. It was a little different in the beginning, but I'm getting into the swing of how things work around here."

"So I've noticed, and it's part of the reason I asked to speak to you," Mr. Ages said. "Persia, I know how it can be when you're the new kid in school. Sometimes you find yourself doing things you wouldn't normally do, because you want to fit in. I get it, but don't let new people, places, and things change your priorities."

"And what's that supposed to mean?" Persia asked.

"What it means is you're not like your little friends." He nodded to the doorway, where Ty had her nose pressed against the glass, making funny faces. "Karen only comes to school half of the time, Ty is a lost cause, and Meeka has been here almost as long as I have. There's actually a pool going on in the teacher's lounge as to how many of them will actually finish high school. You"—he jabbed his finger at her—"have the potential to not only finish high school, but go on to college and be successful in the world, but you have to apply yourself."

"Mr. Ages, I do apply myself," Persia said.

"So you call coming to my class high out of your skull applying yourself?" Mr. Ages asked. Persia looked surprised. "Don't give me that look, Persia. I used to smoke a little pot in my day, so I know the signs. The difference is, I wouldn't have dared come to school high. I understood the importance of education and put that before my vices."

"I apologize, Mr. Ages. It won't happen again," Persia said.

"Let's hope not, Ms. Chandler. I don't think your parents would appreciate hearing that you've been getting high before school. I'd hate to have to call them, but I will if you don't pull it together."

"I promise, Mr. Ages. No more weed for me," she lied. Persia had no intention of giving up weed. She'd just be sure not to smoke before school anymore. "Can I go now?"

"Yes, Ms. Chandler. You can go, and please tell your friend Meeka if she's going to cut my class, at least be smart enough not to loiter outside the door where I can see her. Damn slackers," Mr. Ages grumbled and went back to shuffling his papers.

"What did old sour puss want?" Ty asked when Persia finally came out of the classroom.

"Nothing, he was on my back for being high in class," Persia told her.

"His old ass needs to get some pussy in his life so he can stop being so fucking mean all the time. I hate that nigga," Meeka said.

"I think the feeling is mutual," Persia half joked. "Let's go get something to eat. I'm hungry, tired, and ready for this day to be over. I been up almost all night and just wanna go home and take a nap."

"What were you doing all night that kept you up?" Karen asked suspiciously.

"Nothing, just talking to my cousin from down South on the phone. She's always got some drama going on," Persia lied.

"I thought you might've been getting your back dug out." Ty laughed.

"Unlike you, I don't have sex on the brain twenty-four-seven, but I get mine when necessary," Persia shot back.

"Or give it." Karen snickered.

"Very funny, bitch," Persia said, picking up on the dig Karen was taking at her. She had made the mistake of confiding in Karen how she had recently tried oral sex with the boy who lived next door and found that she liked giving head. It was the first time she had ever gotten off without being penetrated. She wasn't ashamed at sucking dick, but she didn't like how Karen tried to put it out there.

"Y'all chicks knock it off, and let's make a move. I heard it's a hookie party in the Bronx that's supposed to be off the hook," Meeka said.

"Who's throwing it?" Persia asked. She really couldn't afford to miss two days of school in a row, but if the rewards justified the risks she might entertain it.

"That kid Nitty and some of his peoples," Meeka told her.

"Nitty from sixth-period math? Nah, I'm gonna pass on that," Persia said.

"Stop acting like that, Persia. I heard they got all kind of liquor and weed at the spot. Let's go get right," Meeka tried to convince her.

"Girl, please, knowing those lames we'll probably end up drinking forty-ounces and smoking ditch weed. Holla at me when a real nigga is having a party," Persia said.

"Listen to this one here." Karen looked Persia up and down. "We've drank plenty of forty ounces and smoked dirt when we didn't have it, so why you acting like you're above that now?"

"Because I'm trying to prioritize, Karen. I missed the whole day yesterday and if I'm gonna cut out early today, it's gotta be for better reason that to smoke headache weed and have some thirsty-ass dudes cracking on me for the pussy all day," Persia told her.

"Listen to Miss High and Mighty. You get a little bit of attention from a dude who's handling and now everybody else is beneath you," Karen accused.

"I'm not saying it like that and you know it, Karen. All I'm saying is that I missed a day coming to hang out with you guys yesterday and I don't wanna miss another one unless it's worth it."

"Didn't nobody twist your arm and make you come uptown, Persia. Don't try to put that bullshit off on us," Karen said with an attitude.

"Karen, I never said you guys made me do anything, so I don't know where that's coming from. You need to slow down." Persia matched her tone.

"Persia, you know a party ain't a party unless our whole clique is there. Just think about it," Ty said.

"Don't beg her. If Princess P wants to stay her square ass in school then let her. We don't need her to have a good time. We've been doing this since long before she started slumming with us," Karen said, rolling her eyes.

"Karen, you've been acting real shitty since yesterday. What the hell is your problem?" Persia asked. Karen had been giving her major attitude since the day before and Persia was getting tired of it.

"My problem is phony-ass broads who only fuck with us when they feel like it. Only loyal bitches run with this crew."

"Oh, so now I'm not loyal to the crew because I don't wanna cut school to run the streets? You sound silly," Persia told her.

"Not as silly as you looked when your thirsty ass was all on Chucky's dick yesterday," Karen spat.

"Now I get it. You're acting funny toward me over some dick that doesn't belong to either one of us? I thought we were better than that," Persia said in a disappointed tone.

"Nah, we ain't better than that, but you think you're better than us. Everybody has noticed it, Persia. You come around trying to walk like us, talk like us, and act like us, but you ain't really like us. When you're done getting your kicks in the ghetto you go back to the suburbs and sit around the dinner table with your nice family, talking about how fucked up it is for us in the slums," Karen said venomously.

The statement hit Persia like a slap. "That's not true and you know it. I'm from the same place y'all are from. It's not my fault that my family moved away because they wanted better for us."

"See, it's just like I said. She thinks she's better than us," Karen told Meeka and Ty, trying to get them riled up.

"Karen, you're trying to twist my words," Persia said.

"I ain't gotta twist nothing, Persia, because it's all out there for everybody to see. You ain't from what we're from and the only reason that the hood shows you love is on the strength that you hang with us. You're wearing a mask and it's time that you took it off," Karen told her.

"Karen, you're going too far," Ty said.

Karen turned on her. "You siding with this bitch over me?"

"I'm not siding with anybody, Karen. I'm just saying we shouldn't be arguing among each other. We're supposed to be a crew," Ty told her. She was the most non-confrontational of them and was trying to keep the peace.

"Crew my ass. Had it been you or Meeka neither of you would've been trying to throw the pussy at Chucky knowing we had history."

Persia had to laugh to keep from crying. She was hurt, but wouldn't give Karen the satisfaction of showing it. Instead she struck back. "Spoken like a true washed-up bitch. You know, I wasn't gonna give Chucky any pussy at first, but I think I just might. I gotta know what it is he's working with that got you out here playing yourself."

Karen's eyes flashed rage and she lunged for Persia. Had it not been for Meeka and Ty, she would've whipped Persia's ass in that hallway. "I'm gonna knock your head off, you bourgeois ho!"

"Better a bourgeois ho than a broke ho. When I suck Chucky's dick tonight, I'll ask him which one of us does it better," Persia spat and walked away. Karen hurled insults and threats at her the whole time, but Persia just kept it moving, with her head held high. It wasn't until she was alone in the stairwell that the tears she had been holding back came. In less than twenty-four hours she had been hurt by two people she cared about and it dug into her chest like a knife. She knew that she was too emotional to finish out the school day, so she decided to cut the day short after all. The question was, where was she going to go? It was too early in the day for her to go home and have to explain why she wasn't in school in the middle of the day, and she didn't have any money so wandering the streets aimlessly was out of the question. She needed somewhere to clear her head, and get a meal and a blunt, in no particular order, and had an idea where she could get all three.

CHAPTER 16

"Now this is a pleasant surprise," Marty said when she opened her front door and found Persia standing on the other side. She was a pretty white girl with strawberry-colored curls, a small waist, and curves like a black chick. Some speculated that she'd had work done, but Marty was all natural, courtesy of her mother, who was Argentinean, but could pass for white and didn't bother to correct people who assumed that she was.

Marty and Persia had been friends, and occasionally rivals, since they were five years old and Persia was new to the neighborhood. Even at that early of an age the girls were always in competition, who had the best Halloween costume, who could build the biggest snowman . . . They were always trying to outdo each other. When they became preteens and discovered boys, the rivalry intensified. For as competitive as Persia and Marty were, they were also very close and knew each other's darkest secrets.

Marty and her parents were the only people in the neighborhood who knew what Persia's father really did for a living, and they were there for Persia and Michelle when Face had gone to prison and they stumbled upon hard times. Marty knew things about Persia's life that not even Karen knew, and no matter how much they argued she had never thrown any of it in her face.

The same way Marty knew Persia's business, she was also aware of her secrets. The prim and proper white girl, who lived in the big house, had a wild side that you had to see to believe. Marty was what some might call rebellious and what others might've called a problem child. She was into bad boys, hard drugs, and good times. In Marty's head she was a rock star, so she moved like a sexually liberated young woman, who lived for the day with no care for tomorrow and made no excuses about it.

In Marty's defense she wasn't totally responsible for the woman she was becoming. Her father owned a lucrative car service, which allowed them to live a cut above everyone else, but he spent more time with his mistresses than he did with his family, and substituted money and gifts for love. Marty's mother was like an older, wilder version of Marty. She loved a good time so much that she spent most of her time chasing them.

She was a socialite who kept vampire hours and suspect company.

"What's good?" Persia asked, giving Marty an air-kiss on each cheek.

"Life, what else?" Marty spread her arms, motioning at her expansive house. Persia and her family lived in an impressive home on the next street, but Marty's place is was like a mini-mansion. "Come in." She stepped aside and allowed Persia in. "I must admit, I was surprised to hear from you and even more surprised that you actually showed up."

"I told you I was coming," Persia said.

"Yes, but it wouldn't have been the first time you said you were coming and didn't show up. We haven't seen much of you since you started going to that new school with your *other* friends."

"It isn't that, I've just been busy," Persia told her.

"So I've heard."

"And what's that supposed to mean?" Persia wanted to know.

"I overheard my mom talking to that nosey old hag, Mrs. Peterman, who lives next door to you. She said she heard someone fighting at your house last night. I tried to call you for hours, but your bedroom line was busy," Marty told her.

"I hate that nosey old bitch," Persia huffed. "Me and my mom got into it last night because I had been sipping a little bit while I was out." She left out the part about her mother forbidding her to go to Harlem because she didn't want Marty to know about her travel restrictions. "Speaking of mothers, is yours home?" she changed the subject. "I was hesitant about calling at first, because I didn't want to blow your cover if you were ditching school today."

"Yeah, she's in her usual spot, face down and drunk across the bed. I don't think she'll mind that I didn't go to school today. Let's go in the bedroom. Sarah is back there."

Marty led her up the spiral stairs to the second floor where her bedroom was. Sarah was sitting near the window packing a tall glass bong with weed. Unlike Marty, Sarah was an average-looking blonde with little to no curves, but she had the best drug connections. Her father was a pharmacists and she made a killing selling what she could filch from his inventory to the rich pill heads in her school.

"Looks like you're right on time, Persia." Sarah hunched over the bong, preparing to light it.

"You greedy bitch, I can't believe you were about to smoke without me," Marty said with an attitude.

Sarah ignored her, and lit the bong. The small bowl sizzled when the lighter touched it, and the glass chamber filled with grey smoke. Sarah inhaled deeply, clearing the smoke from the bong and holding it. Within a few seconds she was coughing and choking.

"That's what you get for being a fiend." Marty snatched the bong. She took her time with it, taking delicate pulls, and letting them flow from her nose. The last pull she held, and held the bong out to Persia, along with the lighter.

Persia lifted the bong to her mouth, but hesitated. She thought something smelled off, but when she sniffed it the second time it just smelled like weed. Persia fired the bong up and took short tokes until the chamber was full. In one mighty breath she cleared the chamber. The smoke hit her chest like icy fingers, trying to pump the air from her lungs. She immediately broke into a violent fit off coughing. She was barely able to pass the bong to Sarah without dropping it, when she scrambled to Marty's wastebasket and started dry heaving.

"I guess that weed is a little bit stronger than that ditch weed you're smoking up in Harlem." Marty laughed, firing up the bong again.

"Jesus, what the hell was that?" Persia asked, wiping her mouth with the back of her hand.

"That was some of California's finest. When we get high, we go to the moon with it," Sarah said proudly.

"Whatever." Persia waved her off. "Can I get something to drink? That weed gave me the cottonmouth."

Marty went to the mini-fridge that sat in the corner near the window, and rummaged around for a few seconds before she came up holding a bottle of wine, and a bottle of vodka. "Pick your poison, because I'm not going downstairs to the kitchen."

"Happy time." Sarah snatched the bottle of vodka. She didn't bother with a cup, sipping straight from the bottle. "Here." She extended it to Persia.

"Well, damn, don't you at least have a chaser for it?" Persia asked.

"Chase it with your spit." Marty snatched the bottle from Sarah and took a swig. "On the phone you said you were having a shitty day, so what better to take the edge off than a strong drink?"

Persia usually didn't drink that early in the day and especially two days in a row, but Marty was right, she was having a shitty day. "Fuck it." She took the bottle and took a sip. The vodka burned at first, but by her third sip it wasn't as bad.

For the next hour or so the girls watched videos, laughed, and talked about boys. Persia was having a good time with Marty and Sarah. They weren't as catty as Karen and her cronies, and they weren't always looking for Persia to spend her money on the drinks and drugs. It was nice to be able to just have fun without the bullshit. Marty's cellular phone rang. While she chatted on the phone, Persia entertained herself watching Sarah try to mimic the moves some girls were doing in the video that was playing. The girl didn't have one ounce of rhythm, but she thought she was killing it. When Marty was done with her phone call, she had a big smile plastered across her face.

"What did you just hit the lotto or something?" Sarah asked sarcastically.

"Almost as good; found out where there's going to be a bunch of rich rappers tonight and how we can get in," Marty said coolly. "That was Jenny Hunter, she's tending bar at some club tonight where they're having a hip hop showcase. There's supposed to be lots of rappers there, including the Big Dawg crew!"

"What's a Big Dawg?" Sarah asked.

"Trouble from the way I hear it," Persia said. Big Dawg was a name that she was familiar with, being from Harlem, which was the place where the company was birthed. It was one of the most successful, and notorious, rap labels in the music industry. It was run by a retired crack dealer turned music mogul, who called himself Don B., the self-proclaimed Don of Harlem. Big Dawg was known for producing a string of number-one albums, as well as the people who seem to meet their mysterious and untimely ends in the shadow of the company.

"Trouble or not, I know there's going to be bottle popping and drugs, so I wanna go," Marty said. "Jenny says once we're in she'll let us drink without carding us."

"Won't we still need ID to get in? I mean, it is a nightclub," Sarah pointed out.

"If we make our faces up and put on some tight clothes, ID is the last thing anybody is going to be thinking about asking us for." Marty winked. "Persia, you're coming with us."

"Great idea, Marty! Those rappers are gonna take one look at Persia's big ol' ghetto booty and wanna put her in all their videos," Sarah slapped Persia on the ass playfully.

"Shut up." Persia shoved her. "I'd love to, but I don't think it's gonna happen. My mom has been on some bullshit lately about my comings and goings. I don't think she'd let me go."

"Ye of little faith, and limited lies." Marty shook her head. "Tell her that after the big blowout you guys had, you want a little space to clear your head so we're going to have a sleepover. It's the weekend, so it should be cool. If she gets suspicious, I'll have my mom call her to back the story up. She'll either be passed out again or out partying somewhere so she won't know if we snuck out."

"Sounds good, but I don't have anything to wear," Persia told her.

"Not a problem. You and my mom are about the same size, so we'll see what we can find for you in her closet," Marty told her.

"You've got it all mapped out, huh?"

"Of course I do, Persia. This is going to be a night to remember and I want you there with us. Now stop worrying and let me handle everything."

CHAPTER 17

Monk was dead tired when he got home that evening. He had been out robbing, stealing, and getting higher than an airplane for the past few days and he was ready to crash and sleep, before getting up to do it all over again. His old friend Face would be ashamed to see what he had let his life become, and he wasn't too happy with himself either.

When Face went away, and Charlene was killed, everything changed. Face had been his heart and Charlene his soul; with them gone he slipped into a dark place. Monk was still getting money on the streets, but his heart was no longer in it. He had become a shell of the man he was and life held no more joy for him. If it hadn't been for the fact that he was the only person in the world Li'l Monk had left, he would've probably swallowed a bullet years ago. To cope, Monk substituted love with drugs. He spent his nights binging on cocaine and pills, while partying with random women, leaving others to take care of his business. His so-called friends bled him slowly, and Monk was so coked up half the time that he didn't even notice it. By the time he realized what was going on, their operation was nearly in shambles and over half his soldiers had either gone to work for someone else or struck out on their own. Monk had a lifestyle and a habit so he had to find a way to keep money coming in, so he started robbing to make ends meet.

He hooked up with Scooter and his sister Sissy, and concocted a scam that would net him a nice haul with each lick. Sissy was always on the arm of one hustler or another and she started setting her dates up to get robbed by Monk and Scooter. In the beginning it was sweet and it kept the three of them in money, cocaine, and booze, but it didn't take long before their habits got in the way of their business. Sissy had set cut into some players from Atlanta who were in New York on business, and set them up to be robbed by Monk and Scooter. The plan was for Monk to rob the dudes in their hotel room and Scooter was to be waiting for him in front in the getaway car. Scooter was so coked up that he got the instructions wrong and was parked in front of a different hotel two blocks away. Monk ended up fleeing on foot, but the police caught him five blocks from the scene. The dudes from Atlanta were drug dealers, so they didn't report the robbery, but Monk had a gun on him at the time of his capture and was given two years for it. When he got out of prison, what little bit he'd been holding on to was gone, and the only things waiting for him were his son and his demons.

When he opened the door to his apartment, the first thing he noticed was the smell. It didn't have its usual scent of faint musk and lingering nicotine. It smelled of bleach and pine. Curious, he went into the kitchen and found that the dirty dishes, which had been sitting there for days, were washed and put away. When Monk snatched the refrigerator open and found it full of food, he figured he had to have come into the wrong apartment.

"What the fuck is going on?" Monk wondered aloud, making his way to the back of the apartment, where Li'l Monk's bedroom was. He didn't bother to knock before pushing the door open and what he saw tickled him.

Li'l Monk was sitting on his lumpy mattress, back against the wall and his eyes rolling back in his head. Between his legs was a girl with her big yellow ass pointed heavenward and her lips wrapped around Li'l Monk's cock. Within spitting distance of them at the other end of the mattress, Omega had one leg out of his jeans and held a brown-skinned girl in what looked like a wrestling move, while he thrust in and out of her. The four teenagers were so busy going at it that no one noticed Monk standing in the doorway.

"Make sure you save a taste for your old man," Monk finally announced himself.

"What the fuck, Monk!" Li'l Monk pushed the girl off him and awkwardly stuffed his sausage into his jeans. "I asked you not to just bust up in my room like that." He got off the mattress.

"I called your name, but I guess you were too preoccupied to hear me," Monk told him, glaring lasciviously at the two girls who were scrambling into their pants. "I see you finally cut them nappy-ass braids." He rubbed his hand over Li'l Monk's head, which was now cut low. "Looks good."

"Thanks, now can you step out for a minute so my people can get straight?" Li'l Monk asked.

Monk took one last hard stare at the girls, committing their nude flesh to memory. "A'ight, meet me in the living room. I need to holla at you." He left the room.

A few minutes later, Li'l Monk led his group from the bedroom to the front door. The girls looked embarrassed and kept their eyes glued to the floor. "Wait on me, O. I'll be out in a few," he told his partner.

"Do your thing." Omega gave him dap.

"We still going out tonight, right?" the light-skinned girl who had been performing oral sex on Li'l Monk asked.

"Yeah, Sophie. I told you we are. Just give me a little while to handle some business and me and Omega will come through your block and scoop y'all," Li'l Monk told her.

"Okay." Sophie puckered her lips for a good-bye kiss.

Li'l Monk was hesitant. He could see his father watching him from the living room and it made him uncomfortable, so he kissed her on the nose instead. "See you in a few, ma."

"It's like that?" Sophie asked with an attitude.

"Sophie, just let me take care of this and I'll get with you." He ushered her away. When he closed the door he could still hear Omega laughing at him from the hallway.

In the living room, Monk lounged on the couch, drinking one of the beers he'd found in the refrigerator and smoking the blunt clip Omega had left in the ashtray. "That Marcy Jean's daughter, from 'round 147th?"

"Yeah," Li'l Monk answered.

"I remember her mama from back in the days. That bitch could suck loose change from a parking meter, and from the slob job I seen Sophie putting on you earlier I can tell the apple doesn't fall too far from the tree." Monk laughed.

"Can you watch your mouth?" Li'l Monk sounded offended.

"That your girl?" Monk asked.

"No, me and Sophie are just cool," Li'l Monk lied. The truth was, Li'l Monk and Sophie had lost their virginity to each other a few years earlier. They had never been in a relationship to speak off, but they could come to each other to fulfill certain needs. Li'l Monk always respected Sophie because she was still willing to hang out with him even when he didn't have a pot to piss in. They had spent more than a few broke days together, which was why he made it his business to invite her out when he came up on a few dollars.

"Does she suck the dicks of every nigga she's just cool with? If that's the case, maybe it's a good thing it's not your girl," Monk said.

"What the fuck is your problem?" Li'l Monk asked, tiring of his father's taunting. It was always like this when they were in the house together, which was why Li'l Monk was always in the streets.

"I ain't got no problem. I'm still the same old Monk; looks like you're the one who's changed." He looked over Li'l Monk's new sneakers and haircut. "New gear, food in the pad, and you cleaned up. You must've had one hell of a good night."

"We paid Sophie and Tasha to clean up, and I caught the sneakers on sale on 125th. Ramses put a few extra dollars in my pocket at the end of my shift so I could get a haircut and something to wear," Li'l Monk told him.

"And what does Ramses care about your appearance? You ain't gotta be at the height of fashion to stand on no corners and sell crack for another nigga," Monk taunted his son.

"I don't stand on corners anymore. Ramses gave me a new position." Li'l Monk brushed past him and went into the kitchen. His father followed.

Monk leaned against the counter, arms folded, watching Li'l Monk rummage around in the refrigerator. "Less than twenty-four hours and you've already gotten a promotion? That's a mighty quick climb, even by the best's standards. What did you have to do for this promotion?"

"Nothing, just held Omega down when shit got a little crazy. That's all." Li'l Monk twisted the top off the beer and took a sip.

"Just held shit down when it got crazy, huh?" Monk asked. There was something not quite right with Li'l Monk, but he couldn't place his finger on it.

Li'l Monk shrugged his broad shoulders. "Ramses says he's taken a liking to me, so he wants to take me under his wing."

"More like under his thumb. People like Ramses don't show kindness to nobody, unless they plan on using them," Monk said in disgust.

"Just because you've always got an agenda when you get close to people doesn't mean everybody else thinks like that," Li'l Monk told him.

Monk laughed. "So what, you think you're gonna be Ramses's little play son, like Chucky and them? He tell you how he's gonna make you rich if you stay loyal?"

Li'l Monk didn't reply, but his facial expression spoke for him.

"Boy, you're greener than I thought. If you believed that shit then maybe you should put down the gun and pick up a pen so you can fill out some job applications. The game ain't for you, son."

"I think you're just pissed, because Ramses is trying to drop game on me instead of bullshit, like you always do," Li'l Monk said.

"Ramses ain't teaching you the game; he's running it on you. He keeps dumb little niggas like you around to do shit he wouldn't do himself. You'll pop off without question, and never think twice about the consequences. Murder is a dirty, dirty business, Li'l Monk, and you don't want that kind of stain on your soul. Right now you're straddling the fence, but once you cross over to that side there's no coming back. You ain't ready for that, son. You're my kid, and I know you better than anybody."

Now it was Li'l Monk's turn to laugh. "I never realized until just this second how fucking clueless you are as to who I am." He turned his back and returned to his bedroom. He had barely crossed the threshold when he was violently shoved from behind. Li'l Monk tripped over his feet and dropped the bottle, spraying beer and broken glass all over his bedroom floor.

"How dare you give me your back?" Monk stormed into the room. His nostrils were flared and the veins in his neck bulged. Even strung out, Monk still had a very intimidating appearance.

"Don't put your hands on me again," Li'l Monk warned. He grabbed a towel off the chair and got on his hands and knees to clean the beer up off the floor.

"What you gonna do, tell Ramses I slapped you around? Go right ahead. And if he wants to make something of it, we can get to it. You might be his new play son, but you're my *real* son. I brought you in this world and I can damn sure take you out, you hear me?" Monk grabbed Li'l Monk's shirt to get his attention.

In a fluid motion, Li'l Monk was on his feet and had one of his massive hands wrapped around his father's neck. He slammed Monk into the wooden closet door and it splintered. Li'l Monk placed a piece of the broken glass from the beer bottle to Monk's neck with enough pressure to prick him. Looking into the cold expression on his son's face, Monk now realized what was off about Li'l Monk that he hadn't been able to place earlier. The innocence was gone from his eyes.

"It's too late, ain't it?" Monk asked, sounding hurt. It was the closest to compassionate his son had seen him in years. "You plan to add my life to your list too?"

Li'l Monk blinked as if he were waking from a dream. Slowly, he released his father and took two cautionary steps back. "You ever put your hands on me again and the next time I'm gonna go through with it."

"Ramses made you kill for him tonight, didn't he?" Monk shook his head sadly. "I had a feeling the blood of them boys they found in the lobby was on your hands when you vanished all suddenly, but I didn't want to believe it. I wanted to believe . . . I *needed* to believe that I didn't pass my sickness on to my baby boy."

"You don't know what you're talking about." Li'l Monk grabbed his jacket and a plastic shopping bag before heading for the door. Monk didn't try to stop him, but he did follow him.

"Do you know what's waiting for you behind that door you're about to open?" Monk asked.

"Not really, but it's gotta be better than what's waiting for me here," Li'l Monk spat and left the apartment.

CHAPTER 18

Li'l Monk shoved the door of his apartment building open with so much force that it hit the wall and the glass cracked. As usual his father had managed to get into his head, and in doing so he forced Li'l Monk to face something that he had been trying to block out of his mind. Once meant you killed somebody; twice made you a killer.

He had recounted the story for Ramses, and again for Chucky during the ride back from the Bronx, but Li'l Monk hadn't had a chance to process it yet. The scene had been playing on repeat all night and throughout the day in his head, the deafening bang of the pistol, the smell of gunpowder, the blood. It was the blood that stuck out more than anything. Li'l Monk could remember looking at the hallway floor and wondering who was going to clean up all the blood. Initially he thought that he'd be burdened with guilt after committing murder, but strangely enough he wasn't. He felt neither good nor bad about the deed. It was simply something that happened, like stumbling on a broken piece of sidewalk, but not breaking your stride. What he'd learned was that the more you took life, the less complicated it became. It was the second person he had ever killed, and he knew he could do it again without reservations.

On the corner of his block, he saw Omega talking to Chucky. Chucky was one of the last people he wanted to see at that point. It was bad enough that Chucky already disliked Li'l Monk for reasons he wouldn't say, but things seemed to get worse after what happened to Benny. Chucky hadn't come out and said anything, but the way he glared at Li'l Monk and Omega the whole ride back from the apartment said that he held them responsible for what had happened to his friend. Li'l Monk walked up on the tail end of their conversation, but he didn't miss the sharp tones being traded back and forth.

"Chucky, how many times you gonna ask me about this shit? I told you everything that I told Ramses," Omega was saying.

"Maybe there was something you left out . . . something that you maybe told Ramses when you called to tell him about the murders," Chucky said in an accusatory tone. When Chucky saw Li'l Monk approaching, he visibly tensed. He seemed jittery and his eyes were glassy. Li'l Monk had seen the look before, but kept the observation to himself.

"What up, killer?" Chucky asked sarcastically.

Li'l Monk fought back the urge to slap Chucky. "You tell me. I didn't mean to interrupt your little chat."

"Nah, you ain't interrupting nothing. As a matter of fact, I'm glad you're here. I've been trying to get ya man Omega help me to fill in some of the blanks about what happened to Benny," Chucky told Li'l Monk.

Li'l Monk shrugged. "It's like my man told you, we've been over all this already."

"Well, if I wanna go over it one hundred more times, muthafucka, we will!" Chucky snapped. His eyes were wild and the corners of his mouth were white with dry spit.

Li'l Monk took one look at Chucky and knew without a doubt that he was high off more than weed and not in total control of himself. He would be mindful of it, but he wasn't going to allow Chucky to disrespect him any further. "Chucky." He set his bags on the ground and gave Chucky his undivided attention. "I'm gonna tell you like I told Ramses, and let's hope that's the end of it. Some niggas came through to rob the spot, and me and O laid 'em down. Unfortunately, one of them was connected to your peoples. Now I can understand you being upset, but your problem ain't with me. You need to direct that anger at whoever it is you're really mad at because neither me nor Omega has done anything to you."

Chucky's face twisted angrily. "What you dropping your bag for like you wanna do something?"

"Chucky, I ain't trying to do nothing. I'm just trying to tell you what it is. I don't want no problems," Li'l Monk said in as calm a voice as he could muster. His patience was wearing thin with Chucky, but he didn't want problems with Ramses. He was too new to the crew to make waves. It seemed like his attempt at diplomacy only made Chucky more agitated.

"You're damn right you don't want no problems. I don't care who you killed, I'm still the top gun around this muthafucka," Chucky sneered. "You think because Ramses gives you a pat on the head like a good little dog, you got a voice at the table? I've seen a hundred little punks like you come and go and they all thought they would be Ramses's new number one, but I'm still holding that spot! You ain't shit but a soldier and that's all you'll ever be, just like your daddy!"

"Fuck you say about my father, nigga?" Li'l Monk took a step toward Chucky, but Omega stepped between them.

"Be easy, my nigga. Chucky is on one right now. He don't mean nothing by it," Omega whispered to him.

"Fuck that, don't hold him back. Let him go so he can come get some of what I got for him." Chucky pulled his gun.

"You think yours was the last gun they made?" Li'l Monk drew the gun his father had given him . . . the gun that had cut the man down in the lobby. He could almost hear it pleading with him to feed it more bodies.

Before the confrontation could go on an unmarked police car slowed alongside them. The window rolled down and Detective Wolf glared at them. "Everything okay, boys?"

"Everything is fine." Chucky hid the gun behind his back. "Me and the young boys are just talking a little shit. Ain't that right?" He turned to Li'l Monk.

"Yeah, just talking shit," Li'l Monk agreed. His gun was pressed to the back of his thigh, ready to give it to Chucky or the cop, if either of them moved funny.

Wolf's thick lips parted into a grin and he nodded, like he knew something that he wasn't

telling. "Why don't y'all go talk shit on somebody's corner? This corner belongs to me. Ain't
that right, Chucky?"

"You got it. I got shit I need to be attending to
anyway," Chucky told him. He turned back to Li'l
Monk. "We're gonna continue this conversation
another time," he promised and hopped in his
car.

"I'll be looking forward to it," Li'l Monk called
after him as Chucky pulled off. A few seconds
after he'd gone, the police car left too.

"What the hell is wrong with you? Chucky is a
lieutenant out here!" Omega scolded Li'l Monk.

"I wouldn't give a fuck if he was the president.
If Chucky ever pulls a gun on me again I'm gonna
kill that dude and take it up with Ramses after,"
Li'l Monk said seriously. "What the fuck is his
problem anyhow?"

"He's probably going through the motions
over what happened with Benny. That was some
made-for-TV shit that went down."

"True story," Li'l Monk agreed. "What would
make a nigga who is already in a good position
fuck himself up like that?"

"Greed," Omega said flatly. "It's greedy niggas
who are fucking the game up. A nigga like me, I
ain't hard to please. Pay me what I'm worth, according to what I bring to the table, and I'm good.

It's when niggas start feeling like they're entitled to more when shit gets twisted and muthafuckas find themselves tied to chairs and shit."

"I can't even lie, I thought Ramses was gonna have that dude killed. I was surprised when all he did was exile him. Where do you think Benny is gonna relocate to?"

"Potter's Field." Omega laughed. "If I know Ramses, Benny is probably being committed to an unmarked patch of dirt as we speak."

"But he said—"

"I know what he said, but with Ramses what he says and what he does can sometimes differ. That shit was mostly for Chucky's benefit. I'm fucked up about what went on with Benny too, but at the end of the day he broke one of Pharaoh's cardinal rules: he stole. To Pharaoh, a thief is damn near as bad as a rapist."

"You think Chucky knows?" Li'l Monk asked.

Omega thought about it before answering. "In his heart, he probably does and I'll bet it's fucking him up. That would explain his behavior."

Or whatever he's on, Li'l Monk thought but he didn't voice it.

"Let's get up off this corner and make a move before Officer Dickhead comes back and gives us grief. I got a shorty who doesn't live far from here, and we can shower and change at her crib, before we go pick Sophie and Tasha up," Omega said.

Li'l Monk laughed. "Damn you on your pimp shit, huh?"

"Nah, I'm just living fast and young. We only got one life and mine will be lived with no regrets."

"So, where we gonna take them?" Li'l Monk asked. He had never really been on an official date and wasn't sure what the etiquette was.

"I know a spot downtown where they're having a music showcase. One of the bouncers is a friend of mine, so we don't have to worry about showing ID or getting in with our pistols," Omega filled him in.

"Sounds good to me. Do you think I should hit Ramses up and let him know what went down between me and Chucky?" Li'l Monk asked.

"Man, fuck that shit for right now. When Chucky sobers up and crawls out of his feelings everything will be back to normal. Stop worrying so much, my nigga. Tonight is all about having a good time. Whatever troubles you've got will still be waiting for you tomorrow."

Li'l Monk nodded in agreement with his friend. They had been promoted and it was cause to celebrate and he shouldn't let other people's bullshit steal his joy; still, he couldn't help but to think of Chucky and how he had been acting. Had Chucky been anyone else, Li'l Monk would've given him a good beating already, but Chucky was a part of Ramses's inner circle and laying hands on him might put him out of favor with Ramses. Li'l Monk saw the writing on the wall and Chucky was a disaster waiting to happen. He had already made it clear that he was going to be a problem, and Li'l Monk knew he would have to deal with him sooner or later, he just had to figure out how.

CHAPTER 19

Chucky zigzagged in and out of Manhattan traffic, with his music blasting and his face screwed up. From the time he had come back on the streets that day he had been in a foul mood and taking his anger out on anyone he came in contact with.

That morning he had come closer to death than he could ever recall, and it was his own fault. Ramses had been good to him, and in return Chucky was looking to rip him off and use his best friend as a pawn. For as savvy as Benny was with numbers, he wasn't built to be a leader, which was why he and Chucky ran the strip together. When Chucky got the idea to strike out on his own, it was only natural that he went to his friend Benny with it. Benny was hesitant at first, but Chucky was eventually able to convince him, just like he always did. The plan was foolproof: hit a few of Pharaoh's spots for a little at a time and build the foundation of their empire off what they'd stolen, and pay Chucky's debt off at the same time, but Benny got greedy. Chucky warned him against doubling back and hitting the same spot twice, but he had scored so big with the first lick that he just had to go back for another taste, and that was his undoing.

Turning his back on Benny at the apartment was the hardest thing he ever had to do. The saddest part of it all was that Benny really believed Ramses would let him live and Chucky had allowed him to believe it. Ramses talked big about just banishing Benny from New York, but Chucky knew better. Benny had embarrassed them so he had to die. It was a cold piece of business, but no matter how you sliced it, someone was going to get killed in that apartment. For as relieved as Chucky was to have lived through it, his heart still mourned for Benny.

Chucky hated Ramses for what he'd done. He understood his position as their leader and knew that examples had to be set to keep up appearances, but he seemed to take joy in torturing Benny and fucking with Chucky's head. Chucky kept thinking back to the smirking faces, of Ramses, Huck, and Boo, and couldn't decide which one of them he hated more. Benny was wrong, but he was still Chucky's friend and somebody would answer for his death. Ramses was untouchable, so that took him off the dinner menu, but the same rules didn't apply to Boo and Huck. In due time they would see him again and Chucky's would be the last face they saw before they left the world. He was going to kill them for Benny.

Benny's death and feeling responsible for it weighed on Chucky. He locked himself away in Yvette's apartment all day, drinking Jack Daniels and snorting blow. Chucky was going so hard that even Yvette warned him to slow down, but that got her a slap in the mouth and cut out of the rest of the cocaine. Chucky snorted until his nose dripped blood, and when it was all gone he hit the streets in search of more.

When he bumped into Omega on the corner, he was speed balling and his paranoia levels were on ten. Seeing him brought back thoughts of Benny, and Omega's role in his fate. Omega had been Chucky's and Benny's little protégé, and he was supposed to come to Chucky first when he discovered the identity of the robber, yet he went to Ramses. This made Chucky look at Omega like he had an agenda. Could he possibly have been trying to knock Chucky out of the box like he and Benny had tried to do to Pharaoh?

Then there was his new best friend, Li'l Monk. Had it not been for Detective Wolf's untimely arrival, Chucky would've likely shot him dead on that street corner for talking to him like he wanted to do something. To him, Li'l Monk was a bottom feeder, a lifetime soldier, and Ramses was making a mistake by putting so much stock in him so early. If Chucky had things his way, he would've killed Li'l Monk after the lobby shooting, and let the secret die with him, but Ramses wouldn't allow it. Ramses claimed it was because Li'l Monk had shown loyalty and was down to bust his gun, but Chucky had known Ramses long enough to be able to see through his bullshit. In Li'l Monk, Ramses saw the chance to shape the perfect soldier: loyal, fearless, and down to do whatever. Li'l Monk was like an un-flawed version of his father, and that's probably what Chucky hated about him most. Every time he saw Li'l Monk, he was reminded of Monk and the part he'd played in fucking his life up.

Chucky spun through Harlem, wondering where he could get his next fix from. Normally he would've just rolled through one of the stash houses and pinched off what he needed from the supply, but after what had happened Ramses was sure to see to it that every last gram was accounted for. He couldn't even send Yvette to cop for him after the way he'd treated her before he left. Chucky needed to get high in a major way, so he did something he promised himself he'd never do: copped off the street.

It was a short ride from heart of Harlem to Washington Heights. In the Heights, it snowed all year around. You couldn't go half a block without someone trying to give you a deal on some grams, and it only took a few seconds before Chucky was approached. Chucky made sure he didn't know the face of the young dude before beginning the negotiations. As it turned out they were out of soft and only had hard. If Chucky wanted soft he'd have to wait around for a few minutes. Chucky was uptight, but he was also desperate for a certain kind of high. Free-basing wasn't his thing, but he'd done it on several occasions, and could make do with it in a pinch. The money and product had barely exchanged hands before Chucky was peeling off. The last thing he needed was someone to see him uptown, buying coke on the street like a common crackhead and getting the ghetto news networking against him.

Replaying the events of the day made Chucky agitated all over again. He needed to get high and take the edge off. He parked under a tree on a dark street where he knew he wouldn't be disturbed for a while. He quickly twisted a blunt of weed laced with the crack rocks and fired it up. The drugs crackled and popped louder than a bowl of cereal when the flames hit it. There was a distinct difference between smoking coke and smoking crack, with crack being the harsher of the two. The smoke burned his eyes and nose in the close confines of the car, but Chucky refused to let the windows down, wanting to get as high as possible as quickly as possible. The hit was so powerful that Chucky heard bells and whistles in his head, or so he thought. It was just his cell phone ringing.

Chucky started to ignore the call and continue enjoying his blast, until he saw the name that was flashing across the screen. Tone never called unless it was about money. "What's good?" he answered.

"You," Tone replied. "Dig, I know it's kind of short notice, but I need a delivery. My boys are performing at this spot downtown and we need a li'l frosting to go with our cake, ya heard?"

Chucky knew that by frosting Tone meant coke.

"I got you, my G. Just give me the particulars and I'll bring it through," Chucky assured him.

Tone gave Chucky the address to the spot and told him how much coke he wanted to buy. Chucky took down the information and ended the call, smiling like the cat who had swallowed the canary. This was just the call he needed.

Chucky and Tone went way back, to the days when Tone was still hustling in the streets before he went legit. Tone was now the manager of a high-profile rapper and was making more money than he knew what to do with, but he had kept his street ties. Though Tone didn't do coke, at least not that Chucky knew of, he liked to keep some on hand for the groupies and members of his entourage who indulged. Whenever Tone and the rappers he managed were in town and looking to score, it always meant that Chucky could expect a big payday.

Chucky first hit one of the stash houses and grabbed an ounce of cocaine. It was more than Tone had asked him to bring, but he figured between the Big Dawg entourage and whoever else was in the club, he'd be able to get rid of it all. Next he went to his house to change his clothes and grab some extra cash. When he looked at himself in the mirror, he was pleased at the reflection starting back at him. His eyes were red and glassy, and his nose felt raw, but he looked good and was sure every chick in the spot would be on him. With any luck, he would not only be able to drop a bag full of cash in Ramses's lap the following morning, and earn his way back into his good graces, but he might just make some lucky young lady's night by taking her home after the club.

"Game on, muthafuckas." Chucky popped his collar and headed out.

CHAPTER 20

Just as Marty said it would, the plan went off without a hitch. When Persia called her house, she lucked up and Richard answered. She fed him a story about needing a little space after the argument and was going to spend the night at Marty's. Richard gave her the okay to spend the weekend at Marty's and promised to smooth it over with her mother, provided that Persia agreed to go to church with them on Sunday morning and afterward discuss what had happened so they could come to some type of resolution.

For the next few hours, Persia, Marty, and Sarah smoked more weed, put a dent in the bottle of vodka, and had completely gone through the wine. When it was time for them to get dressed, Marty had everyone covered.

Sarah had managed to find a dress in the back of Marty's closet that she hadn't been able to wear since puberty kicked in and she filled out. It was a cute silver drop-waist number that stopped at mid thigh. Sarah slipped on the shoes that Marty had to match the dress, but her feet were about a half size bigger than Marty's, so her toes came dangerously close to hanging over the front. She rocked them anyway.

Marty looked like she'd aged five years when she was done getting herself together. Her face was made up to near-professional quality and her hair was pinned on top of her head in a lazy bun, with a few stray strands tickling her pale neck. Marty's black sequined mini cocktail dress had a steep V down the middle, showing off her cleavage and flat stomach. The heels on her black stilettos were so steep that most women would've had trouble walking in them, but Marty's mother had her practicing in heels since she was five, so she navigated them with little trouble.

For the evening Persia had borrowed a black mesh dress that hugged her breasts and hips like it was made for her. Persia had more ass than Marty's mother, so the dress hiked a bit in the back, but not enough to show anything, just to draw attention to her ample rump. When all three of them lined up in front of Marty's wall mirror to take a group picture for their Myspace pages, there was no doubt in any of their minds that all eyes would be on them that night.

Instead of taking a taxi into Manhattan, Marty called one of the drivers from her father's car service. Marty had several of them who she kept on standby when she needed a ride somewhere. She never worried about it getting back to her father, because none of them wanted to be exposed for trading sexual favors with a minor.

The driver who had come for them that night was named Julio. He was a Hispanic gentleman with oily black hair and shifty eyes. Marty greeted Julio with kisses on both cheeks, before sliding into the passenger's side of the black Lincoln Town Car. When Julio held the back door for Persia and Sarah to climb in, Persia could feel him staring at her ass. He gave her the creeps.

Once they were out of their residential neighborhood, it was time to get the party started. Sarah was charged with the task of pouring drinks for all of them from the minibar, while Persia rolled a blunt. Marty fumbled with the car radio, looking for a station playing something good. The new jam "You" by Lloyd and Lil Wayne came bumping through the speakers, making all the girls dance in their seats.

Marty leaned and whispered in Julio's ear. "Are you holding?"

"I'm always holding," Julio said, without taking his eyes off the road. He was hip to Marty's routine.

"Can me and my friends get a little something so we don't have to go in the party sober?" she asked.

"You've already helped yourself to the liquor. What more do you need?" Julio asked.

"Stop acting like that." Marty moved closer to him. Her hand found its way to his thigh and up to his dick, where she tested his girth in her hand. "You know I'm not talking about alcohol." She tugged him gently. "Take care of me and I'll take care of you."

This time Julio did look at her. It was always the same thing with Marty. She would get him to chauffer her around all night, use up all of his drugs, and leave him with nothing but a hard dick and hope. The closest he had gotten to sex with Marty was when she'd given him a hand job one morning when he drove her to school. He hated the way she toyed with him and always vowed that he wouldn't let it happen again, but he wanted her so bad that he always gave her another chance, in hopes that it would finally be his time to claim the prize. That night he was determined to stick to his guns.

"You wanna get high then I'm gonna need to get off." Julio pulled his dick through his zipper and let it rest on his lap.

Marty looked at the shriveled worm he called a dick and found it just as repulsive as the last time she'd seen it. There was no way she was adding that to the list of guests who had visited her pussy, but she was going to have to give him something if she wanted what he had in his goodie bag. Next to Sarah, Julio always scored the best drugs. She had to shit or get off the pot.

"I got you, just set it out," Marty said in her sweetest voice.

Julio reached into his inside jacket pocket and pulled out a pill bottle, which contained two rolled joints and some loose pink pills. Marty greedily snatched the bottle from his hand. She dry swallowed one of the pink pills, and fired up a joint before handing the second joint and pill bottle to the back seat.

Sarah popped one of the pills in her mouth and washed it down with a gulp of vodka. "You want?" She offered a pill to Persia.

"What is it?" Persia asked.

"Those are called Joy Rides, they're all the rage at parties these days," Julio said over his shoulder.

"You mean like ecstasy?" Persia had taken pills before, but those were valium or prescription drugs that she and Marty had stolen from her mother's medicine cabinet on random days when they wanted a quick buzz and couldn't score any weed. She had never danced on the side of the fence that Julio was trying to show them.

"Almost, but not with as much kick. These are like uppers, so the worst that'll happen is you might find you can't stop dancing when we get to the club," Sarah explained.

"Drop one of those happy fuckers and all your troubles will seem like a thing of the past, but if it's out of your league then I'll take yours too," Marty said slyly. She was challenging Persia, just like she did when they were kids.

"Anything you can do, I can do, Marty," Persia capped and popped the pill.

"That's my girl." Marty smiled. "Here's to a great night with my favorite bitches." Marty raised her glass in salute, and the girls toasted.

About twenty minutes into the ride, Persia's pill started to kick in. She was slouched in the back seat, staring aimlessly out the window. The passing streetlights on the freeway made pretty patterns and she found herself trying to count the colors. The air conditioning was on, but it still felt warm. She rolled the window down to let the fresh air hit her face, but then she found she was cold and rolled the window back up, only to be hot again. Persia kept sending the window up and down, making music in her head with the noises from the window motor. She was in a pretty place, and just as Marty had said, all of her problems were now things of the past.

In the front seat, Marty leaned over and started whispering softly into Julio's ear. Persia watched as her hand slipped over into his lap and started fondling his dick. Marty spat in one of her palms and started stroking him until he became erect. Her handling felt so good that Julio's leg trembled and he accidentally tapped the gas pedal, causing the car to lurch.

"You're gonna make me crash. If I crash this car your father is gonna kill me." His eyes kept flashing from the road to her grinning face.

"Then for your sake, you'd better keep the wheel steady," Marty said mischievously.

Persia watched curiously as Marty's hands glided up and down the shaft of Julio's dick. Marty ran her fingers over her pussy until they were wet, then smeared them on Julio's throbbing muscle. Persia could see the veins in Julio's neck bulge when Marty locked her thumb and index fingers of one hand at the base of his shaft and stroked him feverishly with the other one, causing Julio to whimper in pleasure. Persia wasn't sure if it was the pill or the way Marty was working Julio, but she was getting turned on by the show. Without even realizing she was doing it, she dropped her hand between her legs and started toying with the lining of her damp panties.

All Julio could do was bite his lip and mumble in Spanish as Marty worked. She had the most gifted hands he'd ever felt. Her strokes now became aggressive and she squeezed his dick hard enough to hurt him, but he dared not tell her to stop. Julio's face flushed red and he looked like he was having trouble catching his breath, which only made Marty stroke him harder and faster. The cruel expression on her face said that she was enjoying his discomfort. Julio could feel the buildup, but he was determined to hold it in for as long as she could, but when she dipped her head and ran her tongue ever so gently across the head of his dick, he lost it. Marty moved her face out of the way just as Julio shot his load on the steering wheel and his pants.

When the show was over, Persia released the breath she hadn't even realized she was holding. A thin sheen of sweat had formed on her forehead and her panties felt soggy. She looked up at the rearview mirror and saw Marty's eyes staring back at her. She wondered how long she'd been watching. Persia was embarrassed, but Marty seemed amused, giving her a playful wink.

"Damn you, Marty," Julio said when he was finally able to compose himself. There was cum everywhere.

"You complaining?" Marty asked, wiping her hands with some McDonald's napkins she'd found in the glove compartment.

"Not at all, baby. I ain't never came that quick before," Julio lied. "Listen, since that hand job was just a warm up, how about I pull over somewhere so I can get at you properly."

"Aww." She patted him on the cheek with the same hand she'd just wiped the cum off. "As much as I would love to, I don't want my dress ruined before I get a chance to show it off." Before Julio could press the conversation, Marty busied herself engaging her friends in small talk.

A few minutes later they were in Manhattan and turning onto the block of the club. Traffic was bumper to bumper and it took them almost five minutes to make it halfway down the block. The sidewalk outside the club was teeming with people. A line went from the entrance to the next corner and seemed to keep getting longer. The street looked like a car show, with foreign and domestic cars, fitted with rims, tints, and loud sound systems lining the block. Dudes talking loud and wearing gaudy jewelry trolled the sidewalk, spitting game at women who were dressed in little to no clothes. The whole scene was one juggling monkey short of a circus.

"This is insane," Persia said, looking out the rear window.

"There're always huge turnouts at Big Dawg events. I heard once they had to call in the riot squad because things got so out of control," Sarah said.

"I wonder how long we're gonna have to wait on that line?" Persia thought out loud.

Marty gave Persia a look. "Sweetie, for as long as you've known me, have I ever waited on line for anything? You've been hanging around the washed-up and impoverished for too long. Let me remind you how the young and privileged do it. Let us out right in front, Julio," she ordered.

When Marty and her girls stepped onto the curb, they turned more than a few heads. Dudes tried to spit game at them and females rolled their eyes. Marty soaked it all up, hate and praises alike. She loved to be seen. With her head held high, and her walk confident, she strode up to the front of the line, where a burly man wearing a tight black jacket stood holding a clipboard and checking IDs. Marty flashed him her winning smile, expecting the rope to part like the Red Sea for her and her friends, but it didn't quite play out like that.

"Line starts back there, ladies," the bouncer told them.

"We're on the list, I'm Martina Slaughter," Marty introduced herself.

The bouncer scanned the clipboard. "Sorry, I don't see your name, which means you'll have to get on line."

"My name has to be on there. I'm a guest of Shorty's; he's with the group," Marty said, blinking innocently. She had no idea who Shorty was, but she figured there was somebody in the Big Dawg entourage by that name. Every rapper knew someone named Shorty . . . or so she hoped.

The bouncer frowned. "Who the fuck is Shorty?"

"He's with the group. How do you work here and not know who's performing?" Marty snapped.

"Look, I don't know who Shorty is and I don't know you. If your name isn't on the list, your ass is on the line." He turned his back to her.

"Maybe we should just go home. Julio couldn't have gotten too far, call him and have him pick us up," Sarah suggested.

"Fuck going home, we're going to have a good time like we set out to do," Marty told her. "If you think I'm going to let that minimum-wage goon ruin our night, you've got another think coming. We're getting in that club; we just have to be creative about it."

Marty fired up a cigarette, so it would look like they were standing outside for a reason other than not being able to get in, while her devious mind worked on a way to get them past the bouncer.

A red BMW pulled up to the front of the club and the valet stepped off the curb to greet it. Persia thought the car looked familiar, but couldn't remember where she had seen it before, until the driver stepped out.

With a devilish smile on her face, she turned to her girls and said, "Ladies, it looks like our luck might've just changed."

"Is this fate, or a coincidence?" Chucky asked when he saw Persia approaching him. She looked good enough to eat in her form-fitting dress and heels.

"I waited for you to call, but you never did," Persia lied. She hadn't even been home to know if Chucky had called her after school like he promised.

"My fault, ma. I've had my hands full all day with work," Chucky told her.

"You could've had your hands full with me," Persia said playfully.

Chucky was a little thrown off by her directness, which made him take a hard look at her. He hadn't peeped it at first, the dilated pupils, the fact that she was having trouble standing still. Persia was high off of something, but what he couldn't be sure. It didn't matter, the fact that she was willing to experiment with more than weed was a feather he would stick in his cap and use at a later time.

"Looks like somebody is feeling themselves," Chucky said jokingly.

"And why shouldn't I be? I'm young, fine, single, and ready to mingle." Persia did a little dance.

"From the way you're rocking that dress, you might not be single for long." Chucky licked his lips.

"I don't know about all that, Chucky. I've yet to meet a man who could tame my wild heart," Persia told him.

"That's because you haven't met the right one yet."

"So you're saying you're the right one?" Persia asked.

"I ain't saying I'm the right one, but I'm not the wrong one either," Chucky said. He had a good mind to blow off his meeting and take Persia somewhere where he could fuck her high-ass brains out, but he had to be cool about it. He didn't want to overplay his hand too early and ruin the game. "Why don't you come inside with me and let me buy you a drink?"

"I would love to, but I've got my girls with me." Persia motioned toward Marty and Sarah, who were standing off to the side watching the exchange.

Chucky looked at the two white girls, with his eyes lingering on Marty. She was taking slow drags off her cigarette and giving Chucky a look that could've been taken one of several ways. "Fuck it, bring them too. I got all of y'all."

With his arm draped around Persia, and her friends in tow, Chucky marched up to the front of the line, where the same bouncer who had turned Marty away was still at his post. Chucky gave him his name, which the bouncer found on the VIP section of the list. Realizing that Chucky was a guest of the group performing, the bouncer hurriedly opened the velvet rope to let Chucky and his guests in. One by one he stamped each of their hands with the special emblem reserved for important guests. When he went to stamp Marty's hand, he had a flash of recognition.

Marty took her time, finishing the last few drags of her cigarette, before tossing the butt at his feet. "I trust you'll get around to taking care of that. It's so hard to find good help these days." She flipped her hair and walked into the club laughing.

Marty looked uncomfortable, thinking the last few days of her marriage. I believe I was the butt of his joke. I bet you'll get nigged to taking care of that. I've a bird to find good trip those days.

She turned her face and looked at Nick, she still laughing.

CHAPTER 21

The stop by Omega's shorty's crib took a bit longer than expected. Omega's shorty lived in a two-bedroom apartment in Wagner Projects on the east side. Li'l Monk had never been to those particular projects, but they were familiar by reputation. It was a less-than-friendly place to outsiders.

The taxi let them out on Second Avenue, and they trooped through the projects. The unfamiliar faces drew a few curious glances, but no one said anything to them. In front of the building they were going to, about six or seven dudes were posted up, all with hard faces and larcenous hearts. Omega moved through the group like he belonged, nodding to those he knew and breezing past those he didn't. Omega had a way about him where he seemed to be able to blend in anywhere.

Omega's shorty had a two-bedroom apartment on the second floor, which she shared with her roommate and the five kids they had between them. She was a shapely Spanish chick, who was slightly older than Omega, but still had the body of a young girl. Li'l Monk was shown to the bathroom so he could shower, while Omega was led to the bedroom so she could show him how much she missed him.

Considering how many people lived in the house and the fact that they had popped up unexpectedly, the bathroom was surprisingly clean. Li'l Monk showered and dried himself with the T-shirt he'd just taken off, since neither Omega or his chick had bothered to provide him with a towel before they went off to handle their business. From the shopping bags he'd brought with him, he pulled out a crisp pair of black jeans, black Gore-Tex boots, and a black button-up shirt. It had been quite some time since Li'l Monk had been able to treat himself to something to wear and the new fabric felt good against his skin, but the gun tucked down the front of his jeans felt better.

Li'l Monk sat in the living room watching the news while Omega finished handling his business and went to shower. There was a story being reported about three bodies found in the lobby of a Harlem apartment building, which made Li'l Monk sit bolt upright and pay attention. They didn't release the names of the victims, but they didn't have to for Li'l Monk to know they were talking about the messes he and Omega had left behind. He continued to watch, nervously, just waiting to hear his name or Omega's in connection with the crime, but the police didn't seem to have any suspects, at least as of yet. Ramses had told them not to worry about it, that he would take care of everything, but Li'l Monk still felt like he was walking on eggshells.

Omega eventually came out. His chick had twisted his dreads into three large plaits, and he traded in his street clothes for jeans, a blazer, and a graphic T-shirt beneath. "Why are you sitting there looking all crazy in the face?" Omega asked, noticing something seemed to be troubling his friend.

"Nothing, I'll talk to you about it outside," Li'l Monk told him and got up to leave.

"Do you have to go?" the chick whined, pawing at Omega's jacket.

"I told you I gotta bust some moves, but I'll be back to finish knocking the bottom out of that later on tonight," Omega said coolly.

"Omega, that's the same bullshit excuse you give me all the time when you promise to come back and never do. I'm gonna stop opening my door for you," she threatened.

"When one door closes another one opens. You keep that in the back of your mind while you're talking slick," Omega capped. "Let's roll, my nigga." He led Li'l Monk from the apartment. The chick called after him, telling him that she was just joking, but Omega never turned around to respond.

"That shit was on the news," Li'l Monk finally told Omega once they were in the elevator.

"What shit?" Omega asked.

"The shooting."

"What they talking about? They got any suspects?" Omega asked anxiously.

"Nah, they're clueless as to who did it," Li'l Monk told him.

"See, Ramses said he was going to take care of it and he did." Omega smiled.

"We splattered those cats in the middle of the evening, and I know the old head who came out of her apartment saw our faces. You don't think anybody is gonna go to the police with information?"

"Not if they know what's good for them," Omega said. "When you work for Pharaoh, you're protected. Nobody is gonna say shit because they know if they do, them and everyone they love will likely be dead before we ever see the inside of a jail cell. We good, stop worrying."

When they came out of the building the dudes were gone, and there was a police cruiser sitting in the middle of the projects. Li'l Monk tensed when they passed it and the cops started staring at them, and talking among each other. Their eyes felt like high beams on them and the gun in Li'l Monk's pants suddenly felt very heavy. Li'l Monk kept his eyes down and kept walking, not daring to take a breath until they were out of the projects and in a taxi on their way to pick up their ladies.

Sophie and Tasha stopped traffic when they came out of Sophie's building. Tasha was wearing a tight jumpsuit with a leopard print and black thigh-high boots. Her dark face was made up smooth and flawless and there wasn't a hair out of place. Tash was only sixteen, but that night she could've easily passed for twenty-something. Sophie kept it a bit simpler, but looked no less radiant. Red hot pants hugged her ass and thighs like they had been airbrushed on. Outside of a little lipstick, she wore no makeup, but she didn't need any. Sophie was a little hood and rough around the edges, but she was a very pretty girl. Li'l Monk jumped out and held the door open for the ladies to get into the taxi.

"At least one of you has got some manners." Tasha climbed in the car, rolling her eyes at Omega, who hadn't so much as looked up from the blunt he was sitting in the passenger's seat rolling.

Truth be told, Omega had just met Tasha that day, through Li'l Monk, and she had already let him hit it, which lost points for her in his book. Girls with loose pussies usually had loose mouths to go with them. In Omega's chosen profession, secrecy could be the difference between life and death, so any girl he claimed he would have to know that he could trust her, which was why he didn't have a steady girlfriend yet. Tasha was cool, but their relationship wouldn't go beyond entertainment.

Li'l Monk didn't hear her. He was too busy staring at Sophie. "Wow, you look really pretty."

"Thanks." Sophie blushed. "You clean up pretty nice yourself." She fixed his collar.

"You two lovebirds get in the cab so we can make a move. I wanna get there before it gets crowded," Omega said from the passenger's seat.

Before heading to their destination, Omega had the cab stop by a liquor store, where he grabbed a pint of Hennessy for him and Li'l Monk and a pint of Long Island Iced Tea for the girls. On the ride downtown, they fired up two blunts of some Black weed that Omega had scored, to wash down the liquor. It smelled like burning wood, but it was high-powered pot. Everybody was feeling groovy, especially Sophie. She nestled close to Li'l Monk, eyes low and red, gazing out the window. He was surprised by the gesture, but receptive to it. He put his arm around Sophie, and pulled her a little closer.

"Y'all make a cute couple," Tasha remarked.

"We ain't a couple." Li'l Monk withdrew his arm.

Sophie felt slighted, but she didn't show it. "Yeah, we're just friends."

Tasha shook her head. "You two have been playing this game for as long as I've known you. Y'all always together, you're fucking and neither one of you wants to see the other one with anyone else. It's like you're in a relationship already, so why not just make it official?"

"I got too much going on in my life right now to focus on a girlfriend," Li'l Monk said.

"Boy, you sound crazy," Tasha said.

"Leave it alone, Tasha. Ain't nobody sweating Li'l Monk. Besides, his heart belongs to someone else already," Sophie said.

The remark stung. Sophie was one of the only people Li'l Monk had ever confided in about his feelings for Persia. She knew it was a sensitive subject and had said it to hurt him, the way his rejection had hurt her.

For the rest of the ride, Li'l Monk didn't say much and neither did Sophie. The earlier conversation had raised a wall of tension between them and for the first time things were awkward. This was another reason why Li'l Monk had never pursued a relationship with her. Sophie thought that Li'l Monk being in love with Persia was the reason that he refused to officially date her, but that was only partially correct. Next to Charlie, Sophie was his best friend and commitment would change that. He would rather not have Sophie as a lover than to lose her as a friend.

The cab let them out up the block from the club and they walked the rest of the way. Li'l Monk was surprised to see how many people were lined up outside. In addition to the club security there was also a noticeable police presence. He thought about stashing the guns, but Omega assured him that they wouldn't have a problem getting them in.

At the door Omega greeted the bouncer with a smile and handshake, during which he passed the bouncer something Li'l Monk couldn't see. The bouncer looked at whatever was in his hand, nodded, and opened the rope for them. When Omega and his group were directed around the metal detectors instead of having to go through like everyone else, Li'l Monk understood what the exchange was about.

The inside of the club was crowded and dark, except for the few lights at private tables and the spotlights focused on the stage where a rap group was performing. Li'l Monk recognized the group Bad Blood from their videos, but couldn't say he was a fan of their music.

"It's packed in here," Sophie said, startling Li'l Monk. It was the first time she'd said more than two words to him since their conversation in the taxi.

"Yeah," Li'l Monk replied. It was all he could think to say.

"Yo, let's hit the bar and get some drinks," Omega called over to him, pointing at the bar on the other side of the room.

"With all these people in here, it's going to take forever for us to reach it," Tasha said. They couldn't move more than a few feet without bumping into someone.

"I got this." Li'l Monk began bulldozing a path for them through the crowd to the bar. "What you drinking?" he asked her, hoping she asked for house-brand liquor instead of something exotic. He had been doing the math in his head, and between the new clothes and bullshitting around he had already eaten up a good chunk of the money Ramses had given him.

"Everything is on me tonight," Omega told him with a wink. He didn't say it, but he was aware of Li'l Monk's financial situation and didn't want his friend to be embarrassed.

"Since it's on you, let's get some champagne," Tasha suggested.

Omega shot her a look. "How about we start off with a few shots and move from there." He turned his back to her and ordered the drinks.

"Your shovel is showing, gold digger," Sophie whispered in Tasha's ear.

"Child please, these goodies don't come for free," Tasha said with a roll of her eyes.

The bartender came back with four shots of tequila and four Coronas and set them on the bar. Omega divided the drinks among them. "I'd like to propose a toast." He raised his glass.

"Hey now." Tasha snatched her drink up.

"What are we toasting to?" Li'l Monk asked.

"The world, because soon it's gonna belong to us." Omega downed his shot.

CHAPTER 22

Walking inside the club was like stepping into another world for Persia, especially since she had never been. Seeing clubs in movies and music videos was one thing, but to actually be in the thick of it felt surreal to Persia. The people, the music, the glamour . . . she loved everything about it.

Chucky led them across the dance floor, where there were throngs of people humping and grinding on each other. To her left, two girls were engaged in a lip lock and feeling each other up like they were about to go at it right there in front of everyone. Overhead the strobe lights began blinking in different colors and patterns, making it hard for Persia to focus. She was suddenly overcome with vertigo, and stumbled. Thankfully, Chucky caught her by the arm and kept her from falling and embarrassing herself.

"You okay?" Chucky asked, steadying her.

"Yeah, my heels just got caught on something," Persia lied. Truth be told, it was a side effect of the Joy Ride she'd popped. Something about the flashing lights was making the drugs in her system spike, and Persia felt like she was on a roller coaster with no safety belt.

"I could carry you if you want?" Chucky offered.

"That's sweet of you, but I'll be fine. I just need to sit down for a minute," Persia said.

"Then let's get you a seat and a drink." Chucky took her by the hand and pulled her along.

In the back of the club there was a section that was separated from the main area by a thick gold rope. There was a sprinkling of tables and booths, some occupied and some not, and each had a bottle of champagne on it. Waitresses scurried back and forth to cater to the needs of those privileged enough to occupy that side of the rope, while groupies with no shame performed strange acts for men with long paper and larcenous hearts. This was their destination.

"Give me a second," Chucky told Persia, and approached the rope to speak with the bouncer guarding it. They exchanged a few words, before a man wearing a sweat suit and a long gold chain interceded. The man in the sweat suit motioned to the bouncer that Chucky was "good," and he was allowed to step inside the gold rope, where he was greeted with a handshake and a hug.

"That dude looks familiar," Marty said, trying to place his face. She didn't have to wonder who he was for long because a few seconds later they were all whisked inside the roped-off area by security.

"Ladies, this is a friend of mine, Tone," Chucky introduced them.

"I know I'd seen your face somewhere before. You're signed to Big Dawg, right?" It finally hit Marty where she had seen him before. He was in a few of the rap videos she had seen.

"Yeah, I'm down with Big Dawg, but not signed to them. I don't rap, I count money," Tone boasted. "But enough about me, you guys are guests of Chucky, which means you're guests of the Dawg House." He motioned around the VIP area. "Let's get you pretty ladies situated so we can begin the festivities."

Tone showed them to a private table, which had an excellent view of the stage. The group, Bad Blood, had just finished their set and were lounging at the table, drinking and smoking weed. They had some girls with them, but the females were quickly forgotten when the fellas saw Persia and Marty.

"Damn, I think I just caught a mean case of Jungle Fever," one of the men in the group said, eyeballing Marty like she was the Last Supper.

"Fall your thirsty ass back, Pain. You ain't entitled to every piece of flesh that comes through here," Tone told him.

"Why not? We're dawgs and share everything don't we?" Pain asked jokingly.

"Excuse this ignorant muthafucka. His mother dropped him on his head when he was a kid and he hasn't been right since," Tone told Marty.

"You cuffing already, Tone?" another of the group joked. He was called Lex. He was Pain's partner in crime, but not quite as abrasive.

"You know cuffing ain't in my vocabulary, Lex, so knock it off. I'm just trying to make sure you thirsty-ass niggas don't frighten our guests off before we've had a chance to get properly acquainted."

"Don't worry, Tone. We won't be too rough with them," Pain said sarcastically.

"Sometimes I like it a little rough," Sarah spoke up. She already knew that Persia was going to hook up with Chucky, and Tone had eyes for Marty, but she was sizing up the quiet dude in the corner with the big chain on. Weighed against what was left over, Pain was the next best option so she figured she might as well put her bid in early.

"I think I like you, white girl. Why don't you come have a seat by me and get some of this liquor." Pain patted the seat next to him. Fearlessly, Sarah went over and took the spot he'd patted, making it a point to bump the girl over who had been sitting closest to him. She held her cup out while Pain filled it with straight vodka. He offered her a chaser, but she declined.

"You've got some live-ass lady friends, Chucky," Tone said.

"So I'm noticing." Chucky watched in amazement as Sarah downed the vodka and held her cup out for another round.

"Is that crazy-ass Chucky?" The quietest of the young men asked abruptly, jumping to his feet. He hadn't said much since they'd come over. The diamond-encrusted Rottweiler medallion hanging from his chain clanged against his chest when he moved. The girls who had been hanging on him quickly scattered, thinking there was going to be an altercation, but instead he and Chucky embraced each other. "Damn, I ain't seen you in a minute."

"That's because you're too busy being famous to come back and visit us niggas in the slums, True," Chucky said with a smile. True was the biggest act signed to Big Dawg. He was quickly making the ascension from underground rapper to celebrity, and the country was rocking to his music. But for as much as a star as True was becoming, to Chucky he was still the same bad-ass kid who used to sell crack on Eighth Avenue.

"I ain't never too big to visit the hood that birthed me, but I'm wise enough to make my visits as infrequent as possible and only when necessary. It's an unfortunate thing when niggas get so bitter from you trying to reach the stars that they get to scheming on how to put you in the dirt," True said solemnly. "But enough about that bullshit, what brings you out tonight? I know you ain't no fan of crowds, and this place is a zoo."

Chucky shrugged. "Just came to handle some business with Tone and grab a drink."

True was smart enough to read between the lines. The only business Chucky dealt with was the business of cocaine. True shook his head. "Same old Chucky."

"We can't all be blessed enough to go platinum," Chucky shot back.

Their conversation was interrupted when a young man joined their group. He was tall, standing about six feet four inches, with rich chocolate skin and innocent eyes. He went around the group giving everyone dap, but when he turned and saw Persia he paused. When their eyes met it was as if everything else had faded away and she was the only woman in the room. He tried to say something, but couldn't find the words. It was as if she had stolen his breath and all he could do was stare.

"See something you like, homeboy?" Chucky asked, snapping him out of it.

"Sorry, I didn't know she was with you," the boy said apologetically.

"Well, now you do, and you might wanna keep your eyes to yourself. Some people might take that gawking as disrespectful," Chucky warned.

Tone placed his hand on Chucky's shoulder. "Relax, he didn't mean anything by it. My little cousin, Vaughn, can be a bit naïve about certain things, but he's not a disrespectful kid."

"Wait, this is the same little dude who used to be in the park, practicing throwing footballs through the tire swings?" Chucky asked in surprise.

"Yeah, that was me," Vaughn said shyly.

"Man, I haven't seen you since you were like ten years old!" The last time Chucky had seen Vaughn he was a rail-thin little kid with a big head, but he had grown into an Adonis of a man.

"Vaughn's been in Virginia for the past ten years or so," Tone began. "He got himself into some trouble up here, so his mama sent him down there to live with our aunt and go to school."

"That's what's up! You still playing ball?"
Chucky asked.

Tone laughed. "Chucky, I can tell you're not
into sports. Everybody knows Vaughn Tate,
starting quarterback for Virginia Tech. My little
cousin is gonna be in the NFL one day," he said
proudly.

"Tone, I wish y'all would stop saying that.
Maybe one in every ten thousand kids actually
makes it to the pros, which is why I'm busting
my ass to graduate in case football doesn't work
out."

Tone draped his arm around Vaughn. "It's
gonna work out, trust your big cousin on this
one. Listen, I got some business to handle with
Chucky, so I'm gonna skate for a minute. Get
yourself a drink and mingle. I'll be back in a few."

"Okay, Tone." Vaughn nodded.

"I trust you ladies will be okay in the company
of these wolves?" Tone asked Persia and her
friends.

"Every dog can be tamed." Marty slipped onto
the seat next to True. She ran her finger along
his gold chain. "You boys go do what you have to
do. True was just about to tell me all about how
many albums he sold." She picked up his cup
and sipped from it.

"Damn, you don't beat around the bush do
you?" True asked with a smirk.

"Not really," she said honestly.

Leaving the girls in the care of the rappers, Chucky and Tone disappeared to the bathroom to talk money. The guys from Bad Blood weren't that bad once the girls got to know them. They freely shared their liquor with the girls and every time they turned around it seemed like someone had lit another blunt. Though the rappers treated Vaughn like he was one of them, it was obvious that he didn't belong. They were loud and obnoxious, whereas he was quiet and polite. Vaughn didn't hit the weed, but he partook in the alcohol. Every so often Persia would catch him looking at her, but whenever she turned in his direction, he looked away. She had to admit that Vaughn was a good-looking guy, but he wasn't her type. Persia like bad boys and Vaughn seemed a little too pure for her taste.

Persia was a little tense at first, but she eventually loosened up. True ordered a bottle of chilled tequila, and poured rounds for everyone in black shot glasses with the Big Dawg logo on them. Persia had heard horror stories about the effects of mixing liquor, but she was going to do it anyway. If they were pouring she was drinking, and if blunts were being rolled, she was smoking. Only God knew when she'd have another night like this before twenty-one and she wanted to

make it memorable. Being out at the club, surrounded by pretty people and money made her
feel like a different person. There was nobody
to harass her about her grades, and she and her
mom weren't beefing. All that existed at that
moment was a good time.

"Don't drink that," Vaughn told her when
Persia reached for the shot glass.

"Why not? I'm trying to get my drink on like
everyone else." Persia told him, holding the glass
mid-shot.

Vaughn shook his head. "Everything that
glitters isn't gold, shorty."

"Vaughn, stop talking the girl's ear off and let
her do her shot," Pain barked.

"Yeah, Vaughn, stop being such a wet blan-
ket," Sarah half slurred. "As a matter of fact, I
don't see a drink in your hand." She thrust her
shot glass at him, splashing liquor of Vaughn's
pants.

"I'm cool on that Devil's Brew. I'll stick with
what I know." Vaughn held up the bottle of beer
he was sipping.

"Shorty, you drinking or not? Because you're
holding up the toast," Lex asked, eyeing Persia
like a hungry predator.

Feeling like everyone in the club was watching,
Persia threw the shot back. The tequila stung, but

only for a second before sending a calming numbness through her chest. She ran her tongue along the roof of her mouth and it felt gritty, as if the glass hadn't been properly washed. She wiped her tongue with a napkin and resumed her drinking. What she didn't know was that that the residue she felt on her tongue were from the crushed pills sprinkled in the bottom of each glass.

After the last act preformed the DJ cut loose. He had the crowd going crazy, playing a mix of all the most popular raps songs that were out at the time. Persia was swaying back and forth, in her chair, to the beat. She thought after consuming the different liquors and smoking so much weed, she'd be sick by then, but she actually felt great. So great in fact, that she got up and started dancing.

Marty joined her on the dance floor and the two of them started dancing together. At first they were just clowning, but the deeper into they got, the more intense the dancing became. At some point they moved their little dance-off to a tabletop, and were putting on a show for the members of Big Dawg. Marty was dancing so close to Persia that she could smell the liquor and weed on her breath. Staring into Marty's eyes Persia realized that she had known Marty nearly all her life and never realized how beautiful they were. They were as green as summer leaves, and Persia found that she could stare into them all night.

A trail of sweat rolled down the side of Persia's face. Marty reached up to wipe it away, and when her hand made contact with Persia's skin, is sent an electric shock through her entire nervous system. Marty picked up on it, and ran her fingers gently over Persia's spine, causing her to shudder. Everything around Persia became a blur . . . the whistles, the flashes of cameras, the stray hands on her legs . . . She blocked it all out. She was too far gone in the rapture drugs, music, and Marty's touch to care about anything else.

CHAPTER 23

After having a few drinks, Tasha convinced Omega to get out on the dance floor with her. To all their surprise, Omega was a pretty good dancer. Sophie tried to get Li'l Monk to join in, but he declined. He had never been very coordinated and refused to go out there just to make a fool of himself.

"You're no fun." Sophie tossed a napkin at Li'l Monk.

"I'm plenty of fun, I just ain't no dancing-ass nigga. As big as I am, I'd look like a damn fool out there pop-locking." Li'l Monk imitated one of the moves he'd seen Omega do on the dance floor, which made Sophie laugh. "See, I told you I'm fun."

"You a'ight, I guess."

For a few seconds there was an uncomfortable silence.

"You want another drink or something? If the shots and beer are too harsh, I can get you something softer, maybe some wine?" Li'l Monk suggested.

"You know damn well I don't drink no wine, and you don't have to keep offering to buy me drinks, Li'l Monk. I'm not here with you because you buy me drinks, I'm here with you because I like being around you."

"I couldn't tell from the way you were giving me the cold shoulder in the car," Li'l Monk said.

"I was giving you the cold shoulder because you had hurt my feelings. And speaking of that, I owe you an apology. It was wrong of me to take something you told me in confidence and throw it in your face because I was in my feelings."

Li'l Monk shrugged as if it was nothing. "You know we can speak our mind to each other, that's how it's always been with us. You're my best friend."

Sophie sighed. "How come you can make 'friend' sound like a dirty word?"

"Okay, how about homie?" He laughed.

"Cut it out." She punched him playfully.

Li'l Monk grabbed her by the wrists and pulled her close to him. "Don't me spank your li'l ass in here." He patted her on the butt.

"Watch those hands." She moved out of his reach. "I can't just be having random niggas touching me like that."

"Oh, so I'm just a random nigga now?"

"You ain't my nigga, so what else can you be? That's the problem with you guys; girls are always giving you the milk without making you pay for the cow and that's why you think you can treat us like shit."

Li'l Monk frowned. "You know good and well that I don't treat you like shit."

"No, you do treat me really nice when you're not being an insensitive asshole. I swear, sometimes you make me feel like my sister. She's thirty-five, been the bridesmaid at four weddings and doesn't even have a boyfriend, let alone a husband."

"Whoa, slow up with all that marriage talk, ma. We're still trying to figure out dating versus friendship," Li'l Monk said. He meant it as a joke, but Sophie didn't laugh.

"Don't be a dick; nobody is trying to march you down the aisle. I'm not talking about marriage. I'm talking about feeling wanted, and knowing that somebody only has eyes for you. Li'l Monk, sometimes being with you fills every void in my life, then you pull away and I feel empty again. That shit is like being on an emotional rollercoaster."

Li'l Monk could hear the pain in her voice. "I'm sorry, Sophie. I don't mean to make you feel bad."

"And that's the thing, you're not even conscious of what you're doing so I can't get mad at you. You just don't get it." She shook her head.

Li'l Monk sighed. "What do you want from me, Sophie?"

"I don't want anything that you're not willing to give me freely," she replied. "Li'l Monk, I know you feel like you've got too much going on in your life to have a girlfriend and I respect that, but it wouldn't kill you to sometimes let me know that I'm more than just a fuck-buddy."

Before the conversation could progress, Omega and Tasha returned from the dance floor. Both of them were sweating and breathing heavily.

"Your boy has got some skills," Tasha told Li'l Monk of Omega.

"I told you that I knew how to move, but you had to see for yourself, which is why I had to take you out there and burn you right quick," Omega capped.

"You didn't burn shit; I was just getting warmed up. Let me go piss out some of this liquor and we can go for another round. Sophie, come with me to the bathroom."

"Sure, since there's nothing going on over here." Sophie rolled her eyes at Li'l Monk. She grabbed her purse off the bar and went to the bathroom with her friend.

"What's good with you and shorty?" Omega asked after the girls had gone.

Li'l Monk shrugged. "Sophie is just tripping right now. She'll be over it in a little while."

"She's tripping because she's trying to get you to wife her and you're acting like you don't know what time it is," Omega clued him in. "Sophie is fine as a muthafucka and from what I can tell she's cool as hell. Why is it again that you don't wanna snatch that sexy muthafucka up?"

"Now you gonna start in with that shit?" Li'l Monk asked with an attitude.

"No need to get an attitude with me, I'm just asking. From what Tasha was telling me you and Sophie have history."

"That fucking Tasha is always volunteering information. She needs to mind her business," Li'l Monk said angrily.

"Calm your ass down, man. Come on, let's get you a drink." Omega tapped on the bar and ordered two Hennessy sours.

The two men leaned against the bar, sipping their drinks and watching the crowd while waiting for their ladies. Near the VIP section there seemed to be some kind of commotion going on, so they decided to go over and be nosey. There were two girls, one black and one white, dancing on the table and making out while the crowd cheered them on. Those standing close enough slapped the girls on the asses and urged them to take their clothes off. People had even started gathering around the VIP area and snapping pictures of the show. Li'l Monk was about to go back to the bar when the light caught the black girl's face.

"Persia?" Li'l Monk gasped.

"Oh, shit, you know them chicks?" Omega asked excitedly.

"I know one of them," Li'l Monk said. From the spaced-out look in her eyes, he knew she was blasted and not in her right frame of mind. He watched in shock and disgust while Persia danced on the table and allowed herself to be groped by strange hands. Li'l Monk wanted to kill every man in the club at that point, but for what? He had no claim to Persia, and what she did or didn't do shouldn't have bothered him, but it did.

"Whoever them broads are, you can bet your ass them rapper niggas are gonna be running the D-train on them before the night is over," Omega said.

"Not on my watch," Li'l Monk grumbled and stormed in the direction of the VIP.

***

Security was so busy watching the show Persia and Marty were putting on that they didn't even notice when Li'l Monk slipped under the gold rope and invaded the VIP section.

"Persia, what the fuck are you doing?" Li'l Monk approached the table.

Pain stepped between them and placed his hand on Li'l Monk's chest. "Hold on, who the fuck are you?"

Li'l Monk looked down at his hand. "I'm the nigga who is gonna break that greasy-ass hand of yours if you don't get it off me."

"Hey, Li'l Monk." Persia waved down at him from her perch on the tabletop.

"Persia, you know this dude?" Pain asked over his shoulder.

"Sure, we've known each other since we were kids. Isn't that right, Li'l Monk?" Her words were slurred.

"Persia, you need to come down off that table," Li'l Monk told her.

"For what? I'm just having a little fun."

"You're playing yourself; now come down off that table before I come up there and get you," Li'l Monk warned.

"Sorry, I don't think there's enough room up here for all three of us," Marty said. She too was faded.

Li'l Monk ignored her and kept trying to coax Persia off the table. "Persia, you are making a damn fool of yourself. Now bring your ass down from there."

"Why don't you chill, my nigga. The ladies are good," Lex told him.

"I wasn't talking to you, shorty," Li'l Monk snapped.

"Pay Li'l Monk no mind, he thinks he's my bodyguard. He's been following me around trying to keep me out of trouble since we were five years old and as you can see, he hasn't done a very good job of it." Persia giggled. "Did you guys know that our dads used to be best friends? They sold crack and killed people together."

"Persia, you're twisted and talking out of your ass right now. You need to come down and get your shit so I can take you home," Li'l Monk said, trying his best not to lose his cool.

"Persia isn't going anywhere, but you need to walk your ass out of here before you get carried out," Pain threatened. Li'l Monk ignored the threat, and tried to step around Pain to pull Persia down. When he did, Pain grabbed him by the shirt and paid for his offense.

Li'l Monk's fist sounded like a slab of meat being dropped on the floor when it connected with Pain's jaw. Pain blinked twice, as if he was trying to figure out what had just happened, before falling into the chair behind him. Lex tried to creep up behind Li'l Monk, when Omega popped up seemingly from out of thin air and broke a beer bottle over his head. It took several minutes for security to separate the warring parties and snatch the girls off the table, but by then the damage was already done. The DJ had stopped spinning the music and the house lights came on.

"What the hell is going on here?" Tone asked, pushing his way through the crowd. Chucky was close behind him.

"Sorry, Tone. These two troublemakers slipped past us," one of the bouncers said apologetically.

"Well, well, well, if it ain't the newest pups in the litter," Chucky said, seeing Li'l Monk and Omega being held back by security.

"You know these two?" Tone asked.

"Yeah, they work for me . . . Correction, they work for Ramses now," Chucky said scornfully. "What's this shit all about?" he asked Li'l Monk and Omega.

"This ain't got nothing to do with you, Chucky. I was just trying to make sure that my friend got home okay, and these cats tried to form on me," Li'l Monk explained.

"Which friend would that be? You mean this friend?" Chucky pulled Persia from the group. Her eyes were glassy and she looked like she was having trouble standing up. "Now what would make you think anything riding with me needs anything from your slum ass?"

Li'l Monk blinked in confusion. "Persia, you came here with this nigga?"

"Yeah, my boo Chucky is showing us a good time." Persia draped her arms around Chucky's neck.

"That's right, Persia is in good hands." Chucky ran his hand up her skirt and palmed Persia's ass for emphasis. "So why don't you take your ass back to the block where you belong, before I take my belt off and discipline you for being a disobedient dog."

The remark got a laugh from everyone standing close enough to hear it. Li'l Monk's eyes narrowed to slits, and his jaw clenched.

"You standing there grilling me like you wanna do something." Chucky moved his jacket so that Li'l Monk could see the gun tucked in his pants. "Ain't no police here to save you now. You got some frog in you? Nigga, jump!"

Li'l Monk reached for his gun, but Omega stopped him by throwing him in a bear hug. "Not here and not like this," he whispered in his friend's ear. If he had let Li'l Monk draw on Chucky, right or wrong he knew both of them would be dead when word got back to Ramses, if Chucky didn't kill them first. Reluctantly, Li'l Monk allowed Omega to pull him away.

"That's the last time you're gonna front on me, Chucky," Li'l Monk promised as he backed away.

"That's right, run along, little boys. Hurry on back to the block and see if Ramses has got something for you to do. I'm sure there's an old lady somewhere who needs her purse snatched," Chucky taunted them.

When Li'l Monk turned around the first face he saw was Sophie's. "I saw what happened. Are you okay?"

"I don't wanna talk about it; let's just go." Li'l Monk took her by the hand and pulled her along toward the door.

Li'l Monk didn't say much during the cab ride back to Harlem. To say that he was mad would've been an understatement; he was feeling murderous. Between Persia acting a fool, and Chucky violating him in a club full of people, he was ready to hurt something. Chucky had come at him sideways for the last time and as far as Li'l Monk was concerned. He was living on borrowed time. He would play nice for now, but as soon as the opportunity presented itself, he was going to either kill Chucky or put him in the hospital for a very long time. The trick was doing it without finding himself suffering a similar fate at the hands of Ramses. Chucky was a piece of shit who deserved everything Li'l Monk was scheming on giving him, but he was still Ramses's right hand. He knew that if he truly wanted to be rid of Chucky, he would have to prove himself more valuable than his nemesis in Pharaoh's army.

When the taxi pulled up in front of Sophie's building, Tasha said her good-byes and gave Omega a kiss on the cheek before getting out. Sophie on the other hand got out without saying a word.

"You gonna sit there looking stupid or are you going to make sure she's okay?" Omega asked.

Li'l Monk mumbled something under his breath, before getting out and going after her. "Hold on, Sophie," he called, jogging up the stairs to catch up with her before she made it inside the lobby.

"I'll wait for you by the elevator," Tasha told her, giving Li'l Monk and Sophie their privacy.

"You okay?" Li'l Monk asked her.

"Considering that I just watched the dude I was on a date with nearly get into a gun fight over another bitch, I'd say I'm just fine," Sophie said sarcastically.

"Sophie, let me explain. I was just—"

"You don't even have to say it, Li'l Monk. You were just trying to make sure Persia was good. You know, after seeing her for the first time tonight, I have to admit that I can't blame you for being head over heels for her. She's a very pretty girl."

"It ain't like that, Sophie. Me and Persia got history," Li'l Monk explained.

"And we don't?" Sophie shot back. "Just forget it, Li'l Monk. I am so done with this situation."

"Don't go to bed mad at me, Sophie."

"I'm not mad, Li'l Monk, just a little disappointed." She turned to go inside the building but stopped short. "If anything, I can chalk this whole night up to a learning experience. You wanna know what I learned?"

"What?" Li'l Monk asked, not sure if he really wanted to hear the answer.

"That you and I are more alike than either of us wants to admit."

"How do you figure that?"

"Because the both of us are in love with people who don't even see us. Good night, Li'l Monk." She disappeared into the lobby.

CHAPTER 24

After the brawl in the VIP it was a wrap for the club. Police shut it down and kicked everyone out. Tone invited everyone back to the after party they were throwing in their hotel suite, but Persia was in no condition to do any more partying. She was done with a capital D. Marty and Sarah wanted to keep the party going, but they didn't want to abandon their homegirl, so Chucky promised to take her somewhere to sleep it off and pick them up when they were ready to leave the after party. It didn't take much convincing before the two party girls were off with the Big Dawg entourage, leaving a very intoxicated Persia with Chucky.

Persia and Chucky looked like the picture of a drunken couple, staggering out of the club arm in arm. It was a wonder that the valet even allowed them to drive in their condition, but the extra fifty dollars Chucky slid him ensured that he wouldn't cause trouble. Chucky took his time driving back uptown, admiring Persia's visage. Even drunk and sweaty she was still beautiful. Persia turned her dreamy eyes toward him and smiled. Whatever she was on had her touchy-feely, because she kept running her hand up and down Chucky's pant leg while he drove. She was twisted, but Chucky didn't need her getting too twisted . . . at least not just yet. He pulled over at a store, and hopped out to grab a couple of bottles of water and a ginger ale.

While Chucky was gone, Persia tried her best to compose herself. Her head was spinning, but there was still a part of her that wanted to keep cutting loose. She wasn't sure what was in those black shot glasses, but she knew it wasn't all booze. She finally managed to get herself into an upright position and cracked the window. Her mouth watered up like she was going to vomit again, but it was a false alarm. In the ashtray she spotted a half-smoked weed clip. That would be just the thing she needed to settle her stomach. Persia didn't have a light, but she spotted a book of matches on the floor of the car. Striking two at a time, she lit the weed clip and took a deep pull. Something about the weed tasted off, like there was a second flavor intermingled with it, but it didn't stop Persia from filling her lungs with the smoke. When it settled, her whole body went as rigid as a statue. She couldn't be sure, but Persia thought she heard cannons going off in her ears. Persia could barely part her lips enough to cough out the foul smoke. For a minute it she thought she was having an out-of-body experience, and it was the greatest thing she'd ever felt.

When Chucky got back to the car, he found Persia sitting up, staring off into space, with the smoldering weed clip in her hand. "What the fuck are you doing?"

Persia turned to him and her eyes looked almost vacant. "I found it in the ashtray. I didn't think you'd mind."

Chucky looked at Persia closely. From the whole set of her jaw, he could tell that her bells were ringing. "You okay?"

"I think so." Persia touched her fingers to the seat she was sitting in and found that it was damp. "But I might've just had my first real orgasm," she said without an ounce of shame. "You got any more of that?"

When they arrived at Chucky's apartment, Persia was a little surprised. It was a cute one-bedroom that was sparsely decorated and immaculately clean to be a bachelor pad. "Make yourself at home and I'll get us something to drink." Chucky directed her to the couch, while he tossed his jacket over one of the armchairs. He disappeared into the kitchen and came back a few seconds later holding two glasses, one of which he handed to Persia.

Persia sniffed the glass and frowned. "This is orange juice, don't you have any liquor?"

"Trust me, you need that more than you need liquor right now," Chucky said as if he was genuinely concerned with her well-being. What he knew that Persia didn't was that the citric acid in the orange juice would boost the effects of the pills she'd taken. Chucky watched Persia as she downed the orange juice. When he saw the flicker in her eyes, he knew she was rolling again. "Better?"

"Umm hmm." She nodded with a goofy smile.

"You know, for as much as I was looking forward to this moment, now that it's here I don't know how I feel about it," Chucky said.

"What do you mean?" Persia asked.

"Persia, you're a good kid. From the minute I saw you, I knew you weren't like Karen and them. You're special and a special girl should have a special guy. Not some street nigga like me," Chucky said as if he was ashamed of his chosen profession. "For as much as I hate to admit it, your friend Li'l Monk might've been right; you don't belong around men like me."

"Pay Li'l Monk no mind. He's just overprotective of me," Persia said, thinking of how over the years he had always been the one coming to her rescue, whether it was when she scraped her knee when she fell of her bike, or to give a good beating to the school bully in kindergarten for messing with her. "I'm grown and I can take care of myself."

Chucky laughed. "Persia, you're mature for your age, but in reality you're still a kid. Me, I'm in a whole different league. Only a certain kind of chick is fit to deal with a man like me, and I don't know if that's you."

Persia set the empty orange juice glass on the table and looked Chucky in the eyes. "Everybody thinks I'm this prissy-ass girl from Long Island City, but what they forget is that I was born in Harlem Hospital and raised right on 143rd and Seventh Avenue. My father used to run those corners, so I'm not stranger to the criminal element. I knew that you had to be mine and I had to be yours from the first time I saw you. You think you lured me over here, but I wanted to come. I wanted to be with you."

"That's sweet of you, Persia, but any chick with me has to be ready to accept the good, the bad, and the ugly. You sure you ready for this?" Chucky asked.

"I've never been more sure about anything," Persia said emotionally. She didn't know why she felt the need to bare her soul with Chucky, but it felt better to get it out. It was like a weight being lifted off her soul. Persia thought she was having a moment, but it was actually the drugs playing hell with her nervous system.

That was all Chucky needed to hear. He walked over to his jacket and dug in his pockets until he'd gathered all the things he needed. He pulled out what he had left from the crack he'd bought in Washington Heights, some weed, and a cigar, which he laid on the table.

"Is that crack?" Persia asked in shock.

"Crack is for fiends, this is base. There's a difference," he lied.

"I'm down for pretty much whatever, but I don't know about smoking that," Persia said skeptically.

"That's not what you said when you were sucking this down in the car and asking for more."

"You let me smoke free base?" Persia asked in shock.

"I didn't let you do anything, baby. You invited yourself to that meal, remember? Listen, if all this is too intense for you then maybe I should just take you home. I knew this was a mistake." He stood.

"Don't kick me out, Chucky. I wanna stay; I'm just not sure about this. What if I get hooked?" She thought of the broken addicts on the streets of Harlem and wonder if this was how their slow falls to hell started.

"Only weak bitches get hit off toking a little bit. Are you a weak bitch? Because if you are then you've got no business with me. I'm a boss, so any broad on my arm has got to be a boss bitch."

"I can be a boss bitch, Chucky. I know I can. I'm just scared," she admitted.

Chucky stared at her for a few minutes as if he was weighing it. "For as long as you are with me you'll never have to fear anything." He sat back down. "Let me tell you the story of Pleasure, Pain, and Joy," he said, separating everything. "Pleasure and Pain were a god and goddess." He started breaking the green buds up on a magazine. "Pleasure"—he motioned toward the weed—"was an easygoing god. All he cared about was sunshine, music, and laughter. He wanted to make the world happy. But Pain"—he pointed to the small broken rocks—"she didn't care about happiness; she wanted to be worshipped. For years they clashed, with each gaining ground over the other here or there, but neither really winning the war. One day this old dude comes up with an idea." He produced a cigar. Chucky swiftly cut the cigar down the middle with his fingernail and emptied the contents into the wastebasket. "He proposed a marriage between the god and goddess to bring about balance to an insane world." He intermingled the crushed crack and weed in the hollow cigar. With the skill of a seasoned blunt roller, he sealed the ends of the cigar and the deal. "And from that union"— he lit the blunt and took several deep drags and exhaled the stink smoke—"was born Joy." He extended it to her.

Persia accepted the blunt with the delicacy of a thousand-year-old Egyptian scroll. Had you told her that morning that she'd be sitting on her crush's couch, zoned out of pills, and about to smoke laced weed, Persia would've called you a liar, yet there she was. She could hear her mother's voice in her head warning her about the ills of drugs and fast-talking men, but it was like white noise at that point. She looked at Chucky, sitting there, watching her, looking handsome as ever and thought of how much she wanted to be his. "Just once ain't gonna kill me," she whispered to herself before taking a hit.

Persia was in a magical place. The laced weed made her feel like she was dancing on clouds to the music of chirping birds. Through dreamy eyes she watched Chucky standing over here. He looked like the god Pleasure, standing there glowing radiantly. It was at that moment she decided that Chucky was the most beautiful man she had ever laid eyes on and she would do any and everything to be with him.

"Take your clothes off," Chucky ordered, and Persia happily did as she was told. He had to take a few minutes to admire her nude form. Persia's body was perfect.

Persia watched from the bed as Chucky slowly came out of his clothes. He was a handsome physical specimen, with a broad chest, flat stomach, and toned arms. The real treat was when he slipped off his boxers. Chucky was hung like a porn star. She pleaded for him to enter her, but Chucky wouldn't be rushed. He had waited too long for this moment.

Chucky grabbed her legs and forced them back until her knees touched her shoulders. He looked down at her neatly shaved, fat pussy, and found it already moist and inviting. Without warning, he clamped his mouth over her love box and began pleasuring her.

Persia's back arched at the feel of Chucky's mouth on her. It was an unexpected but welcome surprise. The last boy who attempted to go down on her was a complete ogre about it, all lips and teeth, but Chucky had style. He let his tongue slowly inspect every inch of Persia's womanhood, paying special attention to her clitoris. When Chucky pinched the flap of skin between his lips and began sucking gently, Persia could feel herself cumming over and over.

When he was done tasting her, Chucky flipped her over on her stomach. Persia reached her hand between her legs and started playing with herself in anticipation. Even though Persia was soaking wet, Chucky had trouble entering her. She was tight, which told him she hadn't been with many men. He worked himself inside her a little at a time until he was able to fit the whole thing, then he paused, savoring her warm walls.

Persia loved the way Chucky felt inside her. His stroke was aggressive, but he wasn't a brute about it . . . at least not in the beginning. Chucky gradually sped up his pumping, digging inside her a little harder with each stroke. Holding her waist with one hand, he used the other to grab a fistful of her hair and went from stroking to pounding.

"Damn, take it easy, baby," Persia said over her shoulder. If Chucky heard her, he showed no signs of it. She tried to scoot away, but he wrapped his arm around her waist and pulled her back.

"This dick is good ain't it?" Chucky breathed in her ear, while thrusting in and out of her. Persia found herself somewhere between pleasure and pain, as Chucky rode her like a jockey at the Kentucky Derby. When he felt himself about to bust, he pulled out of Persia and pulled her by her hair so that she was kneeling in front of him.

"Wait a minute . . . my hair." She struggled.

"Just take it, just take it," Chucky panted, stroking himself feverishly. With a groan he exploded, painting Persia's face with his seed. When he was empty, he released her hair and allowed her to fall back onto the bed. "Damn, that was good." He flopped down next to her.

"You didn't have to get it all in my hair," Persia complained, trying to wipe the semen out of her hair with a T-shirt she'd found on Chucky's floor.

"My bad, I was caught in the moment," he said, still breathing heavily. "Come here." He pulled her down next to him and tucked her in the crook of his arm so that her face was resting on his chest. "You really impressed me today," he said, tracing his finger along her side.

"I'm glad, Chucky. All I wanted to do was show you that I could make you happy," Persia told him.

"And you did a good job of that. I think I can fuck with you, Persia. I mean really fuck with you, but I'm still not sure. How do I know you're down for me and not just after my money like the rest of these bitches?"

Persia perked her head up and looked at him. "Chucky, I'm not after you for your money. I've got my own money. I told you that my father used to run those corners and when he went away, he didn't leave us broke."

This got Chucky's attention. When Face went away to prison and Monk ran the business into the ground, there were more than a few rumors floating; the most popular was that besides the house they lived in, Face hadn't left Michelle with any money, but now Persia was telling him different. Face had always been a very smart man and from the kind of money he was clocking in the streets, it was very possible that Persia and her mother could've been sitting on a small fortune. It would be the answer to his prayers.

"Tell me more about your father."

Chucky and Persia lay in bed talking until well into the night, before both of them dropped off to sleep. Sometime around first light, Persia had a nightmare, which startled her awake. Careful not to wake Chucky, she slid out of the bed and went to use the bathroom. On her way back, her eyes landed on the crack and weed that had been left out on the table from the night before.

Persia sat on the table and plucked one of the little rocks between her fingers. She couldn't believe that the seemingly harmless pebble in her hand had been credited with destroying so many lives. Granted, when she smoked, it had been one of the most intense highs she'd ever felt, but hardly the big bad monster that she had expected it to be. Maybe Chucky was right and only weak-minded people got hooked. She was strong.

Without even realizing she was doing it, Persia had picked up a cigar and began cracking it open. She wasn't the best blunt roller, but she did a fair job of twisting it. She could feel the lumps along the blunt from the rocks inside, as she held the lighter to it. Persia sat on the couch, smoking the laced weed, and listening for the sounds of cannons and birds chirping.

When Persia woke up, it was dark outside. She was lying on the couch, where she must've fallen asleep when she was smoking. She looked at the table for the blunt she'd rolled, but it was gone along with the paraphernalia. She got up and went into the bedroom looking for Chucky, but there was no sign of him.

Persia gathered her clothes and went into the bathroom to take a shower. She was so tired and sore that even washing herself was a task, but it was all worth it. She thought about the magical night she'd had with Chucky and it made her smile. Since she was a little girl and her father had gone away, all she ever dreamed about was having a man like him, a hustler who would do whatever it took to keep his lady laced and take care of his family. She hoped she had found that in Chucky.

After her shower Persia dried off and put her clothes on. Just as she was coming out of the bathroom, Chucky was coming in the front door holding bags of food.

"I see you're awake," he said, setting the bags on the table. "I bought you some food because I figured you'd be hungry after last night. I thought I'd put you down after the first round, but you surprised me when we went for two more."

"Two more?" Persia was confused.

Chucky looked at her. "You mean you don't remember? I came out here last and found you on the couch smoking. We talked for a while more about your father then we had sex, again and again. You had me calling for my mama by the time you were done with me. If you don't remember that then you must've been more twisted than I thought."

"I guess I was," Persia said, trying to put the pieces of the night back together in her mind. There were only vague flashes of her dirty deeds. "What time is it?"

"About six or six-thirty," Chucky told her, pulling a Styrofoam container full of chicken from one of the bags and setting it to the side.

"The sun will be up soon. Maybe we should head over to the hotel to see if Marty and Sarah are ready to go."

Chucky looked at her to see if she was joking or serious. "Persia, it isn't six in the morning, it's six in the evening. You've slept the whole day away."

"Holy shit," Persia said nervously. She had been missing for hours and Marty was probably worried sick. She just hoped that her mother hadn't been trying to reach her or else she was going to be in some serious trouble. "I've gotta call Marty, can I use your phone?"

"Sure." He handed her his cell phone.

Persia dialed the number to Marty's bedroom and listened while the phone just rang and rang. She was about to hang up when somebody picked up on the other end. "Marty?"

"No, this is Sarah. Persia, where the hell have you been, we've been worried sick!" Sarah told her.

"I'm sorry. I got caught up here with Chucky and lost track of time. I've been sleeping all day long. Has my mom been looking for me?"

"Yes, her and everyone else in the neighborhood. We tried to feed her excuses all day long, but when she popped up at the house and you weren't here, shit hit the fan. We had no choice but to tell her that we didn't know where you were."

"Jesus, why would you do a stupid thing like that?" Persia asked with an attitude. She knew when she finally got home her mother was going to kill her then ground her until she graduated college.

"What were we supposed to do? You disappeared with some strange dude for an entire day. For all we know he could've done something to you."

"Well, I'm fine, but I had a wild-ass night. Call Marty to the phone so I can give both of you the dirty details at once," Persia said proudly.

Sarah got quiet.

"Sarah, what's wrong?" Persia asked.

"Marty doesn't feel like talking right this second," Sarah said in a depressed tone.

"What do you mean? Sarah, what's wrong with Marty?" Persia asked frantically.

"Persia, I can't really talk about it right now, but something happened. Call me at my house when you get home and I'll fill you in."

"All right, I'll be there in a little while." She ended the call. "Chucky, I need to go."

"Okay cool, just have something to eat first."

"I don't have time. I've got to get back to Long Island City."

"Is everything okay?" he asked.

"Just some bullshit. My mother is tweeking because I stayed out all night and something happened to Marty. I need to go see what's going on. Can you drop me off at the nearest train station?"

"Nah, my lady don't take no trains. I'll drive you there myself," Chucky told her.

Persia felt good hearing him call her his lady. "So I'm your lady now?"

Chucky stood and hugged her. "Girl, from the way you put it on me last night, I'd kill another nigga for coming anywhere near your pussy. You belong to me now, understand?"

Persia just smiled and nodded. As she and Chucky embraced, her eyes landed to splotches of red on his tan Timberland. "Is that blood on your boot?"

"Nah, I must've stepped on a ketchup packet or something when I was in the chicken shack," he lied. "But forget about my boots; let's get you home so that your parents don't worry."

CHAPTER 25

It was colder than Persia had expected when she came outside, and the skimpy cocktail dress she had one wasn't helping. She cursed herself for not having the good sense to bring a jacket with her when they'd left Marty's house, but that was almost twenty-four hours prior and she didn't know she'd end up needing it.

"You wanna wait here while I go get the car?" Chucky asked, seeing that she was cold.

"No, I'm okay. I just hope you're not parked too far."

"I'm just around the corner." He took her by the hand and led her down the street. As they were passing the bodega on the corner, three girls were coming out. When Chucky saw who it was he sped up, hoping he could make it across the street without being spotted, but he had no such luck.

"Persia!" Ty called, running over to give her friend a hug.

"Hey, Ty." Persia hugged her back. A few feet behind Ty she saw Meeka and Karen. It was her first time seeing her friends since she and Karen had the argument. "Hey, y'all," she spoke to Karen and Meeka.

"What's good, Princess P? You're rocking the shit out of that dress," Meeka complimented her.

"Thanks, girl," Persia said graciously. "Hey, Karen," she greeted her, trying to be the bigger person.

"A little early in the day for a cocktail dress," was Karen's reply.

"I know, but I've got on the same clothes from last night, and haven't been home to change yet," Persia told her, hugging Chucky's arm.

Karen couldn't hide the hurt on her face. "It's like that?" she asked Chucky.

"Be easy, Karen," Chucky said coolly. He didn't feel like dealing with one of Karen's scenes, especially not while he was with Persia.

"Karen, leave that shit alone," Meeka told her.

"Fuck that, Meeka. This nigga and his bitch are playing themselves!" Karen said heatedly.

"Karen, take a walk and I'll holla at you later," Chucky told her.

"Oh, you sending me on walks? I ain't good enough to ride no more?" Karen was working herself up.

"Karen, let's just go smoke," Ty said. She smelled the storm coming.

"You got some balls on you, Chucky." Karen got in his face. "You got me out in the streets covering your dirt, and this saditty bitch lying up in your bed like she's the queen of Harlem?"

Chucky took a calming breath. "Karen, I ain't gonna tell you again—"

"Nigga, you can't tell me shit!" Karen cut him off. "You think you the shit because you're strutting around with a fake rich girl on your arm, but she ain't built like me. Let's see if Persia is still riding with you when you're asking her to dig your holes and keep your secrets."

Chucky's eyes flashed anger. He took two steps toward Karen, intent on knocking her head off, but Meeka stepped between them. Her hand was hanging down at her side, and in it was a box cutter.

"Chucky, you and Karen can argue all you like, but you know I ain't gonna let you put your hands on her," Meeka said. It was more of a fact than a threat.

Chucky thought about testing Meeka, but he knew better than anyone she would give as good as she got.

"Let's just go." Persia tugged at his arm.

He gave the girls one last, hard look before letting Persia pull him away. "Fuck all you crazy bitches. Let's go, baby." He hugged Persia to him and they walked off.

"Fuck you too, you closet junkie!" Karen called after him. "You got him for now, Persia, let's see how long you can keep him! Ask him where he was earlier when you were getting your beauty sleep!"

"Don't even sweat that shit, Karen. Chucky is a slime-ball-ass nigga and Persia will see for herself, sooner or later," said Meeka.

"I'm just tight about how he tried to play me. I was always down for him and whatever he needed me to do, and I don't have a pot to piss in to show for it." She was emotional. Quiet as kept, Karen had been playing this game with Chucky since she was thirteen years old, and he was the cute new dude on the corner. She was a naïve young girl and he always said the right things. Karen loved Chucky, and she thought that he loved her, but as she got older she began to see Chucky for what he really was: a silver-tongued dog. Still, she found that no matter how hard she tried, she couldn't stay away from him.

"Niggas come a dime a dozen," Meeka was saying. "Fuck that nigga Chucky. Eventually karma is going to fix him for the games he plays with young girls' hearts."

"I couldn't agree with you more," Karen told her and started walking down the block.

"Where are you going? I thought we were gonna smoke!" Ty called after her.

"Y'all go ahead and get high without me," Karen called back. "I'm going to see if my mom has got karma's phone number."

For the whole ride to Queens, Chucky was tense. He chain-smoked Newports and gritted his teeth, while navigating New York City traffic. Someone kept calling his cell phone, but every time Chucky ignored the call.

"Who was that, Karen?" Persia asked sarcastically.

"No, and why are you trying to be funny?" Chucky asked with an attitude.

"I'm not trying to be funny. I'm trying to be informed. What was that all about with you and Karen?"

"It wasn't about nothing." Chucky dismissed it.

"It looked like it was about something. Chucky, is there something going on between you and Karen that I need to know about? You know she's a friend of mine."

"Persia, don't give me that because your friendship with Karen didn't matter when you came home with me after the club last night," Chucky said.

"Don't try to make this about me, I'm talking about you! Chucky, it's obvious to a duck that there's some kind of connection between you and Karen. I know what the streets are saying, but I wanna hear it from your mouth."

"Persia, what you want me to tell you, that me and Karen fucked a few times? That's all it was. She was a bitch I could call on when I wanted some pussy. You satisfied?" he snapped.

"Are y'all still fucking?" Persia asked.

"No," Chucky said, a little too quickly for her taste.

"Then what was all that stuff she was saying about asking you where you were when I was sleeping?"

"Persia, you know for yourself that Karen will say anything to cut a muthafucka. I did see her when I went out to get the food and we did sit in my car for a second and smoke a blunt, but that was about it," Chucky said, telling half the story.

Persia gave him a disbelieving look. "Yeah, right."

"What? You trying to call me a liar? Check this out, Persia, I ain't been explaining myself to no chicks and I ain't gonna start now," Chucky capped.

"So now I'm just a chick? Earlier I was your lady. What a difference an hour or so makes," Persia said sarcastically.

"Being my lady and being my mama are two different things, Persia. I'm a nigga who is always gonna do what I wanna do, and as long as I'm taking care of me and my shorty I don't expect to get any grief about it. Now, if you don't think that's something you can handle, after I drop you off you can go back to your life of broke-ass teenage niggas and dirt weed in high school hallways."

Chucky's words hurt, as they were meant to. Persia hadn't intended to upset Chucky, yet she didn't want to play the fool either. She wasn't dumb, she knew Chucky had fucked Karen and there was a good possibility that they were still fucking, but it was Persia he had chosen to wear on his arm. Chucky was a dog, to be sure, but Persia was sure that she could tame him.

An hour later, they were turning onto Persia's block. She had him let her out a few houses down instead of pulling up in front of hers. He double parked and let the engine idle, staring straight ahead without so much as even looking at Persia.

"I'm sorry." She broke the silence.

"It's all good," Chucky said. He knew she would break first if he waited long enough.

"No, it's really not. I don't want you thinking I'm some crazy, jealous-ass broad who just wants to question you. The only reason I was even pressing it is because me and Karen are friends."

Chucky looked at her. "Persia, I'm about to give you some cold truth and I hope you grow from it. Bitches like Karen don't have no friends. They go from person to person, using them for whatever they can. And when shit doesn't go her way, she wants to either fight or kick dirt on their names. But I'm sure I don't have to tell you this, because she's done it to you twice already."

Chucky did have a bit of a point. Karen had always acted jealous over what Persia had, be it from boyfriends to new gear, she never seemed to be truly happy for anything she did. Persia had been seeing it for years, but having someone call her on it made it seem more real.

"I guess you're right," Persia mumbled.

"Of course I'm right. Persia, I ain't gonna tell you nothing wrong. Bitches like Karen are poisonous bottom feeders and fucking with her is only going to bring you down. Now let's kiss and make up." Chucky leaned in and puckered his lips. Persia kissed him passionately and just like that she wasn't even mad at him anymore.

"Call me later and let me know that everything is okay."

"I will." Persia reached for the door handle then paused. "Chucky, I need a favor."

"What you need, baby?" He dug in his pocket and pulled out his bankroll, prepared to break her off.

"No, I don't need any money, but thank you. I know that between whatever happened with Marty and hearing my mother bitching, it's going to be a long night. When it's all said and done, I know I'm gonna need something to calm my nerves."

"Say no more, I know exactly what you need." Chucky reached in the glove box and pulled out the bag containing the weed and the last few crumbs of crack. "Take that with you." He handed it to her.

"Thanks, baby." She kissed him, before stuffing the bag into her purse. "Let me go and deal with the mess that is my life."

"If it gets too crazy, you call me. I'll have you jump in a cab and come back to my crib. I owe you for last night anyway." Chucky smiled.

"Thanks, boo." Persia smiled and got out of the car.

Persia had barely made it onto the curb before Chucky was pulling off. She couldn't help but to wonder if he was in a rush to get back to Karen to try to smooth things over with her. At one point Karen had been her homegirl and Persia wanted that back, but when she extended her hand, Karen spat in it. That was one time too many as far as Persia was concerned. They were now on opposite sides of the playing field. Karen was welcome to try to compete for Chucky's affections if she liked, but Persia had something she didn't: new pussy.

She was walking up the path to her house when a voice in the darkness startled her.

"Good evening, Persia." She hadn't even noticed Richard sitting on the steps of their house. The porch lights were off so all she could see was his silhouette and the burning cigar he was smoking.

"Oh, hi, Richard," Persia said.

"Nice dress; a little much for a sleepover though, don't you think?" he asked, looking at her outfit.

Persia tugged the dress down. She'd forgotten she was still dressed from the club. "Richard, before y'all start tripping, let me explain—"

"Persia," he cut her off. "You don't owe me any words because your words don't mean anything, so I wouldn't take them seriously anyhow. Your mother on the other hand is worried sick."

"I'll talk to her," Persia said.

"And who was that?"

"Who was who?" Persia asked as if she had no idea what Richard was talking about.

"The red BMW that dropped you off, who was that?"

"That was nobody. One of my girlfriends dropped me off," Persia lied.

Richard gave her a disbelieving look. "A cold world breeds hard men and it's obvious you're looking to learn that firsthand."

"And what's that supposed to mean?"

"Persia, I can understand being a teenager, but you're getting reckless and I don't like it."

Persia was taken aback, because Richard had never spoken to her like that before. "Excuse you? I'm sorry, but I didn't know that it was for you to like or dislike whatever I do. You're not my father, Richard."

"You're right, and you're lucky I'm not because I'd give you the ass kicking you've been prancing around begging for," Richard snapped. "Your mother and I work hard to give you everything, but you walk around like you're entitled to the world. Your bullshit is tearing your mother, my wife, apart and I'm not gonna stand for it. You need to get your shit together if you plan to stay under this roof."

"Well that's mighty presumptuous of you, considering this isn't your house." Persia snaked her neck. "Don't get it fucked up, you've been good to me and my mom for as long as I've known you, but don't act like you snatched us out of the damn ghetto. We were living pretty good long before you came along, and we'll be living good when my father gets out of prison and you're gone!"

Richard reared back like he had just been punched. "Is that what you think? Your father is going to come home from prison, riding a white horse and pluck my family away from me? Let me enlighten you on a few things, little girl. Your father didn't land in prison by accident because he was a victim of circumstance, he's in there because he's a murderer and that's where murderers go. Since I've been with your mother I've done nothing but try to be a good man to her . . . to you. I never tried to be your father or make you think less of him. I just wanted to be a good man, but that isn't enough for Princess P, is it? I guess it's because you miss your daddy so much that you're trying to land your simple ass in a prison cell next to his."

Persia felt tears well up in her eyes. She had never seen this side of Richard before. "I don't have to take this shit."

"You sure in the hell don't. You'll be eighteen soon and able to strike out on your own, since you think you got it all figured out," Richard said.

"You kicking me out?"

Richard folded his arms. "I'm telling you that if you're willing to act like a respectable young lady and keep your mother happy you can stay, but if you wanna run around like you got a fire burning in your panties you can take it to the streets with the rest of the working girls." Richard had gone too far and he knew it, but what was said couldn't be taken back.

The porch light flickered on, and Michelle opened the front door. "What's going on out here?" When her eyes landed on Persia she breathed a sigh of relief. "Persia, where the hell have you been? Do you know how worried we've been?"

"I'm sorry I worried you, Mom, and it'll never happen again. I'll talk to you about it later, but for right now I think I need to go, since I'm not welcome in this house." She cut her eyes as Richard, before storming into the house and up to her room.

"What the hell is going on?" Michelle asked Richard.

"That girl has a false sense of reality and someone had to be truthful with her," Richard said.

"Richard, what did you say to my child?" Michelle asked.

"Nothing that she didn't need to hear. I might've gone a little far, but no further than she did by telling me that her father was going to swoop in from prison and knock me out of the box. I'm tired of Persia walking around here like she owns the place."

"Technically she does, since Face left the house in her trust," Michelle informed him. "Richard, I know sometimes Persia can be hard to deal with, but she's still a child who's been through a lot in her life. You should sometimes be more mindful of that."

"So I'm supposed to let her pop off at the mouth and not say anything?" Richard asked.

"Of course not, baby. I know you're not Persia's biological father, but you're the only father she's known since she was little. You have a right to set her straight when she's not being respectful to you, but know your limits. Now, I'm going to for sure jump in her ass about this staying out all night, but whatever it is that you said to her that's making her feel like she's no longer welcome in this house, you need to fix it."

Richard wanted to argue his point, but he knew Michelle had a point. His resentment for the things Persia had been doing was building up, but he shouldn't have lashed out like that, especially about her father. If he could he'd fix it. Richard hiked up the stairs to Persia's room and knocked on the door. When he didn't get any answer, he pushed it open and found the room empty.

"Persia," he called, stepping into the room. He looked in her bathroom and walk-in closet, but there was no sign of her. Outside her open window he heard a car door closing. He looked out just in time to see Persia hopping in the back of a taxi. "Fuck," he cursed. He was going to try to catch her, but by the time he made it downstairs to the car the taxi would be long gone. Michelle was never going to forgive him for this.

PART 4

UP IN SMOKE

CHAPTER 26

Li'l Monk was awakened by a heavy banging on his door. Instinctively, the first thing he did was grab the gun from under his pillow. He crept to the door, barefoot and dressed only in his boxers, with the gun at the ready. It was very possible his father had lost his key again and it was him banging on the door, but after all that had happened over the past forty-eight hours, he figured why take chances.

Li'l Monk raised his gun, eye level, and placed the barrel against the door, while he pressed himself to the wall. "Who that?"

"Nigga, it's me, Omega," his friend called from the other side.

Li'l Monk cautiously looked through the peephole to confirm his identity before opening the door. "Fuck you knocking on my door for like the police?"

"Dawg, I've been trying to reach yōu for two hours," Omega told him, inviting himself in. He had a worried expression on his face.

"What's wrong?"

"Ramses needs to see us," Omega told him in a nervous voice.

"About what? Did Chucky tell him what happened last night?"

"I don't think so because he was asking me if I'd seen Chucky, because he can't seem to reach him. Whatever it is, he's pissed off and won't talk about it on the phone. Get dressed and let's go. You don't keep a man like Ramses waiting for too long."

Li'l Monk went into his bedroom and reappeared a few minutes later dressed in jeans, a hoodie, and boots. He and Omega left his building and jumped into a cab to go to the restaurant where Ramses had said to meet him. The whole ride Li'l Monk's stomach was doing flip-flops, wondering what was going on. He worried that maybe he had gone too far with Chucky and Ramses could possibly be luring him to his death, but if Ramses wanted him dead he didn't have to call him all the way downtown to make it happen. He could've had Li'l Monk murdered in his apartment with just a whisper in the right ear. So what was going on?

They got out of the taxi on Fifty-eighth and Seventh Avenue in front of a fancy-looking steak house. The hostess took one look at Li'l Monk and

Omega dressed in their street gear and turned her nose up. Her attitude quickly changed when they gave her the name of the party they were coming to meet. She showed them to a table in the back, where Ramses and Huck sat waiting for them. Ramses was wearing a wrinkled shirt, and hadn't shaved that day. His eyes were red and swollen like he had been crying. Next to him, Huck sat as still as the grave, watching Li'l Monk and Omega like a panther waiting to pounce. Something was definitely wrong.

"Do I have to tell you two idiots how much it irritates me to be kept waiting?" Ramses said in a way of a greeting.

"That was my fault, Ramses. I was asleep so it took Omega awhile to track me down," Li'l Monk admitted. The answer seemed to appease Ramses, but he still looked angry.

"Sit down," Ramses ordered. He waited until they were both seated before speaking again. "Have either of you seen Chucky?"

"Not since last night," Omega said.

"And where did you see him last night?" Ramses asked. His tone of voice made them feel like they were being interrogated.

"Ramses, if this is about what happened downtown, I can explain," Li'l Monk said.

Huck visibly tensed, and he reached for something inside his jacket, but Ramses stayed his hand with a gesture.

Ramses leaned forward and looked Li'l Monk in the eyes. "Then you best get to explaining."

Li'l Monk went on to give him the short version of the two confrontations he had with Chucky the day before. When he was done with his tale, Ramses was giving him a very puzzled look.

"Li'l nigga, you think I called you down here about some pissing contest going on between you and Chucky?" Ramses asked.

"Well, yes," Li'l Monk admitted.

"I should knock your head off for wasting five minutes of my life that I can't get back. I don't know what's going on between you and Chucky, but you better get the shit straight because if it starts to affect my money, the both of you are going to find yourselves covered in dirt. We're supposed to be a team and one of my lieutenants beefing with one of my protégés ain't good for business. Work that shit out, understand?"

Li'l Monk nodded.

"Ramses, if you didn't call us down here to talk about what happened between Chucky and Li'l Monk, what's this all about?" Omega asked.

"Murder," Huck answered for him.

As if on cue, Chucky came walking into the restaurant.

"So I gotta leave you a hundred voice mail messages to get you to answer my summons?" Ramses asked him.

"My fault, Ramses. My phone was dead so I didn't get the messages until late," Chucky lied.

"Seems like your phone is always conveniently dead when something bad happens," Ramses said in an accusatory tone. "You're slipping, Chucky, and I don't like it. Sit down over there with the rest of the little boys." He motioned to the empty seat next to Omega.

Chucky looked at Li'l Monk, who was glaring at him scornfully. It was starting to make sense why Ramses had called him down there. "You couldn't wait to run down here and snitch on me, huh, bitch nigga?"

"Fuck you, Chucky." Li'l Monk got to his feet. "I don't need Ramses to handle my problems. I can deal with you myself."

"Then let's get it on, pussy," Chucky challenged.

"If the both of you don't sit down and be quiet, I'm gonna have Huck put a bullet in both of you, then me and him are gonna walk out of here like nothing ever happened. The waitress is going to swear up and down it was Omega who killed you."

Li'l Monk and Chucky glared at each other for a few seconds more before doing as they were told.

"Though I'm disappointed in you two for making public spectacles of yourselves, that ain't what this is about," Ramses informed Chucky. "Where did you go after you left the club?"

"Huh?" The question caught Chucky off-guard.

"If you can 'huh' you can hear. Where did you go after you left the club?" Ramses repeated the question.

"I don't know, bent a few corners then went back to my crib with this shorty," Chucky said.

"Who? Which shorty?" Ramses pressed.

"Ramses, with all due respect, I don't think who I fuck is anybody at this table's business," Chucky said coolly. He wasn't trying to be disrespectful, but he wasn't ready for Ramses to find out about his secret little lover yet.

Without warning, Ramses leapt across the table and grabbed Chucky by the front of his shirt. He snatched a steak knife from the table and pressed the blade to Chucky's throat. "It becomes my business when one of my oldest and dearest friends is found dead and my lieutenant is the only one with a motive."

"What? Wait, I ain't killed nobody. What are you talking about?" Chucky asked in shock.

"They found Boo's body this morning. Some-body left him stinking in the park near his house," Ramses told him, still holding the knife to his throat. The other people in the restaurant contin-ued eating their meals as if there weren't a man's life being threatened a few feet away. It was as if Ramses's table was invisible.

"And you think it was me? I would never!"

"Bullshit." Ramses pressed the knife deeper. "You think I didn't see how you were looking at Boo after he roughed you up back at the apartment? I know you, Chucky, and I know when you got it in your mind to do something to somebody."

"Ramses, I'd be lying if I said I wasn't thinking about blowing Boo's head off when he put his hands on me, but thinking it and going through with it are two different things. Boo has been with you since the beginning, I know he's got status. Raising my hand to him would've been a death sentence. Maybe one of his enemies got at him," Chucky suggested.

"Boo has been retired for years, all of his en-emies are dead. Everybody in the neighborhood where he was found knew Boo was a made man and what I would have done to them if they so much as looked at him wrong. The only people who could've hated him enough to openly defy me were you and Benny and I think we all know it wasn't Benny," Ramses said.

"Ramses, I swear, I didn't touch Boo. I was with a bitch last night," Chucky swore up and down.

"Then let the bitch verify your whereabouts. Give me a name!" Ramses ordered.

Chucky found himself once again stuck between a rock and a hard place. Ramses had been adamant about him not dealing with Persia, not only because of her ties to Face and Chucky's history with that family, but because of her age and the kind of problems him sleeping with a minor could bring. There was no telling how he would react if he found out that not only had he pursued her anyway, but was fucking her. Still, if he refused to account for his whereabouts there was no doubt in his mind that Ramses was going to kill him.

"Yvette," Chucky blurted out. "I was with Yvette last night." He wasn't sure why he had picked her name of all people, other than she was the first person who came to mind.

"You lying to me, boy?" Ramses asked suspiciously.

"On my life, Ramses, I was with Yvette!" Chucky kept the lie going.

Ramses eased the blade away from Chucky's throat and returned to his seat. "We'll see. Go check it out," he told Huck. Huck excused himself from the table and went to make a phone call. "Chucky, I trust I don't have to tell you what's gonna happen if I find out you're lying to me."

"I ain't lying, Ramses," Chucky said, but his voice sounded unsure. Waiting for Huck to come back was the longest five minutes of his life. The whole time Ramses just sat across the table, glaring at him. Having his whereabouts verified while he was still sitting there was an unexpected turn of events. He hadn't even had a chance to prep Yvette for the lie, and after the way he slapped her around the day before, there was no telling what she was going to say to Huck on the phone. He looked over at Li'l Monk and Omega. Omega kept his eyes on the table, but Li'l Monk was looking directly at Chucky. When they made eye contact, Li'l Monk smirked, letting him know he was happy at Chucky's misfortune. If Chucky was able to worm his way out of this one, his first order of business would be getting rid of Li'l Monk.

When Huck came back, his face was sour, which made Chucky nervous. He whispered something in Ramses's ear, at which he just nodded. "Good looking out. You can wait for me outside. This won't take but a minute."

On Huck's way out he gave Chucky a look that chilled him to his core.

"Seems like your story checks out," Ramses said, to Chucky's relief. "Let Yvette tell it you were in there getting nasty with her until sometime this morning."

"I told you," Chucky said. He thanked the Lord, Jah, and Buddha all for Yvette and promised himself that he would do something nice for her.

"That still don't change the fact that my friend is dead and something has to be done about it," Ramses said.

"Whatever you need, just say the word and I'm on it," Chucky promised.

Ramses ignored him and addressed Li'l Monk and Omega. "I want y'all to get in them streets and put your ears to the ground. Drop word that Pharaoh would look favorably to anybody who can provide us with any helpful information about what happened to my friend."

"We on it," Li'l Monk told him, standing to leave. Omega did the same.

"One more thing." Ramses stopped them. "Any man in my organization who can give me closure on this can write his own ticket. You little niggas wanna move up in the organization? Bring me my pound of flesh."

Li'l Monk stared at him. The hurt in his eyes was evident. This was personal to him. "We got you."

"Word up, Ramses; we gonna put every nigga we got on the streets to crack this case," Chucky said before standing to leave.

"Stick around, Chucky. I need to holla at you for a minute. You two can go," Ramses told Li'l Monk and Omega. When they'd gone he turned his attention back to Chucky. "What's up?"

Chucky didn't understand. "I don't know, you said you wanted to talk to me."

"I mean what's up with you?" Ramses clarified. "Your behavior lately has been real suspect and I'm wondering if maybe there's something you feel like you wanna share with me?

Chucky fidgeted uneasily in his chair. "Nah, everything is good."

Ramses leaned in closer. "You sure? I've noticed you and that broad Yvette have been spending quite a bit of time together. I know she's a great piece of ass, because I've had it, but she's still an addict. I know Yvette keeps our drugs at her pad from time to time, but you're management and don't touch product anymore. So, I've been asking myself, what you two got cooking that requires you to spend so much time with her?"

Chucky shrugged. "If you've had her already, you know nobody in Harlem sucks dick like Yvette. Besides, her crib is in the middle of the hood so it allows me to keep an eye on things for you."

Ramses reached across the table and took Chucky's hand in his. "You know, even though I frown on my people doing more than weed, I understand the stress of the streets can drive a man to unusual vices to cope. If someone who I considered family were to come to me and ask for help in a time of weakness, I wouldn't judge them. We'd work it out, so long as they came to me and were honest. An honest man I can forgive, but a liar I cannot. With that being said, I'm going to ask you for the very last time, is there something you need to tell me?"

Part of Chucky wanted to break down and confess it all to his mentor. He wanted to tell him about his problems with Wolf, addiction, and his role in what had happened to Benny. He wanted to cleanse his soul and beg forgiveness, but he'd known Ramses long enough to know that for as sincere as his words may have sounded he was not a forgiving man, so he lied. "Ramses, I don't fuck with nothing heavier than weed and I might pop a pill or two here and there, but I don't fuck with nothing harder than that."

Ramses looked almost disappointed with his answer. "Okay, Chucky." He patted his hand.

"You need anything else?" Chucky asked, letting him know he was ready to leave.

"No, you can go." Ramses dismissed him. He watched Chucky amble out of the restaurant like he didn't have a care in the world, shaking his head. He had high hopes for Chucky, but lately had been wondering if he had gambled on the wrong horse. Time would tell. His phone jingled on the table next to him. Ramses didn't recognized the number, but he answered anyway. By the time he was done on the phone he found his already-dark mood had become even darker.

Chucky felt like his legs were going to give out on him when he came out of the restaurant. When Chucky got outside, he found Huck sitting on the hood of his car, smoking a cigarette. He was staring daggers at Chucky, and smirking as if he knew something no one else did. Chucky had never been cool with Boo, but he and Huck had always been cool enough. Apparently things had changed.

"How come you looking at me like that?" Chucky asked.

"Because I've never seen a snake walk on two legs." Huck flicked his cigarette butt to the ground and got off the car. "You're a cold piece of work, boy."

"What you talking about, Huck?" Chucky faked ignorance.

"Cut that con-man shit out. It might work with Ramses, but I'm bullshit proof." Huck sneered. "I've always known you were a dirty nigga, Chucky, but over the past two days I've really gotten a chance to see that you ain't just dirty, you foul. First you sell your boy down the river to save your ass, then you kill my best friend."

"I didn't kill Boo. Yvette told you out of her own mouth that I was with her," Chucky countered.

"A junkie will say whatever they gotta say for a hit, you should know that better than anyone else." Huck gave him a knowing look. "I know you killed Boo, or had it done, and soon Ramses will know it too and finally see you for the treacherous little bastard you are. When that time comes, and he gives the word to put your lights out, it's gonna be me who flips the switch." He patted his jacket pocket.

"You're welcome to try," Chucky capped, brushing past him to get to his car. He hopped behind the wheel and fired the engine. He looked out the window and saw that Huck was still watching him and smiling.

"See you soon, Chucky," Huck called after him as Chucky's car merged into traffic.

Chucky's legs were still trembling long after he'd driven away from the restaurant. That was twice in less than a week he had almost found himself on the slab and he had no desire to test the "third time is the charm" myth.

When Ramses had called him down to the restaurant, he had an idea what it was about. He planned to come down, receive the heartbreaking news of Boo's death, and be there for his mentor as he mourned the loss of his friend. Him being a suspect was something he hadn't expected, but he should have.

Ramses was right; Chucky did hate Boo enough to kill him, which was why he did it. Boo had always been on Chucky's shit list, but because of his connection to Ramses he would never go at him. When he put his hand on Chucky all bets were off. Chucky had long ago vowed that another man would never put his hands on him without losing his life and since he was old enough to hold a gun he had kept true to it. Just like Pharaoh had his rules, Chucky had his. Boo's ass was out.

For as long as Chucky had known him, Boo had been a man of routine. He always worked out in the same public park about the same time, in the wee hours of the morning. When Persia had smoked herself to sleep, Chucky slipped out of the house and went to take care of Boo. Sure enough at 5:00 a.m. on the dot, Boo came jogging up the path through the park, where Chucky was lying in wait for him behind a stand of trees. Chucky didn't bother to try to be stealthy about it, he simply stepped out onto the path in front of Boo, with his gun raised.

"Well, well, if it isn't Ramses's pet snake. What the fuck you want, li'l nigga?" Boo asked in an irritated tone.

Chucky chambered a round into the pistol. "You should have never put your hands on me, Boo." His voice was heavy with emotion.

"What, you wanna kill me because I roughed you up a little bit?" Boo asked, with a smirk on his face like the situation was a joke. "You new boys kill me. You wanna run around out here like you John Gotti, but the moment somebody lays hands on you the first thing you do is grab a gun. The only time one of you little faggots even shows an ounce of balls is with a weapon in your hands. You ain't no gangsta, you a punk!"

"Let's see how much of a punk I am when I blow your damn brains out," Chucky said, gripping the gun tighter. All the crack he'd smoked had him jittery. "Beg me for your life like Benny begged for his."

Boo rolled his shoulders and poked his chest out. "Well, if you expect me to beg, you're mistaken. I done looked down the barrels of guns of tougher men then you and never batted an eye. So fuck you, and fuck that thieving-ass nigga who got his ass smoked. If you gonna do something, do it and stop talking about it!" He lunged at Chucky.

The first bullet hit Boo in the stomach. His eyes grew wide with shock as he looked down the growing red stain on his T-shirt. Boo stumbled toward Chucky, hands outstretched reaching for his throat, and Chucky shot him again. Boo fell on his hands and knees, looking up at Chucky in disbelief. "You . . . you . . ."

"Yeah, me!" Chucky said triumphantly and put one in Boo's head. After checking Boo to make sure he was dead, Chucky made hurried steps from the park. There was much that needed to be done to cover his involvement in the murder, but he was pressed for time. He had already been gone longer than he expected and he didn't want Persia to wake up and realize that he was gone.

That would raise questions . . . questions he wasn't prepared to answer.

With Wolf on his ass there was no way he was going to risk going back to his place carrying a gun with a fresh body on it, so he needed to stash it somewhere until he could properly dispose of it somewhere. Against his better judgment he called Karen. She had helped him cover his tracks more than a few times over the years, even once taking a drug charge for him, so it wouldn't raise questions if he asked her to stash a gun for him. Karen had been in love with Chucky since she was a little girl and it was her love for him that he often used to manipulate her when he needed something. He knew he could never have someone like Karen as his main girl, but as long as he let her believe it was a possibility, it would keep her loyal to him. It was a sound plan, until fate once again took a shit on him and Karen spotted him and Persia together that night.

Karen was crushed and Chucky knew it, but there wasn't much that he could do about it at the time. He had to play it cool during their confrontation to keep up appearances in front of Persia, but inwardly he was cursing himself for getting caught creeping. Chucky and Karen had had more than a few fallings-out over the years, but he had never seen her as angry as she was when she saw him with Persia. Chucky might've been an asshole, but he was no fool and knew that there was no telling what a woman scorned was capable of. He was going to pay her a visit to retrieve the gun before she could do something foolish. He would try to buy her silence with money and sex like he always did, but if that didn't work then he was going to kill her.

Chucky was getting sloppy, Ramses was getting too close to the truth, and Wolf was getting impatient. The walls were closing in on Chucky and it would only be a matter of time before he ended up dead or in prison and neither were acceptable choices. There was no doubt in his mind that Chucky had to leave New York for greener pastures, but he couldn't just bolt. He had to continue as if it was business as usual for a while so as not to tip Ramses off to what he was up to. You couldn't snatch your hand out of a lion's mouth, you had to ease it out. He no longer felt safe at his apartment in Harlem so he would need somewhere else to lay his head while he was hustling up some traveling money. He had an aunt and who had a place in Mt. Vernon that she shared with her boyfriend. They were notorious base heads, so Chucky was sure in exchange for drugs they would let him crash for as long as he needed to. It would only be a temporary arrangement. As soon as he got up a big enough bankroll, he was in the wind.

When his phone rang, he almost jumped out of his skin. He looked at the caller ID and recognized Persia's bedroom phone number. He really didn't feel like dealing with her schoolgirl crush at that moment, but it was now more important than ever that he kept her happy and playing his game until he got what he wanted from her.

"What's good, baby? Everything okay?" he asked, faking concern.

"No, not really. Does that offer for you to pay for my cab back to Harlem still stand?"

CHAPTER 27

The weather had started to change, with the cool days of fall giving way to first snowfalls of winter. It had been three weeks since Persia had ran away to shack up with Chucky, and one day shy of her eighteenth birthday. Running away had been an impulsive and emotionally fueled decision, but in her mind she felt like it was the right one. Persia had always felt like a prisoner in her own house . . . the house that her father had built for her.

Persia loved her mother, but couldn't take how she tried to control her life, overreacting to everything Persia said or did. She went out of her way to keep up the image of the upwardly mobile black family to their affluent neighborhood, as if their house hadn't been built by drug money, and demanded the same from Persia, but that wasn't who Persia was. She was a young girl coming into her womanhood and trying to find an identity, not have one forced on her. What

Michelle didn't realize was that the more she tried to reel Persia in, the more she rebelled. The night that Richard had said those hurtful things to her was the knife that cut the reins and sent Persia off into the wild.

She could have only imagined how she'd looked when she showed up on Chucky's doorstep, still wearing the cocktail dress and dragging a hastily packed duffle bag. She was a mess, but he welcomed her with open arms. She'd thought they were going to stay at his apartment in Harlem, but Chucky had other ideas. After that first night he took her to a motel up in the Bronx. Persia didn't understand why they couldn't just stay in Harlem, but Chucky explained that her parents were sure to be out looking for her and Harlem was the first place they would check. With her being a minor, if she was caught in his apartment, he would go to prison. He needed to keep her tucked away at least until her eighteenth birthday and then they could expose their relationship to the world.

The motel was on an out-of-the-way block deep in the heart of the Bronx. The rooms were small, barely clean, and smelled of old beer. It was hardly what Persia was used to, but beggars couldn't be choosers, and it had been she who came to Chucky for help. He promised her that they would move to better lodgings the next day and as soon as things died down in the streets he would start looking for a place for them. Just the thought of them moving in together and building a life made Persia giddy. She had had boyfriends in her life, but never a man . . . someone who would take care of her and who she could take care of. She dreamed of the life they would build together, with him being the king of New York and her being his queen.

That first night, Persia and Chucky made love and smoked weed, laced with the crack Chucky had given her when he dropped Persia off. He was glad that she still had it because he was fresh out and needed a hit. This time when Persia smoked the Woo it didn't hit her as hard. She still heard the cannons, but the not the whistling of birds. Blasted out of their minds, Persia and Chucky had wild animal sex well until sun up, before crashing in each other's arms and sleeping until late that afternoon. For Persia, waking up next to Chucky was something she could definitely get used to. After making love twice more, they checked out of the motel room and hit the streets.

Chucky had to make a quick stop through Harlem before they made moves. Persia was surprised when he pulled up in front of Karen's building. He told her to stay there and he would be right back, before jumping out of the car and going inside the building. Persia immediately caught an attitude, thinking that he was going to see Karen, but then she checked herself. There were dozens of apartments and Chucky hustled on that block, so he could've been going to see anybody. Still she kept her eyes glued to the window of Karen's apartment, trying to catch a glimpse of anything that looked suspicious. Less than five minutes later, Chucky was coming back out of the building and from the look on his face, she could tell that something was wrong.

"Everything okay, baby?" Persia asked.

"I was going to check somebody who was holding some money for me and they weren't home, that's all," Chucky lied.

"Who did you have to see?" Persia asked suspiciously. There was something in Chucky's voice that raised her antennas.

Chucky turned to look at her, his eyes cold and hard. "Persia, don't think that because I'm fucking with you that you can start playing twenty questions when it comes to what the fuck I'm doing. If you feel like that I can always drop you back off at your mama's house."

"No, I wasn't saying all that, Chucky. I just see you're upset and I wanted to know who did it. You know if they upset you then they upset me," Persia told him.

"Don't worry, I got it under control," Chucky told her. "In the meantime, tuck this in your purse for me." He handed her several neatly wrapped packages of crack.

"Where did you get this?" Persia's eyes got wide. It was like just holding it in her hand made her want fire up right there in the car.

"There you go with the damn questions again. Just put the shit up until we get where we're going," Chucky told her and turned his attention to the road, and tried to figure out a solution to yet another problem. He had gone upstairs in search of Karen, but Sissy said she wasn't home and she didn't know where she was or when she was coming back. Chucky knew that Sissy was lying, but there was nothing he could do about it right then and there, short of forcing his way into the apartment. He would have to try to catch Karen on the streets, and if that didn't work he was going to pay Sissy another visit. This time he would have a gun in his hand.

From Harlem, Chucky took her to the place they would call home for the next few weeks until he got his affairs in order: a run-down house that his aunt and uncle owned, located on the wrong side of Mount Vernon, New York. It was on an isolated block that was neighbored by a church. Like clockwork the bells would ring every night at midnight, waking the whole neighborhood up. Persia was skeptical about staying with strangers at first, but Chucky's Aunt Letti made her feel right at home.

Letti was an older chick, about the same age as Persia's mother, but hardly as uptight. She listened to nothing but rap music, wore clothes that were clearly too small for her robust frame, and could drink and smoke most men under the table. Letti didn't treat Persia like a kid, more like one of her homegirls. Letti was what Richard would've referred to as a woman living in her second childhood. For all her flaws, she was a bundle of fun and Persia had grown quite fond of her.

Chucky's Uncle Malcolm was a different story. He wasn't Chucky's biological uncle, but a man Letti had been dealing with for years. From the time Persia had met him, he gave her the creeps. He was always skulking around and looking at Persia funny, and was always looking for a handout. Chucky had broken him off a nice piece of crack the first night they arrived, as payment for letting them stay there, but by the next morning he was back trying to beg for more. Persia reminded him of the addicts she would see wandering Harlem, zoned out and looking for a hit, and he made her terribly uncomfortable.

The first few nights at Letti's house were like a nonstop party. There were always people coming and going, either to buy drugs from Chucky or share drugs with Letti and Malcolm. Persia would stay up until all times of the night, drinking, smoking, and playing cards or listening to music. But like with all good things, the good times came to an end when Chucky had to take it back to the streets.

Persia would sometimes ask if she could ride with him when she went into the city, but Chucky would tell her that things were too hot with her parents still looking for her and she should stay in the house. It was okay at first, but Chucky started being gone more and more frequently, sometimes not returning for days at a time. When Persia would ask about his whereabouts, he would give her a sloppy excuse and feed her more drugs.

It seemed like all Persia did was get high and stress over Chucky and it was starting to show. She was losing weight and her hair hadn't been done in weeks. Being that the next day she would turn eighteen, Persia decided that she wanted to look presentable. With any luck, Chucky would take her out to celebrate. Taking some of the weekly allowance Chucky had been giving her, Persia decided to take the bus to the strip mall to get her hair and nails done. She couldn't wait to see the look on Chucky's face when she came back and saw how pretty she looked. He would be breaking his neck to take her out and show her off.

CHAPTER 28

In the weeks after Boo's funeral, things changed with Ramses and in the neighborhood. Ramses took the death of his friend harder than people expected and became less and less of a fixture on the block. He ran the operation from a distance, delegating the day-to-day responsibilities to his lieutenants.

In a strange turn of events, Ramses had given Omega Benny's old position. Omega had not only proven himself loyal, but he was far more dependable than his predecessors. When Omega was picking his crew, he brought Li'l Monk in as his right-hand man. They would run it together just as Chucky and Benny had; only they wouldn't fuck it up.

Chucky wasn't happy with Ramses's decision, but he was in no position to raise a stink about it. He had one foot in and out, and everyone could see it. Ramses put Chucky in charge of distribution of product just to let him keep earning. Ramses was still looking at him funny from all the bullshit he'd been involved in, so he was letting him back in slowly. It was an easy job, where all Chucky had to do was kick his feet up and just make sure the right people took the right packages to the right places. It wasn't long before packages started coming up short or missing and it got blamed on one of the people working under Chucky. Li'l Monk had seen more than a few dudes become the victims of vicious beatings because of Chucky throwing them under the bus. It was all so suspect that people who had once respected or feared Chucky were now looking at him funny. The streets were talking and the word was that he was falling from grace.

Li'l Monk and Sophie had slowly begun mending fences. It started with an occasional hello, then elevated to smoking the occasional blunt together. They hadn't had sex in quite some time, but they were cool. Li'l Monk missed spending time with Sophie and was glad they were hanging out again. It took quite awhile for them to get back to that point because Sophie kept Li'l Monk at arm's length. He couldn't say that he blamed her because of the way he'd treated her in favor of Persia. Seeing Persia act the way she did in the club opened her eyes to the fact that they weren't cute kids with crushes anymore; they were young adults with two different agendas. Li'l Monk never came out and told Sophie any of this; he let his actions do the talking, and simply treated her like he appreciated her. The subject of relationships was off-limits when they talked. They had both decided it would be best to just let things take their natural course with no expectations.

With Chucky's sporadic behavior and frequent disappearing acts, Ramses leaned more heavily on Li'l Monk. He kept the young boy close to him, running errands or driving him around when he made rare appearances in the streets. Li'l Monk didn't even have a driver's license, but he was pushing Ramses's big truck around town like it belonged to him. Sometimes when Ramses was in for the night he would even let Li'l Monk borrow the truck so he could take Sophie out or joy ride with Omega.

Li'l Monk and Omega had become extremely close, especially since he and Charlie had fallen out. Li'l Monk would've thought that his childhood friend would've been glad to see him in this position, but Charlie seemed resentful. Li'l Monk did everything: pop bottles, put money in Charlie's pocket, and took him shopping when he still had a little extra, but it never seemed like enough. All Charlie did was make negative comments about Omega, and talk shit about Li'l Monk being a slave to Ramses. It came to a point where Li'l Monk was going to have to cut Charlie off or break his jaw, so he stopped fucking with him.

Spending extended time with Ramses also allowed Li'l Monk a chance to get to know him better than most. On the streets he wore the persona of Pharaoh's enforcer and a deranged killer, but Ramses was actually a very quiet man who loved a good book more than he liked going to the club. Of course he could flip the two personalities as easy as a light switch, but the killer was not all there was to him, just like Li'l Monk.

One afternoon Ramses had popped up on the block unexpectedly and summoned Li'l Monk. Li'l Monk was half asleep and partially hung over, but he answered the summons. Ramses was already outside of Li'l Monk's building when he emerged. He had moved from behind the wheel to the passenger's seat, meaning he wanted Li'l Monk to drive. Li'l Monk had been around Ramses enough to pick up on certain things without him having to say it.

"You do that thing I asked you to do?" Ramses asked Li'l Monk as they rode downtown. Li'l Monk was behind the wheel and Ramses was leaned back in the passenger seat.

"Yeah, I took care of it, Ramses. I had him drop the money off to Omega," Li'l Monk told him.

"You know I've been trying to get someone to go squeeze my money out of him for weeks and your little ass manages to collect it in a few hours." Ramses shook his head.

"Maybe it was the way I asked him?" Li'l Monk smirked, looking at the bruises on the backs of his hands from where he had pummeled the dude who owed Ramses money.

"You and those fists remind me of how Chucky was with guns when he was your age. He was another one who used violence as the skeleton key to all the doors of life. A cold world breeds hard men."

"Huh?" Li'l Monk didn't understand the statement.

"It's something a friend of mine used to say. What it basically breaks down to is that the circumstances you grow up in play a big role in what kind of person you turn out to be. People who've been handed everything in their life don't know how to fight, and people who've always had to struggle, all they know how to do is fight."

"I've been fighting all my life," Li'l Monk told him.

"Indeed you have, and it's been taking you places. Life has changed for you since you started running with my team, just as I said it would. Has it not?" Ramses asked.

"Absolutely, Ramses. You know I tell you all the time how appreciative I am of what you and Pharaoh have done for me."

"We haven't done more than what you've earned, Li'l Monk. I have to admit, I was a bit skeptical about you at first, considering who your father is, but I see that you are your own man."

"Thanks," Li'l Monk said.

"You can't thank me for something that was already in you. Not for nothing, I've been paying attention to how much smoother things are going since I bumped you and Omega up."

Li'l Monk nodded. "Yeah, Omega is a natural leader. I'm proud of my nigga."

"Indeed he is, but a good leader is only as strong as his right hand. Omega is charismatic, handsome, and smart. Men like him are easy to put in positions of power, but it's men like you and I who keep them there. It's the same way with me and Pharaoh. He rules, but I command."

"Which one is better?" Li'l Monk asked.

Ramses shrugged. "I guess it all depends on who you ask. Either way, the one with the real power is the one willing to do what other people won't. Are you one of those kinds of people, Li'l Monk?"

Something in the tone of Ramses's voice made Li'l Monk look at him. The OG was watching him closely for his response. "Why do you ask? You got something that needs to be done?"

"A little piece of business that I've put off for too long," Ramses told him.

"Say no more. I'll holla at Omega and we'll take care of it," Li'l Monk assured him.

"No. Not Omega, nor any of your other little homies, are to ever hear of this. Huck is gonna ride with you on this one. It's personal. Do you understand?"

"You got it, Ramses, just tell me what you need done," Li'l Monk said, wondering what it was that required so much secrecy. When Ramses ran the whole situation down to him, Li'l Monk found himself dumbfounded. "Are you sure?"

"No, but it doesn't change the fact that it needs to be done. There's only one stipulation." Ramses reached into the glove compartment and retrieved something wrapped in a paper bag and handed it to Li'l Monk.

Li'l Monk cautiously looked inside the bag at the shiny black 9 mm. He looked up at Ramses with a confused expression on his face. "What's this?"

"The gun that killed Boo."

CHAPTER 29

Persia looked like a totally different person after getting a wash and set and her nails and feet tightened up. The girls at the shop didn't lace like they would've done at her regular spot in Queens, but they did a decent enough job. She was looking good and feeling better.

It would be about twenty minutes or so before the bus came that would take her back to Letti's house, so she had some time to kill. She walked up and down the strip mall window shopping, hoping something caught her eye that she could wear for her birthday. She saw a cute dress in the window of one store that was similar to the one Marty had been wearing the night they'd all gone to the club. Thinking of her friends made her realize how much she missed them. Persia had wanted to call Marty and Sarah sooner, but Chucky wouldn't allow it. He told her that the white girls would likely turn her into her mother and he didn't need that kind of heat on him, or his aunt's house. At that moment, Persia didn't care. She needed to hear a familiar voice.

Persia found a payphone on the corner near the bus stop and fished around in her purse for some change. She dialed Marty's bedroom line and waited, but the phone just rang. She figured Marty might be out or either at Sarah's, so she called Sarah's house. Sarah picked up on the third ring.

"Hey, white girl," Persia said into the phone cheerfully.

"Persia? Oh my God, where the hell have you been?" Sarah asked. It was clear by the tone in her voice that she was happy to hear from her friend.

"I've been living my life like I'm supposed to. For the first time all is right with the world. I tried to call Marty, but she didn't answer. Are you guys together?"

The line was silent.

"Sarah, what's wrong?" Persia asked.

"Persia, I've got something that I need to tell you," Sarah began, but she was hesitant.

"Sarah, you're starting to scare me. Just tell me what's going on already!" Persia demanded.

"Marty is dead!" Sarah finally belted out.

Persia looked at the phone, knowing she had heard her wrong. "Sarah, if this is your and Marty's idea of a joke, it's not fucking funny. Put Marty's ass on the phone before I beat the crap out of both of you."

"I'm not kidding, Persia. She's dead, she killed herself," Sarah explained.

Persia couldn't believe it . . . she wouldn't believe it. Marty was beautiful, rich, and popular; why would someone with everything going on for herself take her own life?

"Persia, are you still there?" Sarah's voice came back over the line.

"Yeah, I'm still here," Persia said, barely able to find her voice. "Why? Why would she do something like that?"

"After the club we went back to the hotel with those guys we met from Bad Blood, to their after party. There were a bunch of industry people there and we were having a good time at first. Marty was wasted and passed out on the couch, so True left with some other groupie and the guy Tone ended up stealing me from Pain. Tone and me went into his room to have sex, and when we were done we came out and . . ." Her words trailed off as she relived the painful night. "When we came out we found Marty on the floor unconscious and naked. Pain and some of the others were taking turns raping her," she said emotionally.

"Oh my God." Perisa covered her mouth.

"I don't know how long they had been doing it or how many of them had been involved," Sarah continued. "When I saw what they were doing to my friend I wanted to kill them and I would've had Tone not grabbed me and snatched that lamp out of my hand. After I threatened to call the police they let us go, and I got Marty to a cab and took her to the hospital."

"What did they say? Did you call the police?" Persia asked.

"Yeah, but they weren't much help. When they questioned the guys from Big Dawg they claimed that the sex was consensual. They even had footage of Marty popping pills and putting on a strip tease in the limo on the way to the hotel. One of the guys had recorded it with his camera phone. The detective told Marty that she could press charges if she wanted to, but if she did the video would have to be submitted as evidence and everyone would see it. Marty didn't want to face the embarrassment so she didn't press charges."

"Why didn't you make her?" Persia was livid. Had she been there she would've not only made Marty press charges, but she would've taken one of Chucky's guns and killed the bastards.

"I tried, Persia, but she wouldn't listen to me!" Sarah shouted back. "Why do you think

I kept asking you to come over? I knew Marty would've listened to you. I stayed with her over the weekend and when I left Sunday night she seemed okay, but when she didn't show up in school Monday I got nervous and went to her house to check on her. By the time I got there the paramedics were bringing her body out. They said she overdosed on her mother's Valium. Her funeral was a week ago. Nobody knew how to contact you to give you the news, but your parents were there . . . Sorry, your mom and your stepdad."

This made Persia feel even worse. She had been so busy with her head up Chucky's ass that she had missed her best friend's funeral. "Do her parents know why she killed herself?"

"They didn't at first, because Marty made me promise not to tell, but when she died I told them everything. I think they hate me now," Sarah said sadly.

"They don't hate you, Sarah. They just need time to grieve. You know you've always been like a daughter to them. They'll come around, just give it a minute." Persia tried to make her friend feel better. "Are her parents going to pursue it?"

"Marty's dad was talking about killing them, but somebody beat him to the punch. Every member of the group who was involved in the rape was killed in a shootout over drugs. How ironic is that? It's been in all the newspapers, I'm surprised you haven't seen it."

"I've been kinda busy lately," Persia said, thinking about how she had been holed up in Letti's house smoking Woos and drinking for weeks and hadn't so much as been outside until that day.

"Persia, are you okay?" Sarah asked.

"I'm fucked up about what happened to Marty. I just need a minute to process all this," Persia told her.

"That's not what I meant. I mean are *you* okay?"

"I'm fine, why do you ask?"

"Well, one of the burnouts who went to school with us said that he was up in Mount Vernon to score some coke and saw you in a crack house."

The statement hit Persia like a slap. Letti's house was a hot spot, so people of all ages and colors came and went all the time, especially since Chucky had started selling crack and coke out of there. It never even occurred to Persia that she might bump into someone she knew way up there. "That's ridiculous. What would I be doing in a crack house?" Persia asked as if the story was so farfetched.

"That's the same thing I said. I mean, we all do a little of this and a little of that, but it's only a weekend thing for us, right?" Sarah laughed.

"Right," Persia said weakly. "Sarah, who else did you tell what he said?"

"Nobody, why would I? For one it can't be true, for two that guy snorts so much powder that he probably sees shit that isn't there all the time. Anybody with a half a brain knows that it'd be a cold day in hell before Persia Chandler would let herself slip that far."

The more Sarah talked, the worse Persia felt. She decided to get off the phone. "Well, it was good talking to you, Sarah. I'll try to call you again soon and please don't tell my mom you spoke to me."

"I won't, but she's worried about you, Persia. I don't know what happened between you guys, and I'm not trying to convince you to go home if you're not ready to, but you should at least give your mom a call and let her know you're okay."

"I will, I promise."

"Oh, and before I forget, there's something else I should tell you. Richard was asking about your friend, the one who got us into the club."

That struck Persia as odd. "Why would Richard be asking about Chucky?"

"I have no idea. At Marty's funeral, he pulled me to the side and was asking me a bunch of questions about the guy you were dating who drove the red BMW. I knew who he meant, but I acted like I didn't know his name. From the way he was acting, you'd think you had been abducted by the devil himself."

Persia sucked his teeth. "Just like Richard to act all concerned when it's his fault I'm gone. Chucky is taking good care of me."

"I hope so."

"Listen, I gotta go, Sarah, but I promise to try to call you again soon," Persia said, wanting to get off the phone. There was too much going on at once and she needed time to process it.

"Persia, one more thing before you hang up."

"What's that, Sarah?"

"In case I don't speak to you again for a while, happy birthday. I love you and I miss you."

"Thanks, Sarah. And I love you too," Persia said before hanging up.

After speaking to Sarah, Persia felt like the world was spinning. She had to press her head against the phone booth to keep from falling over. She couldn't believe that Marty was gone. Her mind went back to all the times they had shared growing from competitive little girls to adventurous young women. Knowing that she would never get to laugh or get in trouble with her friend again, Persia let go the river of tears she had been fighting back. Persia felt broken and there was only one voice that she knew of that could make her feel whole again.

Composing herself as best she could, Persia placed another phone call. This time the phone only rang once and her mother's voice came over the line. "Hello? Hello? Persia, is that you?"

"Mom," was all Persia could manage to say.

"Baby, where are you? Are you okay?"

"Marty is dead," Persia sobbed.

"I know, baby. I'm so sorry to hear about your friend . . . we all were. I know how close the two of you have always been."

"It hurts so bad, Mom." Persia broke down. She just wanted to go home, throw herself in her mother's arms, and cry until it didn't hurt anymore.

"Then come home, Persia. You don't have to deal with this alone," Michelle pleaded.

"I can't."

"Yes, you can. This is where you belong! I know that we've both said and done some things that we wished we hadn't, but we can work through it. As long as we're a family there is nothing we can't overcome. Just come home . . . please."

Persia felt herself caving. For as much as she loved Chucky and being with him, she needed to be around people and places that were familiar to her. She needed to be home.

"Is that her? Are you talking to Persia?" She could hear Richard's voice in the background.

"Persia, just tell me where you are and I'll come get you. The two of us can talk, just like we used to." Michelle ignored Richard, and kept trying to convince her daughter to come home. Before Persia could answer, Richard picked up the other phone.

"Persia, do you know how worried your mother has been? You've been gone almost a month!" He started right in.

Hearing Richard's voice made Persia's mood immediately flip. "Richard, I'm not in the mood for your bullshit right now."

"Bullshit? You run off for a month to God knows where and it's me who's shoveling bullshit?"

"The both of you stop it!" Michelle demanded, but nobody seemed to hear her.

"Fuck you, Richard. I didn't call for this," Persia spat.

"Do you hear how she's talking, Michelle?" Richard's voice was raised. "Persia, I've known you since you were a little girl and this doesn't even sound like you. Who is it, the guy in the red BMW? Is that who's poisoning your mind? You tell that scum bag he better hope to God he gets killed in the streets before I find him!"

All Persia wanted was a little comfort and instead she was getting judgment and orders again. Calling had been a mistake. "Mom." Persia wiped her face. "I was just calling to let you know that I'm okay, and to tell you that I love you."

"Persia, wait—"

The line went dead.

CHAPTER 30

It was freezing outside, but Chucky was sweating like a runaway slave. He had all the windows of his car rolled down and it still felt like he was sitting in the middle of the jungle. He had been snorting and drinking all day long and was as live as a lit match.

Persia had been calling his cell phone back to back, but he didn't have time to talk to her. He was too busy running the streets, trying to hustle up enough money to bust his power move. The last few weeks he had felt the tension between him and Ramses. His mentor still smiled and treated him like everything was all good, but Chucky knew better. When Ramses promoted Omega, it was all the proof that Chucky needed to know it was a wrap for him. It would only be a matter of time before Ramses was ordering someone to dig a hole for him. There was no way in the hell he was going to stick around and wait for it to happen. He was leaving, but first he had to tie up some loose ends, starting with Charlie.

Charlie was the latest pawn in Chucky's chess game. Chucky needed an outlet for the coke he was trying to get rid of, a little bit at a time, and he used Charlie to move it for him under the radar. He was also using Charlie to try to get a lead on his sister, Karen. It had been nearly a month since she had vanished along with the murder weapon he had trusted her to stash, and he was nervous.

Chucky's brain switched to high alert when he hit the neighborhood. Every time he came on the block he had no idea if he would ever make it off again. When Ramses demoted him, he feared the worst but a few weeks went by and he was still alive. If Ramses knew anything, he made no mention of it, but that didn't mean it wasn't coming. He knew Ramses and his methods. He was like a cat toying with a mouse. Once he tired he would devour him. Chucky had no plans on waiting around for that to happen. After a few more moves were made, he was ghost.

Just like the good little soldier, Charlie met him at the Spanish restaurant on Third Avenue as Chucky had instructed him to. He was sitting at a table in the back, sipping a Corona and picking over a plate of chicken and rice. When he saw Chucky walk in, he put on his best tough guy face. Chucky disliked Charlie because he was weak and fraudulent, but dealing with him was a necessary evil. People in the streets were turning their backs on him left and right so he took his allies where he could find them.

"What up, my nigga?" Charlie gave him dap.

"You got that for me?" Chucky asked, skipping the pleasantries.

"No doubt." Charlie reached under the table and pulled out a briefcase, which he placed on the table.

"What the fuck is that?" Chucky stared at the case.

"The money," Charlie said as if it should've been obvious.

Chucky shook his head. "You gotta be the only fool in the world who carries five grand in a briefcase like it's fifty grand." He popped the case open, took the money out, and stuffed it in his pockets.

"So what's up, when are you going to start giving me more than a few ounces at a time to move for you?"

"When I think you're ready and not a minute before," Chucky told him. "Any word on your sister yet?"

"No, my mom claims she don't know where Karen is at, but I don't believe her. I heard her on the phone talking to my aunt down in PA, so I know something is funny," Charlie told him.

"What makes you think that just because she was talking to your aunt it has anything to do with Karen? Maybe it was just family catching up," Chucky suggested.

"Nah, my mother and my aunt hate each other and haven't spoken in years. Lately they've been talking regularly, and my mother is always whispering or leaving the room when she's on the phone with her."

It made sense. Chucky knew that Sissy was just as larcenous as her daughter and she was no doubt a coconspirator in Karen's mysterious disappearance.

"I still can't believe it," Charlie said.

"What's that?"

"That my sister would run off like that because she's carrying your baby and doesn't want to get an abortion."

For a minute Chucky was confused, but then he remembered the lie he'd fed Charlie to get him to be his little spy. Chucky told Charlie that he had gotten Karen pregnant, but didn't want to have any kids and was trying to get her an abortion. Karen was trying to keep the baby to bind her to Chucky, so she ran off so that he couldn't force her to abort the baby.

"That's how bitches do . . . no disrespect," Chucky said.

"Nah, I understand," Charlie said as if his sister hadn't just been insulted. "So, you gonna drop some more work off on me? I got them fiends down on the Lower East Side rocking off that butter."

"Yeah, but not right now. I got some moves to make right quick, but I'll hit you later on tonight. I got some new product that's really gonna blow their socks off," Chucky lied.

"That's what I'm talking about." Charlie rubbed his hands together greedily. "Once we get our weight up, we gonna run this whole city. Fuck Ramses and Pharaoh, it's gonna be Chucky and Charlie. Shit, we should start calling ourselves C and C like the soda."

"I like that." Chucky nodded, humoring Charlie. Little did Charlie know, once Chucky's business was conducted he was going to be left holding the bag. "A'ight, I'm out. If you hear anything else about your sister, make sure you call me immediately."

"I will," Charlie promised.

Chucky left Charlie sitting there and hustled back outside. He had one more stop to make before he headed back up to Mount Vernon to check in on Persia. Lately she had been on his ass about spending time with her and he knew he was going to have to tighten up if he wanted to keep her content and bound to him. He still couldn't believe how easy it had been to rope her into his web. She thought that Chucky was in love and wanted to build a life, but in truth he wanted to destroy her life the same way her father had destroyed his life when he murdered his brother. Chucky could still see that day clearly in his mind as if it has only just happened. Seeing his brother stretched out on a Harlem sidewalk was an image he would never be able to erase from his mind. Persia would suffer for the sins of her father.

Chucky had just made it to his car and was about to get in when he felt someone behind him. The minute he turned around, something crashed into his forehead, splitting it open and dropping him. Chucky made to reach for his gun, but his attacker had the drop on him and he felt the cold touch of steel to his forehead.

"You know how long I've been looking for you, you piece of shit junkie?" Wolf snarled down at him.

"Wait, let me explain—"

"Time for explanations has come and gone." Wolf snatched him to his feet. He reached inside Chucky's jacket and snatched his gun from him, tucking it in his pants. "You think it's a game, so I gotta show you how real it is." Wolf commenced to beating Chucky like a stray dog on the street for all to see. A crowd had started to form, but no one dared interfere.

Chucky knew without a shadow of a doubt that Wolf was going to kill him. Through his bloody and swollen eye he spotted a police car creeping on the Avenue. In a last-ditch attempt to save his life, he broke away from Wolf and ran for the police car.

"Help, he's trying to kill me!" Chucky yelled, throwing himself on the hood of the police car.

The officers got out to attend to the wounded man, just as Wolf came up the block in pursuit of him. When they saw the gun in his hand, they drew theirs. "Drop the weapon!" one of the cops shouted.

"Take it easy," Wolf said, lowering his gun to the ground slowly. The cops moved in and began roughly handcuffing him. "You're making a mistake, I'm on the job," he tried to explain.

The cops took one look at his braids, gold teeth, and sweat suit and laughed. "Yeah, right and I'm the fucking queen of England," one of them said, throwing Wolf against the car to pat him down. They found the gun he had stolen from Chucky and a large bag of weed. After securing Wolf, the cops turned around to check on the injured man, but he was long gone.

CHAPTER 31

By the time Persia got back to Letti's place, it was nearly midnight. After the phone conversations with Sarah, her mother, and then Richard she was numb. She rode the bus in such a daze that she had missed her stop twice. When she dragged herself into Letti's house all she wanted to do was smoke and cry.

Malcolm was in his usual spot, perched by the window, staring out scheming. He cut a glance at Persia then went back to his scheming. Letti was sitting at the table loading a glass pipe with rocks. Once she had it packed, she put it too her lips to light, but hesitated when she saw Persia.

"Damn, looks like you just lost your best friend," Letti joked.

"I did," Persia said.

"Oh, my goodness, I'm sorry, Persia. I didn't know," Letti said, feeling embarrassed.

"I know you didn't." Persia shuffled to the couch and sat down beside Letti. "I need something to take this pain away. You got anything, Letti?"

"I ain't got no weed. I'm waiting on Chucky to bring that back. But I got some hard white. You're welcome to it, if you don't mind getting your fix like the common folks this time." She extended the pipe to Persia.

Persia stared at the pipe for a while. She had never smoked crack without weed, and surely never out of a pipe. She always told herself that so long as she never put her lips to the pipe she couldn't technically be considered a smoker and wasn't too far gone. With the way she was feeling, her principles went out of the window. She wouldn't have cared if she had to smoke out of a fishbowl, as long as she had something to take the pain away.

Persia took the pipe and held it between her lips while Letti lit it for her. The glass pipe fogged with smoke, and Persia sucked it clear like the good little junkie she was turning into. After taking her first official hit, she lay back on the couch, waiting for the cannons and whistling of birds.

From his perch by the window, Malcolm snickered. "Welcome to rock bottom, baby girl. Now pass that shit."

***

Chucky had never thought he'd be so happy to see that raggedy church on Letti's block. The snow had really started coming down and the whole street was white. He had barely made it out of Harlem with his life, thanks to detective Wolf. Chucky looked at his eye in the rearview mirror. It was bruised, and cut from where Wolf had hit him with the gun. Chucky fumed thinking about the ass whipping he had just taken. Wolf was a cop, but he had laid hands on Chucky so he would've have to go; it was Chucky's rule.

What the beating did tell Chucky was that it was finally time to go. He was still strapped for cash, but he had enough money and enough coke to float him for a while, thanks to Pharaoh. After escaping Wolf, Chucky went to the block. He found one of the naïve new dudes that Omega had on the block and convinced him to let him take a shit on one of the stash houses. The boy let Chucky in and waited for Chucky in the hallway, which was a mistake. Chucky stole ten G-packs of crack, which would net him $10,000, and escaped out the window and down the fire escape. A part of him felt bad about double-crossing Ramses, but he reasoned that he wasn't stealing from Ramses directly; the drugs belonged to Pharaoh. He knew when Ramses found out, he would have the kid killed and send a death squad looking for Chucky, but he was a man on the run anyway, so what did one more pursuer mean to him? Besides, nobody knew where Chucky was laying his head those days, and by the time they figured it out he would be long gone. All he had to do was go to his aunt's to pick up his stash, and grab Persia, and they were getting on the road that night.

As he normally did, he rode past his aunt's house twice, with his lights off, before parking. He had just made his second sweep and was about to turn into the driveway when something moving in the shadows caught his eyes. There were two men creeping through the bushes, around to the back door of the house.

His heart leapt in his throat. It was impossible! There was no way Ramses could've found him that quick, unless someone had double-crossed him. And if he had been double-crossed, it could've only been by someone in that house. If that was the case, he would leave them to whatever fate was coming their way. He thought of Persia, sitting inside and oblivious to the shadow of death closing in. Her life was supposed to be his, but someone was going to steal his glory. There wasn't much he could've done about it. Wolf had taken his gun and left him defenseless. For as much as he wanted to be the end of her, he wasn't ready to die to sate his thirst for revenge. With his headlights off, Chucky rode off into the night and left Persia to the wolves.

Persia was in the upstairs bathroom splashing water on her face, when she heard the cannons. This time it wasn't the cannons in her ears from a crack hit, it was the sounds of guns being fired.

She opened the bathroom door, which opened to one of the bedrooms, where there was a couple on the bed shooting heroin. They were so far into their nod that they seemed oblivious to the sounds of panic coming from downstairs. Persia heard the gunshot again. This time it was closer. She tiptoed to the bedroom door and peeked out into the hall. Malcolm was running up the stairs like he had the devil on his heels. He had just cleared the top landing when the back of his head shot off and decorated the ceiling. It was then that Persia saw them.

There were two men wearing masks. One was tall, carrying a sawed-off shotgun and the other short, holding a black 9 mm. There was something about the way the shorter man moved that rang familiar to Persia, but her brain was racing too fast to understand why. When she saw them coming toward the bedroom, she ran in the bathroom and locked the door.

Persia stood with her back pressed to the bathroom door, sweating profusely. A cold chill settled in her bones and her stomach kept lurching as if she was going to vomit. She was going to be sick, but that was the least of her concerns at the moment. Snot dripped from her runny nose, onto her bare feet, but she dared not remove herself from the bathroom door to get a tissue from the sink, so she wiped it with the back of her hand. If her mother could see her doing it, she would surely be on her back about how it wasn't ladylike, but Persia's mind wasn't on etiquette, it was on survival.

Outside the door she could hear voices, one high-pitched and pleading and the other low and cruel. There were the sounds of struggling, followed by the unmistakable retort of a gunshot. She had to clamp her hand over her mouth to keep the scream that had just leapt from her throat from escaping. She tried to be as quiet as possible, but her heart was beating so hard in her chest that she could hear it in her ears and wondered if they could hear it on the other side of the door too.

Persia wasn't sure how long she had been pressed against that door, but it seemed like forever. She listened intently for the sounds of voices or footsteps, but heard none. All was silent. Persia let out a deep sigh of relief, knowing she had once again dodged a bullet. Still leaning on the door, she looked up at the wreck staring back at her from the bathroom mirror. It made her want to cry, but she wasn't sure if she had any tears left. Even if she did, who still cared enough to wipe them? She decided that after that night, she was getting her shit together.

Someone jiggled the bathroom door and her breath caught in her throat. They had found her! Persia thought maybe if she just explained to them that she didn't have anything to do with what was going on they would let her go, but then she thought of Malcolm and his brains on the ceiling. There was no way she was going to die in a crack house. She looked around the bathroom frantically for something she could use for a weapon, when her eyes landed on the window. If she could climb down the side of the house, she might be able to get away. She was three stories up and it was snowing, but her chances out there were better than her chances in the bathroom.

Persia had just managed to work the old window open when the bathroom door came crashing in. The two masked men filed in, guns drawn.

When the shorter one saw Persia, he paused and that was all the time she needed to slide out the window.

"Bring your li'l ass here," she heard one of the men say. A hand clamped around her leg and was trying to pull her back in.

"Let me go. I didn't do anything." Persia began kicking and thrashing.

"Stop fighting and come back in here," the shorter one ordered, trying to get a better grip on Persia by grabbing her shirt.

Persia could feel herself sliding back through the window. If they got her inside, she was dead. With her last bit of strength, she kicked out as hard as she could. Her feet made contact with the shorter one's face. The force tore her shirt, but she was free from his grip. Persia tried to grab on to the storm drain on the side of the house, but it was slick with snow and she slipped.

Persia felt like she was falling forever. The wind felt good, like it was caressing her tenderly. For a few seconds all was right with the world and she was wrapped in her mother's love. That came to a crashing halt when Persia hit the ground and it felt like she broke every bone in her body.

She lay there, in too much pain to move, watching the snowflakes fall across the glare of the dirty yellow streetlight. It made them look like pretty yellow diamonds. She wanted to reach up and grab a handful, but her arms didn't seem to work anymore. As she lay there, feeling her life drain away, she thought about her mother and how she'd treated her. She wished she'd understood that all Persia wanted was a little love and one grand adventure. Persia would've given anything to be able to hug her one more time and tell her that she loved her and wished that she had been a better daughter, but she would never have the chance. She also thought of Chucky, and how he hadn't been there to save her from this horrible fate. She wondered if he would cry when he found out what happened. There was so much that they still hadn't had a chance to do. Tears of regret began to roll down Persia's face. She didn't want to die alone in the snow.

The bells of the church rang loudly. It was midnight . . . her eighteenth birthday.

She began to weep heavily and sang. "'Happy birthday to me . . . happy birthday to me . . . happy birthday, dear Persia . . .'" Her words trailed off as the darkness claimed her and ended her adventure.

EPILOGUE

Persia awoke in a white room. It smelled sterile and clean. She squinted her eyes against the glaring light shining down over her and made out the form of someone dressed in all white.

"Am I in heaven? Are you an angel?" Persia asked groggily.

"No, you're in a hospital and I'm a doctor," the tall blond woman in the lab coat told her. "Do you know who you are?"

"Yes, my name is Persia Chandler."

"That's a good sign. You took quite a blow to the head. All your neuro tests came back negative, but we just wanted to make sure there wasn't any lingering damage," the doctor explained.

Persia took stock of herself for the first time. Her head was bandaged, and right arm and legs were in casts. "What happened? How did I get here?" Persia had a million questions.

"Well, we were hoping you could tell us. About three days ago someone brought you to the emergency room. You had taken a serious fall and for a minute we weren't sure if you were going to make it. If that guy hadn't brought you in when he did you would've probably died from internal bleeding."

"Who brought me in? I'd like to thank them," Persia said.

"He didn't leave a name. He waited until we had stabilized you then vanished."

Persia wondered if it had been Chucky who rescued her, but if so why would he leave? Persia went to try to sit up and realized that her left arm was strapped to the bed. "What's this all about?"

"It's just a precaution, Ms. Chandler. When your blood work came back there were heavy amounts of marijuana as well as crack cocaine. Can you tell me how long you've been an addict?" the doctor asked. She wasn't trying to be insulting; it was a routine question.

"I ain't no damn drug addict!" Persia said indignantly.

"Well, your blood work says otherwise," the doctor countered. "But it isn't my place to judge. The restraint is for your own safety. You're going to find yourself suffering from withdrawal and it may not be pretty. The restraint is so that you don't try to hurt yourself. We can give you something to help take the edge off while you're going through the withdrawal."

"No," Persia said. "No drugs. If it isn't aspirin, I don't want it."

"It could get pretty rough, Ms. Chandler," the doctor warned.

"Can't be any rougher than the last month of my life has been."

The doctor shrugged. "Your choice. Now if you're up to it, there are some people who would like to see you. They've been here around the clock since you were brought in. I'll send them in and give you some privacy." The doctor left.

Persia lay there wondering who could've been coming to see her. She was surprised when her mother, Richard, and Sarah walked in. She was so happy to see her mother that she started crying.

"It's okay, I'm here now." Michelle hugged her daughter, careful not to hurt her damaged body. "Mommy is here."

"I'm so sorry for the way I treated you," Persia sobbed.

"That's the past, let it stay there. Right now we have to focus on getting you well. Richard has contacted a private facility upstate. They have a school program so you can study for your GED while you're getting treatment," Michelle told her.

"Mom, thank you for everything, but I don't want to go to some rehab center like a junkie and I don't want a GED. I want to go home and go back to school like a normal teenager."

"But the doctor said the withdrawal process is rough. Persia, let's at least go check the place out before you make any rash decisions."

"No, she's right," Richard spoke up. "Persia has been through a lot. She doesn't need to be around strangers, she needs around people who love her. If that's what she's decided, that's what we're going to do. We'll beat this thing together . . . as a family."

It felt good hearing Richard stick up for her. She had said some nasty things while she was under the influence, but she knew Richard just wanted the best for her. "Thank you, and I'm sorry for what I said."

"I know, Persia. Don't worry about it. Like your mom said, let the past stay where it is. I'm going to go talk to the doctor to see if we can sign you out and take you home." Richard started for the door, but Persia stopped him.

"Richard, you were right about what you said."

"And what's that, Persia?"

She thought of Chucky and the things he'd showed her during their time together. "A cold world does breed hard men."

***

The doctor had been telling the truth: going cold turkey was harder than Persia had imagined it would be. For days she was racked with cramps and fits of vomiting. It was like she had a flu that wouldn't go away. There were times when Persia felt like she was going to die, but her mother and Richard were always right there to help her through it.

After a few weeks Persia was well enough to go back to school. There was no way her mother was letting her go back to King after all that had happened. Richard pulled some strings and got Persia back into St. Mary's. She had a lot to catch up on and would probably have to pick up some night school classes to catch up, but she was up to the challenge. Persia had a whole new appreciation for life and wanted to make the best out of the second chance she was given.

One day she and Sarah were in her bedroom doing their homework, when Persia's bedroom phone rang. It was a new number that not many people outside of Sarah had, so she wondered who it could be.

"Hello?" Persia answered.

"Hey, baby." Chucky's voice came over the other end.

Persia turned her back so that Sarah couldn't see the expression on her face. "How did you get this number?"

"You know you belong to me and I belong to you, so I'll always be able to get a hold of you when I need you, and I need you now," Chucky told her.

"Chucky, you left me for dead in that house. You didn't even come see me while I was in the hospital," Persia said emotionally.

"It wasn't my fault, baby. Look, just come meet me and I'll explain everything to you," Chucky said.

"I can't," Persia told him, but she didn't sound sure.

"Oh, so now that you're back on your feet, you're too good for me? That's fucked up," Chucky said, faking hurt.

"It's not like that, Chucky. It's just that I'm trying to get my life in order and I don't need any distractions," Persia explained.

"Damn, I've been reduced to a distraction? That's cold, Persia. When you came to me for help I risked my freedom and took you in, but now you're gonna turn your back on me? Don't do me like this, baby. It's a matter of life and death. I'm begging you, just meet me and hear me out."

Hearing Chucky beg was tearing her apart. She knew he was bad news, but she still loved him so much. "Okay, I'll give you five minutes then I'm gone. Where do you want me to meet you?"